THE MOUNTAIN OF MIST

Sean Foster, brilliant RAF pilot seconded to the American airforce to instruct pilots fighting in Vietnam, seems as unlucky in his flying career as he is in his love life. Near-death experiences in the Bermuda Triangle and equally painful love affairs make him redress his life. He has always been interested in UFOs, and it gradually dawns on him that he is being plagued by extraterrestrial forces, a belief reinforced by a meeting with the charmingly sinister Toni Angelini... Pursuit of the truth takes Sean into many varied venues, the Florida swamps, the Grand Canyon, the South Downs of England, the Western Isles and mountains of Scotland, to name but a few. Wherever he goes he has a keen eye for the local flora and fauna and an interest in local history.

A persistent and impossible dream lures him to one of the remoter Western Isles of Scotland where, with the woman destined to be the love of his life, Sean discovers that the truth, though out there, is far stranger and more devastating than he had ever imagined...

The Mountain of Mist is pervaded by a hint of the truth, rather than fiction, and this is reinforced by an Epilogue that suggests even further intrigue...

Educated at Eastbourne College, Patrick Coulcher was awarded a scholarship to the Royal Air Force College, Cranwell. After graduating as a pilot in 1957, he went on to fly many fighter aircraft, including the Hunter and Phantom, specialising in low-level reconnaissance and ground attack. He also served on exchange as an instructor pilot on a USAF fighter squadron. His best-selling A Natural History of the Cuckmere Valley was published by The Book Guild in 1997, and A Natural History of the Isles of Scilly will be published in 1999.

Illustrations are from photographs taken by the author with the exception of 'The scalloped edges of the Seven Sisters....' and the jacket picture which are from paintings by FRANK WOOTTON OBE.

Jacket design by STEPHEN WHEELE DESIGN

THE MOUNTAIN OF MIST

Patrick Coulcher

The Book Guild Ltd
Sussex, England

The Book Guild Ltd.
25 High Street,
Lewes, Sussex

First published 1998
© Patrick Coulcher 1998
Second printing 1999
Paper Back 2006

Set in Baskerville
Typesetting by
SetSystems Ltd, Saffron Walden, Essex

Printed and bound by CPI Antony Rowe, Eastbourne

A catalogue record for this book is
available from the British Library

ISBN 1 85776 311 4

To 'Shona'

CONTENTS

INTRODUCTION

To those readers who enjoyed reading my first book dealing
with the romance and natural history of the Cuckmere
Valley, I hope that this, my first novel, will capture your
imagination and make you think of the great mysteries and
problems of this world we live in.

I also hope that it will appeal to a wider audience who like
to lose themselves in romantic and thrilling events and who
may enjoy the description of the natural beauty of our
planet from the Grand Canyon to the mountains and remote
islands of Scotland.

Be sure to live every day of your life to the full for our
future on Earth is very uncertain and unpredictable.

Many of the events described in the following pages
actually happened.

PATRICK COULCHER

FOREWORD

by Air Chief Marshal Sir Neil Wheeler GCB, CBE,
DSO, DFC & bar, AFC.

This is a fascinating book and covers a wide variety of interests. Indeed, it could be said that the book has something for everybody: romance, excitement, mystery and the scenery of the world around us from the Grand Canyon to remote Scottish islands plus, for good measure, a simple philosophy of life.

I have known the author for some 40 years but it is only in recent years, when I discovered that he was a near neighbour, that I have come to know him well. He is somebody who takes the keenest interest in the world around, particularly in the flora and fauna. His knowledge of wildlife in Britain is formidable and he has already produced an excellent authoritative book about the Cuckmere Valley in Sussex. That book demonstrates his love of nature and the countryside.

Knowing Patrick Coulcher as I do, I suspect that in *The Mountain of Mist* he used romance, excitement and mystery as media to put over his first love – the countryside. Moreover he achieves his aim with remarkable skill.

Patrick and I both spent many years flying in the Royal Air Force. I am, therefore, most interested in his story based on his own exchange tour as an instructor on fighters with the USAF. Whilst, as I have already written, I believe he used this particularly exciting story as a medium for putting over other aspects of his philosophy of life, it nonetheless demonstrates admirably that his fine powers of descriptive writing are not confined to natural life.

The Mountain of Mist is a book that will attract and satisfy a wide variety of readers. Most certainly, I found it very readable and at times, particularly when dealing with the contentious subject of UFOs, very intriguing.

Neil Wheeler

1

Fighter Pilot

The night was dark and humid, flashes of lightning lit up the mangrove swamp that predominated in this near-tropical part of the United States of America. It was July in the late 1960s at MacDill Air Force Base near Tampa in Florida. As duty instructor pilot Sean Foster was making his way to the mobile caravan at the end of the main runway to watch over his students on their first night solo flights on the Phantom F4. He had briefed them all personally only an hour or so ago and warned them to stay to the south and west of the base and not to venture inland. For here, huge towering tropical thunderstorms were building up to give yet another night of torrential rain, so maintaining the ecosystem of the Florida swamps and Everglades.

It was half past eight and the first take off was scheduled for nine o'clock. This was Sean's first stint as duty pilot since he qualified as an instructor on one of the United States Air Force, USAF for short, premier fighter squadrons. Most of the students were young, in their early twenties, and had just completed basic flying training with some 150 flying hours to their credit. They had come to MacDill to graduate as fighter pilots on a course that demanded their all in terms of perseverance, courage, strength and tenacity. Their motivation and stickability would be tested to the full as they proceeded to master the skills ranging from air-to-air combat, ground attack bombing, to night air-to-air refuelling from a giant KC-135 tanker aircraft. Only then after a gruelling and demanding six month course would they be sent on to front line squadrons anywhere in the world. Some

1

would fail the course and occasionally one would be killed in accidents that were inevitable in such an environment.

Sean had been out in the mobile caravan once before in daylight and given instruction on the use of the various communications and safety aspects. He had signed the duty pilot's orders and instructions covering details of all aspects of flying operations and what to do in various emergency situations. He had been warned of the dangers of poisonous snakes, mainly water moccasins and rattlesnakes that were to be found in the tangled mangrove roots and lush vegetation that surround the base. He was advised to draw out a pistol and ammunition from the base armoury just in case.

As Sean drove out to the caravan in the squadron pick-up truck he pondered over his life in the past twenty years and how he had found himself here on an American Air Force Base and to be the first Royal Air Force officer to fly on this squadron.

Educated at an English Public school where his main interest had been natural history, suddenly from the age of fifteen he had wanted to become a fighter pilot. Determined, intelligent and impetuous, he applied for one of the new RAF scholarships and after a vigorous selection procedure was surprised to find himself awarded the first scholarship. Soon after graduating from the RAF College Cranwell at the age of twenty, Sean found himself on No. 1 Fighter Squadron, Royal Air Force, based in East Anglia. After several squadron tours specializing in low level reconnaissance, air defence and ground attack, he had felt huge apprehension and excitement when he learnt of his posting as an exchange officer with an American fighter squadron.

The lights of the pick-up truck shone on the gravel track leading off the main ring road that ran round the perimeter of the airfield. The track, bounded on either side by deep ditches filled with black still brackish water, led for about a quarter of a mile to the remote site of the mobile caravan. The airfield itself was only a few feet above sea level and when the hurricane season started in September, huge tidal surges from the Gulf of Mexico threatened at times to flood the whole area. The ditches were the home of alligators, snakes and huge spiders, all of which petrified Sean. The caravan soon appeared, its metallic silver colour making it stand out starkly against the black night. Strange, Sean mused, the Americans have never had any fear of invasion, for in Europe every military building would be painted in camouflage colours. He stopped the truck and switched off the ignition. As he fumbled with the unfamiliar locking system the keys fell to the floor between the front seats. Instantly Sean felt the darkness close in around him and the caravan was now only dimly visible in the subdued gloom of the vehicle's sidelights. As he got out he was aware of the sounds of the night. No aircraft had yet started their engines and against the background of the gentle lapping waves from the nearby shore he could hear the chirping and low grunts of the many creatures that became active after dark.

Suddenly, as he groped for the keys on the floor a more sinister sound awakened Sean's acute senses. He felt the roots of the back of his hair tingle as he heard the gentle rattle like peas shaken in a glass jar. Frozen with fright he turned slowly, ever so slowly and, straightening his tall, broad frame, he flicked on his torch and pointed it down towards the side of the road. There, only a few feet away, lay a huge rattlesnake in all its stunning beauty with its head arched upwards ready to strike. Sean could see the source of the noise coming from the end of the snake's tail, which was upright and gently shaking from side to side. The rattling noise was made by nine or ten interlocking horny scales making up the last inch or two of its tail. The light from the torch had startled the snake and for a fraction of a second the rattling stopped. Sean knew that any false movement now would mean great pain and possible death, for the venom of this reptile could be fatal. He slowly drew out his pistol and took careful aim. Two shots rang out in rapid succession, piercing the blackness. The head of the rattler blew apart, scattering pieces of flesh on the ground and onto the lush vegetation. The noises of the night ceased and an eerie silence descended.

Sean regained his composure, and having found the keys, opened up the caravan and switched on the main power. Immediately the interior was lit up with a soft light that was sufficient to work by, but not strong enough to distract landing on the well-lit runway only yards away. He flicked on the intercom switch to report to the Base Operations Centre, the hub of the whole station.

'Mobile to Ops, Sean Foster, duty instructor, don't worry about the shots – I had to shoot a rattler.'

'OK. Nobody has reported it. Yankie One has delayed ten minutes and is now due off at twenty-one ten.'

'Twenty minutes to go,' Sean thought as he carried out the many checks in the caravan. The checks were finally completed with the loading of two large pistols, one with green cartridges and one with red. These were used to give final landing clearance to any pilot who suffered a total radio communications failure.

Sean reflected on the past few months. Yankee One was the callsign of his first student, Lieutenant Mike Chapman. A bright young lad with dark quizzical eyes and prone to deep thoughts on philosophy and the world's problems, he proved an easy person to teach. As an instructor pilot on the squadron Sean was expected to know everything about the F4 Phantom, the mainstay of the USAF's front line fighter force, and built by that great aircraft company, McDonnell Douglas. James McDonnell founded the company and was one of the industry's visionaries. He was, though, autocratic and eccentric and was fascinated by the occult. This prompted him to give such names as Voodoo, Phantom and Banshee to aircraft. His ambition as he put it was 'to serve the creative evolutions of life on earth'.

At first Sean found it hard to master the techniques of flying in the USAF. Apart from differences in operating procedures and pilot slang, there was the oppressively hot and humid climate to contend with. He soon became used to consuming large amounts of liquid to prevent dehydration. This was especially important when preparing for air-to-air combat sorties which demanded high levels of

4

exertion to maintain maximum levels of gravity, known as G, in tight manoeuvring turns. This caused pilots to perspire freely. The compulsory wearing of tightly fitting G-suits, designed to prevent the blood flowing from the head, enabled the fighter pilot to withstand higher G loads without blacking out and becoming unconscious.

Sean thought himself lucky to have young Chapman to teach. His background and interests matched his own and with little flying experience and few built-in pre-conceived faults, Sean was able to send him solo on the Phantom after just seven instructional sorties. Chapman soon mastered the intricacies of the aircraft at low speed and he could safely manoeuvre it with the use of rudder alone at speeds around 50 and 60 m.p.h., well below its stalling speed of around 150 m.p.h. This technique was an essential one to learn before any student could be an effective fighter pilot and master of the F4 Phantom.

Sean got on well with the Americans and with his background he was soon accepted as one of the elite members of the USAF. In the late 1960s the war in Vietnam was at its height and most of the graduating students were sent out to that seemingly endless war to gain their spurs. Sean excelled in the challenge and responsibility of training such pilots. He loved the excitement and flow of adrenalin that accompanied each sortie. He learned the difficult art of self-survival and to judge just how far he would let a student make a mistake before taking over control himself with the words 'I have control'. If he took over too early the student would not learn to fly to the limits of his capability; if he took over too late they could both be killed.

Sean tried hard not to enter into the politics of the war and his Cranwell training helped him here. The military was expected to carry out the orders of the government to support the policies it deemed correct. The individual serviceman was not to argue, but to get on with the job and obey the orders of his superiors. In a true democracy this should cause no problem, thought Sean; after all the 'obey orders' excuses made by perpetrators of horrors in war-torn

Germany or in Japan, were not acceptable to us in an autocracy or under a dictatorship. Nevertheless, being an intelligent and thinking person Sean wondered whether politicians really spoke the truth and did they really believe what they said? Was Communism in Vietnam really a threat to a people so primitive compared to those in the industrialized countries of the West? All they wanted each day was a bowl of rice, shelter and a sense of belonging in a community. Was there really a danger that all countries in South-East Asia would fall to a communist one party state like a wall of dominoes?

'Yankee One, taxi.'

Chapman's voice came through the ether of the radio and aroused Sean from his thoughts. The air traffic controller's crisp, clear voice came back immediately, giving clearance for the Phantom to taxi out towards the runway some two miles distant. At the same time the controller gave details of the runway in use, the altimeter pressure setting and other essential information required by the pilot.

Yankee One was cleared onto the runway only some thirty yards away. With the aid of the runway lights Sean scrutinized the exterior of the aircraft through binoculars to see if there were any obvious fuel or oil leaks and, more importantly, if any red flags were showing, for these would indicate that a safety pin had not been removed before flight. These pins were installed in such places as the crew's ejector seats and on the undercarriage wheel struts to prevent inadvertent retraction of the wheels when the aircraft was parked for servicing. Only if Sean spotted something amiss would he interrupt the pilot's concentration as he commenced take-off. The aircraft nosed forward onto its front wheel, held by its main wheel brakes as power was applied. Suddenly there was a deafening staccato roar as the afterburners lit up. Even inside the caravan Sean could feel the vibrations and rumble in his stomach, caused by the awesome power of the two J79 General Electric engines that accelerated the ten ton aircraft down the two mile long runway.

Sean watched his student take off into the dark night and followed the Phantom until the afterburners' glow went out as they were shut down at about 2,000 feet altitude. He hoped that Chapman's first night solo would be uneventful but he knew there was nothing he could do now. He had briefed both crewmen carefully to fly south, keeping well clear of the thunderstorms inland. The rear seat pilot known in the USAF as a GIB (Guy in the Back seat) acted as a weapons' system operator and navigator and was usually a very junior squadron pilot who was eventually upgraded to the front seat.

At ten minute intervals another five aircraft took off, all students on their first night solo flights. With six aircraft now airborne Sean knew he had nothing left to do for about ten minutes until Chapman came back into the airfield circuit pattern to complete several touch and go landings.

His mind wandered over the girl he had met at a squadron party a few nights before. Gayle Cooper was tall and strikingly beautiful, with piercing blue eyes and long blonde hair and a complexion made perfect by an unblemished olive-brown skin. She had obviously been attracted to Sean as she kept close by, giving him more than a 'come on' look many times during the evening. Maybe it was his Englishness or was it his rugged good looks that attracted her? He had bought her a few drinks but he found her conversation somewhat shallow and naïve. He also found it difficult to cope with her sharp nasal and very marked West Coast accent. 'Mind you,' he thought, he was beginning to get used to the various accents and mannerisms of his hosts. He liked deep thinkers, and Sean realized that Gayle would never be a serious companion for him, but she was good fun with an infectious laugh and sense of humour. Her confidence and forewardness made him wary, but he had already learnt that many Americans were like that. They exuded confidence and it didn't necessarily make them insincere. He would see her again and indeed had fixed a date to go to the local beach at nearby St Petersburg over the weekend.

He looked back at his past love life. He had never found

it difficult to attract the opposite sex. Even at school he went out with girls often older than himself, but there were many strict limitations in those days imposed by parents and the male-orientated school itself. It wasn't until his college days in the RAF that love became more serious. Here, apart from restrictions on the use of one's single room in the main college building, life was much less restricted. Although one had to be in by midnight except at weekends, there were always ways of overcoming that problem. The hall porter who guarded the only entrance to the main building could easily be avoided by leaving a bedroom window off its latch. Sean was lucky as his ground floor bedroom was on the quieter north side and looked out onto the bleak, flat Lincolnshire countryside.

Sean recalled his first serious relationship with a girl from his home town in southern England. Sarah shared his serious nature and innermost thoughts and she seldom missed watching him play rugby when the matches were in and around London, where she worked as a secretary. She shared a rented flat in London and Sean often spent exeat weekends at the flat, usually sleeping on the floor when Sarah's flatmate was in residence. At one time, Sean remembered, he had really loved her but soon began to realize their incompatibility. She loved city life, the bright lights, the cosmopolitan atmosphere of parties and the many different and exciting people one met. He was essentially a lover of nature and the countryside. As a schoolboy he enjoyed the rough and tumble of the rugby field in winter, but he eagerly awaited the return of spring when he could again roam the fields, downs and river valleys of his native Sussex. His recollection of finding the rare early spider orchid was as vivid as if it had happened just yesterday. He had searched all day on the rabbit-grazed grassland slope near his home, where he knew from his orchid book the habitat was suitable. In one of the last days of April as the sun shone out of an almost cloudless sky, a pair of peregrine falcons soared high above the white cliffs, their calls of 'zee zee zee' carried far by the gentle southerly wind. An adder with its black zigzag marking, recently awakened from its hibernation, slithered through the cowslips that covered parts of the slope with patches of yellow. He was always afraid of snakes and kept well clear of it. After a fruitless search he decided to return home, and retraced his steps to his bicycle left beside a hawthorn tree at the bottom of the slope.

As he picked up the bike, he saw it. Only a few yards distant on a flat piece of ground grew the object of his search. The beautiful two-inch high orchid of exquisite beauty, with a broad brown labellum, like the body of a bloated spider. Two shiny globules of nectar shone out from the flower, like a pair of eyes. He remembered his intense excitement as he took picture after picture with his battered old Brownie camera.

Yes, Sean realized that now, as then, nature and his love of the wild, lonely places of planet Earth was to him an essential ingredient of life itself. Often in the few quiet periods of his hectic life he would visualize and dream of the wide open spaces of the Sussex Downs and the lush river valleys that flowed from the High Weald to the sparkling blue sea of the English Channel. He recollected too his low-level flights through the magnificent glens of Scotland and he remembered his life-long ambition to rediscover that most beautiful of all plants, the Arctic bramble, on the high regions of Beinn a' Ghlo, the Mountain of Mist.

'Yankee One rejoin.'

The radio burst into life, once again, rousing Sean from his thoughts. Chapman was back only a few minutes later than planned and would now consolidate his night experience with some practice landings. Such practice, Sean knew, was essential to induce confidence in young and inexperienced pilots. His job was to monitor the progress of each student and to criticize constructively their techniques and procedures. As the duty instructor at the end of the runway, he was there particularly to give verbal help and instructions should problems of weather or aircraft malfunction arise.

Air Traffic Control gave Yankee One the atmospheric

pressure setting which was essential for the pilot to enable his altimeter to show the correct height above sea level and such other necesssary information as the runway in use, and the wind speed and direction. Sean looked to the west and he could see the dim lights of the Phantom approaching from over the huge 'Sunshine Skyway' bridge over Tampa Bay linking St Petersburg with Palmetto.

The Phantom approached at 1,000 feet altitude over the end of the runway and turned onto the downward leg parallel to the runway.

As he straightened out Chapman called, 'Yankee One downwind for touch and go.'

Crisply the Controller replied, 'Yankee One clear to finals.'

Sean knew how busy the workload was for the young pilot. All the downwind checks had to be completed within about 30 seconds; gear down, flaps set, fuel sufficient, no warning lights and many others. Turning onto the final approach Yankee One confirmed that his wheels were down and locked, and obtained final clearance from the controller in the main control tower. Sean monitored the progress and noted that the nose wheel and landing lights on the under-carriage were shining brightly, indicating that all was well.

The dark silhouette of the Phantom was now just visible a mile or so from the runway threshold. With an experienced eye Sean was pleased at the angle of approach and the general appearance of the final turn. He knew Chapman was now fully occupied with all his physical and mental senses at high pitch to cope with the degree of concentration required to land this highly sophisticated modern fighter.

'Crump, Crump'. The wheels hit the runway with a good hard thud so dissipating much of the energy of the aircraft landing at 150 m.p.h. The original Phantom was built as a navy aircraft and designed to land on the deck of an aircraft carrier. Its landing was therefore designed to be hard, to enable it to stop in the short space of an angled deck. The Phantom design also incorporated a heavy metal tail hook which when lowered caught on a wire stretched across the carrier's deck, so arresting the landing aircraft and bringing it to a stop quickly. This hook could also be used on land-based airfields where a hookwire was fitted. Yankee One swept down the runway, and then, as full power was applied to the engines, it was airborne again, having travelled only a few hundred yards on the ground; and so into the circuit pattern again.

A clipped downwind call again from Chapman and clearance to finals from the controller.

'Yankee One finals, gear down and . . .' The transmission stopped abruptly and then a somewhat agitated voice confirmed, 'Left gear is showing still locked up.'

Sean felt the adrenalin rise and reacted immediately as his past experience had taught him.

'Yankee One, don't recycle but fly down over mobile control.'

'Will do,' came the reply.

In his excitement Chapman had forgotten to prefix his call with, 'Yankee One' – an essential ingredient to prevent mix-ups in communication, especially when several aircraft are talking on the same radio frequency.

Sean switched on the inspection lights, which sent up a broad beam of light skywards in a direction that avoided shining into an approaching pilot's eyes and destroying his night vision. The Phantom flew through the beam and Sean could see the port wheel door shut and flush with the wing, while the nose wheel and starboard wheel were firmly locked down.

'Yankee One, your port wheel looks firmly up, climb to circuit height and recycle,' Sean said in a calm authoritative voice. He knew that in this case it was worth trying to reselect the wheels, first up and then down, for this might just clear the malfunction. He also knew that if the wheel had appeared to be locked in a position half-down then recycling might do more harm than good.

'Yankee One, have recycled but the port gear still shows locked up.'

Sean, as duty pilot in charge of night operations, now

11

knew he had a problem. He had five other aircraft airborne and they would be returning soon. They had to be directed to another USAF base some 50 miles south near Miami, and he knew that Air Traffic Control and the Base Operations Centre would handle that side of things. He also knew that Chapman would have to land soon, as normally aircraft on such training sorties had fuel for only another twenty minutes or so at this stage. Sean was aware that the crash crews were now in the vicinity by the end of the runway, and the fire tenders were all ready to spray a thick layer of foam on top of the threshold and several hundred yards down the runway itself. This would dampen any sparks and put out any incipient fire that might start as a result of the impending crash landing and ruptured fuel tanks.

Immediate and decisive action was now required.

'Yankee One, orbit the field and try emergency gear lowering,' Sean ordered.

There was a back-up system, that used compressed air that could possibly work, but he knew the chances were slim in an incident that looked like a major mechanical failure of the wheel system.

'Yankee One to mobile,' Chapman's voice sounded calm but there was just a hint of anxiety and tension in his voice.

'Mobile, Yankee One. Go ahead.'

'Yankee One, have tried emergency lowering but no joy. Must land soon only eight hundred pounds of fuel left.'

'Roger Yankee One. Runway is now being foamed, lower your hook and make a long low approach and land in the middle of the threshold engaging hook wire.'

Sean had heard the Base Operations Centre, who controlled all activities on the base, order the fire crews to foam the runway, and he could see the process had already started. With their blue lights flashing these giant fire tenders were racing up and down the first 400 yards of runway, spraying out thick white foam which formed a white carpet layer, like snow, over the black tarmac. A surreal picture presented itself; lightning flashes lit up huge towering cumulo-nimbus clouds while red, orange, green, white and flashing blue lights merged together and reflected off the white foam, as the activity on the runway threshold increased to fever pitch.

'Yankee One, finals, eight miles for emergency landing, hook down.'

Again Chapman sounded calm, but Sean knew from experience the feelings of fear and anxiety that must be racing through his body and mind. His GIB, crouched in the rear seat, must be experiencing the same feelings with an intensity that only such people as pilots and racing drivers, who choose exciting lifestyles, can feel.

'Yankee One clear to land,' the controller replied, knowing the runway was now clear of vehicles.

Swiftly, and almost imperceptibly the crash and fire vehicles left the vicinity of the runway and remained close by, but well clear of the impending crash landing. The Phantom could now be seen some 3 miles to the west of the shore. Sean hoped the hook would engage the arrester wire. Soon he could see the sinister-looking upturned wing tips of the aircraft, reminding him of a huge manta ray that he had seen occasionally swimming in the clear Gulf waters, when he was on a low flying mission. The Phantom was now only a half a mile from the inevitable crash landing. Suddenly he saw the black calm sea burst into ripples of white specks as a surge of power was applied by the pilot to lift the aircraft up over the approach lights and onto the runway. The Phantom smashed down onto the foam with a noise like muffled thunder. The foam was thrown up like flecks of white spume blown about on a wave-battered sea-shore on a wild and windy day.

'Hell!'

Sean saw that the tail hook, as sometimes happened, had skipped over the arrester wire. Now he knew there was a danger of the aircraft wing breaking off and spilling fuel from its wing tanks, but the wing held as it scraped the runway, with the friction sparks easily contained and put out by the foam. The aircraft careered uncontrollably down the runway, slewing off to port and finally coming to rest on the

13

grass. No fire and no horrendous break, Sean thought as he raced his vehicle to the aircraft's final resting place. He watched from a distance as the efficient rescue team swung into action. His mind went back many years to when, in training, he had watched an exactly similar scene involving a Hunter aircraft on an RAF base. Then the pilot was unhurt, but could not open the cockpit canopy and was trapped inside. The crash team, who were proud winners of an efficiency trophy, had practised for just such an occasion many times. The exuberant crew chief had climbed onto the top of the aircraft, smashed the canopy perspex, but in doing so had used too much force and had hit the pilot on the back of his protective 'bone dome' or helmet, rendering him unconscious. Undaunted, he had made the ejection seat safe with pins and unstrapped the pilot. He then lifted him up and over the side of the aircraft and laid him out on the grass, still unconscious. The ambulance had raced up, skidded on the wet grass and the front wheels ran over the pilot's legs, breaking one of them. Sean remembered visiting his fellow student pilot in hospital, with others who were anxiously awaiting his recovery. The student's first words on seeing the assembled throng, which included his instructor were classic; 'What the bloody hell happened? I was perfectly OK until the crash crew arrived, and then I remember nothing!'

As Sean arrived beside the Phantom, he noticed both cockpit canopies were fully open and the crew were busy making the British-made Martin Baker ejection seats safe. This was very important, as any would-be rescuer who inadvertently pulled one of the seat ejection handles would find himself several hundred feet in the air, as the cartridges and rockets of the seat were fired. Sean was soon to discover how much he was to owe the designers of this seat, Sir James Martin and Mr Baker, in saving his life in two horrendous crashes. The Martin Baker Company won the contract against severe competition to fit its seat to the Phantoms of the USAF.

Chapman saw Sean first as he climbed down by means of spring-loaded steps set flush into the side of the aircraft.

'Hope that was OK, sir' he said.

Sean thought for a moment. He didn't want to criticize his first student about an accident subject to an enquiry.

'Fine. Pity the hook bounced over the wire, but that happens sometimes. Not your fault. Nice to see you both uninjured and the aircraft doesn't look to be too damaged. It will soon be repaired. See you both back in the crew-room.'

Sean thought of all the inevitable paperwork, reports, statements and interviews that now had to be completed, all designed to improve the system to see if accidents can be prevented and to reduce damage and injury. Why did the wheel jam in the up position? What other procedures could the pilot carry out to get the wheels down? Could a better landing technique be adopted in such circumstances? The questions were many and the answers varied and sometimes difficult to evaluate as to which was correct.

'Never mind.' Sean waited until the runway was cleaned and cleared of debris and the aircraft jacked up on wheels and towed away for repair. Only then could he return to his duties as instructor pilot of the night and await the return of the rest of the students from their diversion down south. Eventually, they all came back and touched down safely. He heaved a big sigh of relief. It had been a long and eventful night. He locked up the caravan and as he glanced down at the remains of the snake, his thoughts turned to the coming weekend and his date with Gayle on the warm Gulf sands of Sarasota beach.

2

Air Combat

Sean woke up to yet another cloudless hot sunny morning. When he first arrived in Florida seven months ago in January, he began to realize how different it was going to be when compared to the wet, fog-bound and dreary winter of England. The common British practice of greeting people with 'Good morning, what a beautiful day' was an anachronism here in the 'Sunshine State' as every day was beautiful. He wondered what his American colleagues had thought of him in his early days when he greeted them in such an English manner – how polite they were.

After breakfast in the Officer's Mess where he lived in the comfortable, almost luxurious, bachelor's quarters, Sean visited the base supermarket to provide for the picnic he was looking forward to having with Gayle. Drink first, he thought, and saw the line of different wines stacked up just beyond the entrance. He chose a white Gallo wine from the sun-drenched Sierras of California. Next, watermelon and cantaloupe and a few shrimp and crab sandwiches already made up in their cellophane wrappings. Sean was only just getting used to the rich variety of fruit that was available at such ridiculously cheap prices. He wondered how the day would end – would they discover a chemistry between them, linking them forever in a lifelong partnership, or would they find little depth of heart and mind and simply remain as acquaintances while he was on duty in the States? He supposed the latter but was ready to be surprised.

Sean loaded up his red Ford Mustang with its hood folded back. His choice of car had been dictated by circumstances

16

rather than by personal preference. He had never hankered after the fast, sleek and exciting sports cars like the MGB and Jaguar XK140 of his colleagues, but was content to settle for a small saloon, like the Austin or Beetle. Cars always affect their owner's personality and Sean's somewhat cautious and shy nature was probably reflected in these earlier desires. However, on arrival in Florida the aggressiveness and sheer brashness and audacity of his American counterparts warned him that to compete and succeed and, most importantly, be accepted, he should at least give an outward appearance of similarity. On arrival he knew he had to get wheels quickly, for without them he would be confined to the base, with little freedom of independence. His mentor, who met him at the airport and showed him the ropes for the first few weeks, suggested he buy the Mustang that was up for sale by one of the graduating students who was off to Vietnam for a year or so. And that was it. He looked over the car, had a trial drive and bought it for $8,000. In reality he found that he quietly enjoyed the exhilaration and thrill and sheer pleasure of racing down the wide open roads of the 'Sunshine State' with the soft, humid air blowing about his head and shoulders.

He drove along the base roads, sweet with the smell of purple Bougainvillaea, to the officers' married quarters where Gayle lived with her parents, her father, Colonel Cooper, being the deputy base commander. As he turned the corner just past the golf course he saw her house, a low colonial-style gleaming white bungalow with wide overhanging eves. It was set amongst pine trees with a neatly cut lawn and regulation paving up to the front door. Flowering shrubs and plants of all descriptions gave a multiplicity of colours which blended in and complemented the wide expanse of deep blue sky. As he parked outside the house he saw her. Standing at the top of the steps, she looked stunning in her short yellow cotton dress, which did little to hide her beautiful shaped legs and well-proportioned breasts. She waved, her lips parting into a huge smile showing off sparkling white teeth.

'Hi Sean,' she shouted as she skipped down the steps, swinging a beach bag with a floral design neatly matching her dress.

'Wow, you look great,' replied Sean as he ushered her into the leather covered seat beside him. 'Any particular place you would like to go?' he added.

'No, surprise me,' she said, 'as long as there is white sand, blue sea, you and nobody else around.'

Sean felt more confident that the day would work out well after all. He too wanted seclusion and tranquillity and not the popular and crowded beaches near St Petersburg and Clearwater. Here children played with such exuberance and noise, and water-skiers and power boats disturbed the peace and quietness of the Gulf shore. He would go to one of the many sequestered and empty places near Sarasota where small pieces of land, as yet untouched by builders, were tucked away between large homes and led down to little-visited sandy beaches.

'I know some secluded beaches. We'll go over the Sun-shine Skyway bridge just south of St Petersburg and then take one of the side roads off to the west. Have you brought enough to eat?'

'Sure,' she said. 'I have some salad and fruit – that's all I need and of course my swimswuit.'

'Right, let's go,' Sean said as he swept out of the main gate where the duty guard smartly saluted them, recognizing the English pilot and the deputy commander's daughter.

As they drove slowly through the outskirts of St Peters-burg, stopping and starting frequently at the overhead traffic lights, Sean thought how sensible it was not to be following the crowds to the wide expanse of beaches nearby. He hoped that his selected spot on the north side of 'The Bay' would be quiet this weekend. He had been there often before, having spotted the site from one of his earlier aerial reconnaissances just after he had arrived. He found that this was a place he could disappear to at the weekend, where he could relax and read and devour *The Daily Telegraph* news-papers that would arrive by airmail in batches from England

18

every week. He found that he needed to keep up to date with what was going on at home and in the world at large. The American daily papers he found to be somewhat superficial, sterile and very parochial in nature and he seldom discovered much to stimulate him.

'Sure you don't want to stop at a supermarket for anything?' Sean asked, wondering how on earth Gayle could find much sustenance in such a small bag she had brought with her.

'No Sean, I really don't eat a lot.'

'Just lie in the sun and swim eh?' he retorted.

'That and maybe other things if the mood . . .,' she paused for a moment, '. . . and the company was right.'

Sean felt something deep inside him stir, a latent feeling he had not experienced for many years. He sensed emotions swelling up and beginning to take over and he didn't like that, as he always prided himself that he could keep his physical feelings in check. At the same time there was a warning: don't get involved, make sure of her before letting yourself go. He fell silent as the bridge approached.

'You're quiet. What are you thinking about?' she asked, trying to look totally unconcerned.

'Oh nothing really,' he lied. 'Just look at that sight.'

The view of 'The Bay' was magnificent. Large ships swept into Tampa port itself under the huge concrete spans supporting the highway some hundred feet or so above the water. Overhead, the wide expanse of sky with just a few small cumulus clouds beginning to form inland, as the sun climbed ever higher, warming the heavy moist air over the pine-covered landscape. These clouds were the harbingers of the towering thunder clouds that would form as the day progressed and kept Florida's central lakes and swamps filled with moisture.

They turned off onto a side road leading west which Sean knew would lead to the coast. Soon he recognized the track that led to his chosen spot, a clean white beach where a myriad of many-coloured shells, white, pink, purple and yellow with multi-shaded bands of brown and black lay spread about at the high tide mark. Their different shapes and forms scattered the sunlight, mingling with that reflected off the small wavelets that broke on the sea-shore. He was always fascinated by shells and collected a few of them from the more exotic places of the world he had visited. Razors, cowries, wendletraps, smooth buckles – the very names of them were evocative. What stories they could tell of the molluscs that lived inside them and their fight for life against the sea creatures that preyed upon them in the deep oceans. He picked up a large ormer, looked at it and then discarded it.

'Pity it's broken at the edge,' he said.

'Pretty though,' Gayle added, but Sean noticed that she wasn't really interested in shells.

He led her over the beach to a place where some tall palm trees gave some shade. It was noon and the sun was almost at its zenith. It was hot and humid with just a hint of an off-shore breeze.

'It's going to be even hotter soon – thank goodness I packed some ice cubes,' he said, breaking the silence.

'We can keep cool in the sea,' she said.

To clear a patch of sand on which to sit Sean bent down to remove a large piece of wooden planking washed up in some past storm. As he unfurled his multi-coloured beach rug he brushed a small black speck that was moving across the back of his hand. Suddenly Gayle stiffened and her face contorted with intense fear. She raised her hand to her mouth and screamed.

'No, not here, don't sit here! Look at all those black widows.'

Sean's surprise was total.

'What black widows? Where?' he said, but almost immediately remembered the small moving speck he had just brushed off his hand.

'Look around that patch of grass that was under the plank.' Gayle still looked petrified but was slowly regaining her composure.

A white mass of cobweb strands caught Sean's eye and as

he bent down for a closer look he could see the multitude of dime-sized black spiders with long thin legs. They were hurrying hither and thither, all trying to seek shelter and hide themselves again after this sudden disturbance by man.

Sean had heard of black widow spiders in novels but never thought he would encounter them personally. So this small black creature is what strikes fear into man and was the focus of novelists when they wanted to portray terror and excitement.

'Look closely on the underside of the abdomen and see the red hourglass mark' Gayle said, having now recovered almost completely from her sudden horror. 'That is the southern black widow, the same species that bit my younger sister several years ago. I remember that she screamed and screamed in acute pain and experienced dizziness, sweating and nausea. I also recall how her speech became slurred and her face became distorted into a pain-racked grimace. Of course we got her to hospital quickly and she soon recovered after only a few days. You know it is only the female of the species that has a dangerous bite and it delivers a neurotoxic poison that affects the nervous system. The spiders themselves are slow-moving, as you can see, and they avoid the light. So when they are disturbed they retreat into cover.'

Sean, surprised at her knowledge, especially of a subject connected with nature, interrupted her flow of words.

'You're very knowledgeable on spiders. Where did you get all that from? I didn't know it was a subject that interested you.'

'It isn't, but I wanted to find out more about why my sister was so ill. I did some research at a local library. These spiders are not uncommon in Florida, you know. Anyway let's move to the other side of the beach and look carefully where we choose to sit.'

'OK,' said Sean amazed that she had picked up so much information on black widow spiders. 'You know I find it difficult to understand why such a small creature with such an efficient web system should need such a powerful toxin to kill such large animals. It only has to catch tiny insects such as flies to survive, so why has evolution provided it with such a weapon?'

'Don't know,' she said. 'I need a drink after that.'

Sean then realized, as he had already suspected, that she held little interest in natural history and could never share his deep passion for the subject. He decided then that a long-term relationship was out of the question. Companionship, together with shared interests was, he believed, the secret to a long-lasting, happy and meaningful partnership. He knew that he was still searching for that elusive goal. He took out a bottle of wine from the cool box and unwrapped the Waterford crystal glasses.

'Nothing but the best,' he said, uncorking the bottle and pouring out the golden liquid with a flourish.

'What beautiful glasses,' she said. 'Where did you get them?'

'They were a twenty-first birthday present from one of my aunts in Ireland. They are the finest cut glass you can get in Britain. Wine tastes better out of good glasses don't you agree?'

'Cheers, here's to your two years with our air force.'

Their glasses touched and she looked straight into his eyes. He could not help but see into the dark depths of her pupils encompassed by beautiful blue. He saw then her deep passion and feeling for him; but he could not respond. The chemistry was just not there. He felt her touch him lightly on the shoulder.

He broke off his eye contact and said, 'Come on, let's go for a swim. First one in gets a free dinner.'

She did not react immediately, but a look of sad disappointment crossed her face. She then grabbed his hand and led him running down to the sea.

Sean knew that was it for the moment – no love, no romance. He had let that chance go and Gayle knew it too. They swam together in the warm clear water, each with their own thoughts.

They said little as they ate through their lunch of crab sandwiches, cold Gulf prawns, cantaloupe and watermelon.

Sean loved the sea foods and the fresh semi-tropical fruits that Florida provided throughout the year. Gayle surprised Sean during one of the many periods of silence between them.

'What do you think of the war?' she asked.

Sean thought for a moment before replying.

'Well not much really, but I do what I am supposed to do and try not to get involved with the politics of the situation. I have a job to do and that is to train pilots to fight and survive.'

'Yes, but can't you see what this is doing to the people in the streets? They, for the first time in recent American history, are totally opposed to this foreign war waged by our government against a poor people.'

'OK,' Sean replied, taken aback by her forthrightness and vehemence. 'You must understand that, personally speaking, I oppose any war. I repeat, any war where a country with a democratically elected government is attacked and people are killed for purely political reasons, but surely here is a war where an authoritarian form of government unelected by its people is trying to impose its will by force on another country, in this case South Vietnam. Its excuse is that Communism as a social system must be spread across the world. Now you can agree or disagree about Communism, but you must admit that North Vietnam is trying to invade the South against that people's will. You know the only way we will solve armed conflict in this world of ours is to form eventually a world government. I can see a future when groups of countries come together to form large power blocks like a United States of Europe, or a United States of North and South America. Once these power blocks have solved their economic, social and cultural problems then they can form even larger groupings. This may take many decades but eventually a world authority with a world army will develop with a common language – English, or if you like, American – there ain't much difference, is there?'

'Yes I see that, but surely the United Nations is what you really envisage?'

'No, the United Nations won't work for the simple reason that it has been too ambitious. It started by trying to unite together all the nations of this world at the same time. The bureaucracy and cost of trying to solve all the problems at once is too daunting. Much better to encourage small groupings of countries first, and then let them solve their problems before starting the further process of amalgamation into a world body. Such a body will eventually be a world government elected by all the people. We in Europe should start the ball rolling by uniting first and I am certain that this will happen by the end of the century.'

Gayle fell silent and Sean realized that she could not match his vision with any logical conclusions of her own.

They passed the day pleasantly enough, swimming and just lazing in the shade. As the sun sank lower and the sky took on that delicate orange and peach colour so typical of the sub-tropics, they conversed less, their silences became longer and each was left with their own thoughts.

Sean, feeling the tension beginning to build up between them, decided to call an end to the day.

'Well I think it's time to go home. I am up before dawn to brief a four-ship sortie on air-to-air combat.'

Gayle didn't reply immediately, but as she began to pack up her belongings she said somewhat dejectedly, 'Yes, that was lovely, but we've had the best of the day and I have to be at work tomorrow too.'

Sean noticed how sad she looked. Gone was the exuberance and the cheerful self-confidence. He felt disconsolate and blamed himself for prematurely ending the relationship. Why, he said to himself, can't I just enjoy pretending to love someone, and relish the inevitable physical pleasure that this could bring? But he knew he would not be true to himself; he could not do that and hurt someone just for his own ego and gratification. Many years before he had enjoyed the passion of a close friendship which he knew was based on a false notion of love, but he persisted and the affair blossomed and flourished beside the river banks and downland grasses of the English countryside. The end came inevitably as they realized they were two different and disparate persons. The hurt and anguish was so great that it affected Sean for years. He vowed then that next time he made love it would be for real; no more the tears and pain of a broken heart made worse by the knowledge that it affected the other equally and not just himself.

He kissed her lightly on the lips and said goodbye without making any arrangements to see her again.

She, looking more cheerful now with a brightness in her eyes caused by the moistness of near tears said, 'Goodbye now, hope we'll see you again soon.'

She got out of the car, walked up to her front door and turned to wave. Sean waved back and then drove back to the solitude of his room. He felt a great sense of loss. He knew he needed the companionship and warmth of a person close to him. Yes, he wanted love; but he had rejected it and the loss of it hurt him deep down.

Next morning Sean awoke at five, had an early breakfast in the mess and then walked the mile or so down to the squadron to prepare his briefing. The dawn was clear and bright, the sun just peeking through the trees in a cloudless sky. Checking in at the Squadron Operations' desk he phoned the Duty Met Officer to confirm the weather he had obtained off the teleprinter. The weather was seldom any problem that early on a summer's day in Florida, clear skies and light winds, but Sean was meticulous and didn't take any chances, he didn't want to get caught out by a sudden tropical cold front sweeping down from the north. He checked with the Base Operations Centre and briefed himself on airfield restrictions, call signs and runway in use and possible diversion airfields. He then walked down the corridor to one of the briefing rooms specially laid out with maps, charts and a large perspex board on which he could write notes and instructions with a greasepoint pencil. It was 6.20 a.m. The first pilots were just arriving and settling down on the hard seats, each with a flat sideways-folding arm on which to rest their briefing pads. These pads were clipped onto metal backplates and were used as reminders and for taking notes whilst in the air. They were strapped onto the pilot's thigh by means of elastic clips.

When the seven other pilots had sat down Sean strode in, his blue-grey flight suit looking immaculate and his Royal Air Force wings distinguishing him from his American colleagues. But he also wore his USAF TAC (Tactical Air Command) shoulder flash depicting a white sword with golden wings set against a red and blue background. A squadron badge depicting a fearsome termite with green wings was sewn neatly onto the opposite shoulder.

'Good morning, gentlemen,' he said, always politeness itself. 'This morning we are going to complete a two versus two aerial combat mission. Listen carefully to the brief, which is complex, and pay particular attention to the emergency procedures. Any questions at the end, but interrupt if you don't understand anything. Chuck, you are my number two and, Bob, you will lead the second pair as number three with John as your wingman number four.'

Sean was happy to have Major Bob Connor as his number three and deputy leader of the formation. He was an experienced and highly regarded instructor who would cope well in any difficult situations. This was the students, first air combat sortie and each aircraft had an instructor occupying the rear seat.

Sean continued, 'Aircraft tail numbers are shown on the board. Take off is at 0830 hours, landing back at about 0940.'

He went on to outline the mission in detail, explaining the various procedures in case of emergencies such as radio failure, aircraft system failures and even catastrophic events such as ejection. He realized that as leader he carried a great deal of responsibility on this flight. Its success or failure, expensive in terms of fuel, men and machines, depended on his swift and correct decision-making in the air. A poor leader could result in the aircraft never coming into contact within the vastness of the sky.

Sean carefully explained all aspects of the meticulously planned mission. The whole objective, he explained, was to ensure that two pairs of aircraft came into radar contact with each other at 30,000 or 40,000 feet alititude, either head-on or at a slight angle. Until visual or radar contact was positively established, the vertical height separation of 2,000 feet was to be maintained. The students would practice their procedures for the simulated firing of electronically guided Sparrow missiles at several miles distance after a radar lock-on had been achieved. When in visual distance, preparations for the simulated firing of Sidewinder missiles could be made. Unlike the Sparrow, a Sidewinder missile needed to be fired in a line astern position where its built-in heat-seeking system locks onto the hot jet efflux of the opposing aircraft. A growl in the pilot's earphones indicates a successful lock-on.

So the ultimate objective of the fighter pilot was to position his aircraft to the rear of his opponent, using many and varied techniques, such as high G turns, barrel rolls and scissors – all essential tools in the learning process. The final weapon that could be used in close air combat is the integral 27mm cannon firing some 100 rounds per second. On the earlier marks of the Phantom this gun, working on the Gatling principle of rotating barrels, was externally mounted underneath on the belly of the aircraft. On later models, such as the Phantom F4E, the gun was permanently fitted internally as a standard fitment.

After nearly an hour of careful briefing Sean finished off by detailing the diversion and weather situation.

'Any questions?' he asked. There was none and Sean realized his briefing had been thorough. 'Don't forget,' wingmen, if you lose sight of your leader at any stage, yell out. Don't wait for a collision which will be your last.'

This was his parting shot as they filed out of the room, a piece of advice he had learnt from his earlier days when instructing at an RAF Operational Training Unit. He had once not heeded that advice and, having lost his leader when climbing into the sun, he remained silent hoping to regain contact almost immediately. Ten seconds of panic and suddenly there was his leader directly above him on a collision course to disaster. Only his quick reaction and a violent evasive manoeuvre saved him. He said nothing at the debriefing and, as luck was with him, his leader had not noticed his error.

Sean walked out to his aircraft, proud to see his name written on its side below the canopy.

'Good morning, sir,' his crew chief said, smartly saluting him in a typical crisp American style. 'No problems today, the aircraft is fully serviceable.'

'Thank you chief, hope to bring it back in the same condition,' Sean replied.

He liked this particular crew chief who always seemed on top of his job. He was a hard but fair man, always barking out orders, but his crew seemed to love him.

Sean's back-seater, a young first lieutenant hoping to get upgraded into the front seat on his next tour, climbed up into the back to align the Inertial Navigation System and check out the radar and weapons systems. Sean meanwhile walked around the aircraft to see that the many safety pins had been removed and that there were no obvious defects like missing servicing panels or fluid leaks. He tapped the large 270 gallon fuel tanks, one underneath each wing, to listen for the solid thump indicating that they were full. This final check was no slur on the professionalism of the crew chief, but as captain of the aircraft, he was ultimately responsible for its safety. This was standard practice for all military pilots in most countries.

At precisely eight o'clock the engines of the four aircraft roared into life. Sean switched on his radio and pressed the transmit button.

'Hazel Flight check in.'

The response was immediate: 'Two,' 'Three,' 'Four,' they all came back one after the other in a crisp, clear manner. Good, Sean thought, that sounds businesslike, it should be a good sortie. He felt totally in control as he called for taxi clearance to the runway, knowing that the three other multi-million dollar aircraft and crew were now under his command and would follow his directions without question. This

was what he liked, the elation of responsibility and anticipation of an exciting flight. His whole being was keyed up
and he could feel the adrenalin flowing as the four aircraft
spaced themselves on the runway ready for a take-off in
paired formation at ten second intervals.

'Clear take-off,' came the call from the air traffic
controller.

Sean ran up his engines with the brakes fully applied,
looked at his number two who gave him a thumbs up sign.
He gave a vigorous nod forward of his head and at the same
time let go of the brakes and opened up the two throttles.
Simultaneously his number two, seeing his leader's head
signal, did likewise and the pair of Phantoms swept down
the runway at ever increasing speed. Sean pushed the
throttles sideways into afterburner and he felt the 'kick in
the pants' as the aircraft swiftly accelerated to 180 m.p.h. He
glanced to his left to see his wingman still firmly tucked in
formation only a few feet away. Sean carefully avoided not
pushing the throttles fully forward to maximum power so
leaving his wingman some spare in which to manoeuvre. At
about 190 m.p.h. he pulled the control stick back to initiate
a high rate of climb off the runway. Sean had carefully
briefed that numbers one and two would climb away steeply
so allowing three and four to stay low, thus avoiding the
dangers of flying into the massive turbulence caused by the
slipstream of the lead pair. On one occasion in the past Sean
remembered how he had hit the slipstream of the aircraft
ahead and only his quick reactions prevented his wing from
scraping the ground. The take-off phase is particularly
dangerous because the aircraft is at such a low speed that it
is very difficult to manoeuvre and control.

Once he knew they were all safely airborne Sean made a
quick radio transmission.

'Hazel Flight Channel 4 go.'

His GIB confirmed the channel change, 'Hazel check in.'

'Two, 'Three,' 'Four,' they quickly came back one after
the other.

'Pinetree, Hazel Flight just airborne and ready for splitting.'

29

Pinetree was the callsign of the ground radar station that would control the flight to ensure that interception between the pairs of aircraft would take place expeditiously and safely.

'OK, Hazel. One and two turn port onto 180 degrees and stay Channel 4. Three and Four turn starboard onto 260 degrees and go Channel 5.'

Sean now knew that control of his flight had now effectively passed to the ground controller. However, he also knew that he still remained in command of the situation and could change things if he wished. He had spoken to the controller on the phone before take-off and had briefed him carefully on his plans and was confident that the mission would succeed, all things being equal.

As he climbed up through the clear blue sky to 40,000 feet, his thoughts turned momentarily to the grandeur of the scene about him. Looking ahead he could see the first small cumulus clouds forming on the distant horizon which he thought must be Cuba. Looking at his radar scope he confirmed the appearance of that island showing as a bright fluorescent oblong at the top of the radar scope some 200 miles distant. To the east he could see the Atlantic coast of Florida shimmering in the reflected light of the low sun, with sandy beaches flecked with the white of huge ocean waves that were always pounding on that coast. To the west nothing but the blue sea of the Gulf of Mexico, beyond which he knew were semi-desert lands of the Mexican Plateau. He could not ponder for too long as combat was not far away.

'Check oxygen,' he shouted to his GIB over the intercom, at the same time checking the oxygen connector tubes and noting the flow indicator flashing on and off as he breathed.

'Oxygen check OK, sir,' came the reply.

'No need for the "sir" up here,' Sean retorted, reminding the junior pilot that unnecessary words in the air were just a hindrance. In any case there would be enough chatter over the radio once battle commenced.

As he levelled out at 45,000 feet Sean was instructed to

turn back through 160 degrees onto a northerly heading. He glanced over his shoulder and saw his number two comfortably spaced to give rear view cover in case of a sneak attack from behind.

Hazel Three gave a radio call to Sean indicating that all four aircraft were now on the same frequency, thus ensuring that all could speak to one another in case of an emergency or mishap.

Concentrating on his radar scope Sean looked for the tell-tale blips of his approaching foe. He knew they were separated virtually by a few thousand feet for safety reasons. Such a separation was essential since the aircraft were closing at about a mile every three seconds and collision avoidance by visual detection was extremely difficult.

Suddenly his GIB said, 'Contact, range 60 miles dead ahead slightly low.'

'Roger,' said Sean, switching his Sparrow missile switch on and accelerating to supersonic flight.

As the range decreased so the single large blip on his scope became two distinct, albeit smaller, ones. He decided to simulate firing two Sparrows off at maximum range followed by a further two when at optimum range as shown by the expanding Aim circle on his gunsight. Just as he completed this sequence he saw their two grey shapes passing below and just to one side at high speed. Instantaneously he pulled up hard and with full afterburner, knowing that his wingman could keep up with him by turning inside him and cutting the corner.

'Contact, left nine o'clock,' he stated over the radio so that his number two knew what was going on.

He turned hard left, rolled over and dived down onto the opposition. As he did so he felt a sudden sharp pain in the back of his neck at the same time as his G suit inflated with the force of some 6G (six times the forces of gravity). He knew immediately what had happened. His head had become so heavy that one of his neck muscles had stretched to near breaking with the sudden movement. He knew from past experience that the resultant crick in his neck would be painful for several days. No time to think of that now as he forcefully contracted his stomach muscles to prevent the blood flowing down from his head. With the help of his G suit and this sheer physical effort, he was able to prevent any blacking out and unconsciousness.

'OK in the back?' he yelled, not really expecting an answer, as the noise and buffeting of the airframe increased with speed.

He noted mach one point five on his machmeter dial, indicating one and a half times the speed of sound. Looking in his rear-view mirror just above his head he noted his wingman grimly hanging on, almost in line astern. Sean knew the difficulties he must be having at this time trying just to stay with his leader. Straining his eyes into the strong sunlight he caught sight of his opponents some five miles ahead, still keeping on a straight course. 'Good,' he thought, 'they haven't seen us.' As he positioned himself line astern he switched on the Sidewinder missile system.

The Sidewinder was used in fairly close-in situations. He was still out of range but soon a growling noise would be heard through his radio headset indicating a lock-on of the missile. Sean realized that the pair in front had obviously not made radar contact with them on that first pass and they would now be looking for them visually. He would be lucky if they were not soon spotted. Sure enough the number three suddenly broke into a hard left turn.

'Damn, they've seen us,' he shouted. 'Little chance now of a Sidewinder attack. Never mind, try to keep behind, throttle back, airbrakes out, decelerate hard, mustn't get ahead of them, pull up high, keep above, retain the potential energy of height equivalent to speed.'

He found himself talking on the intercom and giving instruction to his back seater who would need to learn from this experience. He turned hard to the left, following his adversaries, noting that the number four had tucked himself close to the inside of his leader. Without warning number three went into full afterburner and pulled up into a tight rolling turn in the opposite direction. Now inverted, the opposing pair were trying to get up behind, but Sean knew this old trick. He followed suit, trying at all times to keep the other pair in sight. He saw that his speed was dropping off alarmingly but he was still overtaking, now down to only 2,000 yards behind. They were inverted in a zero G situation and for a moment he didn't know whether he was upside down or the right way up. There was little horizon to speak of, the blue of the sky merging with that of the sea. What a strange sensation. Thank goodness, there they were as he saw two large aircraft just below him. 'Careful now,' he said to himself as he felt the control stick very floppy with the airspeed now down to 180 just near to stalling. 'Must use my rudder for manoeuvrering, otherwise I am likely to spin out of control.' He switched his gunsight to 'guns mode' and although no external gun was fitted on this occasion, at least he could practise its use in a close combat situation.

He was desperately trying to keep behind the other two by turning as tightly as he could, but with less airspeed. He could just keep control by flying from side to side of his opponent's flight path, in a sort of 'scissors' movement. This was dangerous as there were now four aircraft crossing above and beneath one another at close to stalling speed with limited control and manoeuvrability. The wingmen who had even less safety margin to play with, were in a very difficult situation as the combat progressed. Up till now there had been few radio calls, but Sean knew that intercockpit chatter was at a maximum as the students were given instruction.

A frantic call from number two split the airwaves.

'Hazel two, out of control.'

Immediately Sean realized he had taken it too far.

'Hazel Flight, call it off. Hazel two, keep the stick forward and use tail chute if necessary,' he shouted.

'Hazel two, OK, now recovering.'

Sean scanned the airspace below and saw his wingman just to the right and in level flight. Thank goodness he thought, he didn't have to use the tail chute to recover, so there would be no in-depth enquiry. He could imagine just how it happened. He himself had got into the same situation during his conversion onto the Phantom. At low speed any over exuberance on the use of controls would put you into the first stages of a spin – it was so easy. The first signs were heavy buffeting and then, if not corrected, a sudden flick over and inverted. The nose would either go down into a normal spin, easy to recover from; or the nose would stay up leading to an inverted spin and real trouble.

So the four aircraft recovered to straight and level flight and Sean called 'Pinetree' who had remained silent throughout this time but were following the manoeuvering aircraft on their radar scopes.

'Pinetree ready for further split,' he called.

He knew with luck there was time enough for another three further encounters. He noted on his knee-pad points and lessons to be learnt from the mission so far – all useful for the debriefing.

And so the mission continued and three more encounters were completed, each different and each one having their own lessons. The debriefing would be important and the arguments and discussions that ensued would help to build up confidence and experience, not only for the students but for the instructors as well.

As he led the four aircraft back to base, Sean reflected on how well the mission had fared. 'Luckily,' he thought to himself, 'number two hadn't had to use the tail chute for the spin recovery.' This was in reality a 'last ditch' method for recovery where the chute normally ensures that the aircraft's nose is pitched downwards so that airspeed builds up and control is re-established. As they flew in across Tampa Bay in close formation any observer on the ground could see the typical smoke trails from each of the eight General Electric engines wafting out behind. All four aircraft broke formation at spaced intervals into the circuit and landed uneventfully.

As he climbed out of the cockpit, Sean realized he was soaked in sweat and had probably lost four or five pounds in weight. Never mind, he would soon make that up. He signed off the aircraft with no defects and walked back to the squadron. It was hot, probably 80 degrees Fahrenheit and the sun was beating down fiercely and reflecting off the white hardstanding and white buildings and hangar. Thank goodness for air-conditioning he thought as he opened the door leading to the crew room. Would he have a hot coffee with its soothing powers of caffeine or a cold lemonade? He chose the latter, at the same time helping himself to a couple of salt tablets always available from a dispenser to replace the body salts lost through excessive perspiration. A few chocolate biscuits would also help to replace the energy expended on such a flight.

The debrief was fairly routine and much discussion ensured as to why number two spun out of control. Did the leader let matters go too far? No criticism was made of Sean but all knew from experience that a very frank discussion had to take place, otherwise the proper lessons would not be learnt. All of them knew also that pilots had to expect criticism as well as give it – they had to have broad shoulders!

Sean went off for a lunch break at the mess and on returning to the squadron operations room he looked at the big programme board showing the next day's schedules. Good, he saw that he was to lead a pair of aircraft with two students in the front seats onto the air-to-ground range for live firing of rockets, bombs and the gun. He also saw a prominent notice reminding all pilots of a presentation that evening by the McDonnell Douglas chief test pilot, Jack Spiers, to be held in the huge wing briefing room. It was to be an important briefing about the problems of the Phantom hydraulic control system. Sean was pleased, at last something was being done to solve the problem. Phantom squadrons throughout the Air Force had been losing aircraft due to failures of the hydraulic system that powered the aircraft's controls. At the speed at which the aircraft flew the forces on the external control surfaces were so large that no direct manual system could cope. A powerful hydraulic operated system was therefore necessary to move the controls. If this system failed then, because there could be no manual back up, the aircraft would crash.

A buzz of excited anticipation could be felt in the main briefing room as it filled up with aircrew just before 7.00 p.m. Several hundred students and instructors awaited the arrival of Jack Spiers, a well-known figure in the world of aviation. He strode up to the platform in his white McDonnell Douglas flight suit, his tall frame and craggy sunburnt face epitomized the special breed of men who test flew some of the fastest and most spectacular jet aircraft in the world. He looked all of his 45 years of age, with wisps of grey hair showing on the side of his head.

'Thank you for coming to listen to me.'

His southern drawl was prominent but his presence and authoritative projection carried across to his audience immediately. Sean felt this was a man to be listened to.

'As you all know, we have a problem with the control system . . .'

He went on to describe the system with visual aids and to explain what the company was doing to fix it. He explained how all the aircraft were being modified and that within six months or so there would be no more incidents of failure. The briefing was over in just over 45 minutes and Sean was impressed with the manner in which it was given. All the aircrew were reassured and they now knew fact from rumour and could look forward to a future when the problem no longer existed. But Sean clearly remembered Jack Spiers' parting words.

'Don't forget,' he said, 'until the fix is complete on all aircraft, one or more of you will undoubtedly experience a double power control failure in the next few months. Remember, if the stick makes an uncontrolled movement, then check the hydraulic warning lights. They will almost certainly be on, indicating a total system failure. The stick will either go fully forward with the aircraft hurtling earthwards, so get out quickly if at low level, or it will come back into your stomach and you will be looking at the sky, leaving you a little time to think and perhaps get temporary control of the aircraft with rudders and throttles. But whatever happens, you will never be able to fly the aircraft back to base and ejection is inevitable. Best of luck to you all.'

There were a number of questions dealing with technicalities, but as they all filed out of the room they all knew the problem was with them for a while longer. Sean could almost hear each of them saying to themselves, 'But it won't happen to me, it will be the other guy.'

The next morning Sean made his way down to the squadron to prepare his brief for a 9.30 take-off. Cloudless yet again. 'How I could have done with this sort of weather back in England when I was learning to fly,' he thought to himself, remembering the long delays between flights caused by low cloud, rain and fog.

On this occasion his student was an experienced major who had flown many types of aircraft and was refreshing on the Phantom after a ground tour doing staff work. 'Not much to worry about here,' Sean thought, 'but on reflection maybe I can teach him one or two things he didn't know before.' The briefing was again very thorough, covering in detail the four ground attack manoeuvres they would be undertaking: rocketing, dive bombing, skip bombing and straffing.

'See you on the intercom,' Sean yelled to the major over the deafening high-pitched scream of the mobile generators which the crew chief had switched on to energize the aircraft's systems before engine start. 'Make sure the rocket pods are all safely connected,' he added as he climbed up the ladder to the back seat.

Sean was content to let the student do all the outside checks. Although he himself was captain of the aircraft, as an instructor he had to show his confidence in his student and allow him to carry out the external safety checks. This was standard practice after the students had been through the initial conversion phase of the course.

Just before settling himself as comfortably as possible into the hard padding of the ejection seat, he did a thorough safety check on the parachute connecting lines and other important linkages. He remembered those parting words of the company's test pilot and thought to himself, 'You never know. I may have to use this seat for real today.' He strapped himself in tightly with the help of the ground crew, removed the seat safety pins out of the seat firing handles and commenced the alignment of the Inertial Navigation System.

The flight to Avon Park bombing range situated in the middle of Florida was uneventful.

'Avon range, this is Acorn Flight for rockets, dive, skip and strafe. Joining instructions.'

The major's voice was full of confidence and Sean had hardly touched the controls at all so far.

'Acorn, this is Avon. Clear to join. Right range left traffic. Altimeter One Zero Two One. Confirm.'

'OK, Acorn, acknowledge. Right range, left traffic. One Zero Two One.'

'Sean knew the range layout well, having acted as range safety officer for several short periods of duty lasting several days. As safety officer he directed the pilots while on range and was responsible for all the safety aspects. Particularly he had to warn pilots if they came too low on an attack or if they acted in a dangerous manner. Live weapons were involved and the range officer had wide powers and could send any offender back to base without question for any repeated violations of safety. The overall range layout was simple, with two separate identical ranges situated either side of a centrally placed range officer's building. Each range was complete with its own sets of targets for the various weapons used. There was a right range as the pilot saw it from the air and the traffic pattern for this was always to the left. Similarly, for the left range the flight pattern was to the right.

Often when on duty at the range and when flying was finished for the day, Sean remembered how he used to walk through the surrounding countryside. He marvelled at the abundant and varied wildlife. Three were large areas of coniferous woodland which was not dense but had the trees widely spaced apart. In between were numerous lakes and ponds and areas of swamp. He was amazed at the large number of alligators and wild boar, with the occasional snake which he could not identify but treated as poisonous. Huge spiders made intricate patterns of webs which hung from the branches and kept brushing into his hair. 'No,' he thought, 'no way would I want to eject over here and land amongst this lot, especially if I were injured.'

'Acorn, lead. In rockets, dry,' the major said over the radio as the aircraft arched over into a 30 degree dive at the small white triangle marking the rocketing target. He was at 2,000 feet above the ground 300 m.p.h. and now hurtling towards the ground at an ever increasing speed.

'Acorn, lead. Clear dry,' came back the immediate reply from the range officer who realized that the pilot's first pass was always going to be a practice one where live weapons were not fired, i.e. dry.

Sean had most of the instruments duplicated in the back seat, but his forward visibility was badly restricted by the front ejection seat and canopy rails. Experience had taught him how by glancing quickly to left and right and by peering straight ahead through a small gap between the seat and canopy he could judge the angle of dive and the speed at which the ground was approaching – very important for self-survival in this type of mission. He put his hand lightly on the stick ready to pull it back sharply if he considered the student was making an error of judgement. Occasionally he had come across a student, usually on one of his first ground attack missions, who would freeze on the controls, totally mesmerized by the approaching ground and by the white aiming dot in the gunsight. He had to act quickly on these occasions to prevent the aircraft from ploughing into the ground. That dilemma again: how far should an instructor let his student go in making a mistake before taking over himself? The student had to be allowed to make mistakes and even get a low warning from the range officer – always certain to get his attention as a lot of pride was lost, especially if you got sent home, the ultimate disgrace. No problem here though, as the major started the recovery at just the right height above ground.

'Switches safe,' he said to Sean, indicating that all the firing switches were safe – no chance now of an inadvertent salvo of rockets being fired across the range when the aircraft was not pointing towards the targets.

Sean acknowledged, at the same time tensing his stomach muscles as the G forces built up. The aircraft was now in a hard pull up to gain altitude back to the range circuit height.

'Check fuel and position of number two,' Sean said, reminding his student that fuel checks should be made on every pass and that he should know at all times where his other aircraft was. This was particularly important when on future sorties there would be up to four aircraft in the range circuit at any one time.

'OK, ten thousand pounds of fuel. Number two just turning finals now,' the major replied.

Around the pattern again and onto finals, this time for a hot or live pass.

'Acorn, lead finals hot rockets.'

'Acorn, lead clear hot,' came back the reply,

'Switches on,' the major told Sean. The aircraft once again turned down range and then rolled out straight in a 30 degree dive. 'Switches on,' shouted the major to Sean and a few seconds later, 'Pickling now' as he pressed the firing button.

Sean heard the hiss as a rocket left the tube and he could see the trail of white smoke as it sped earthwards towards the target. For a second or two the aircraft continued its plunge earthwards. Sean spoke sharply to his student.

'Don't try and see it hit or you will surely follow suit.'

Sean knew that with experienced pilots there was a tendency to delay the pull up just to see how close the missile is on target. This was bad practice and the pull up should be started as soon as the rocket is fired. In a real war situation you were probably being fired at by the enemy and if the rocket blows up an ammunition dump, the explosion would send pieces high into the air. Much better to pull up and get away sharply. The major reacted immediately and the G forces built up again as the aircraft rotated skywards. Sean made a note on his pad for the debrief.

'Acorn, lead. Forty at four o'clock,' came the range officer's voice, telling the major that the rocket had missed by 40 yards and to the right.

The same pattern was then repeated a third time, this time with a score of ten yards at one o'clock.

Everything was going well on the fourth and final rocket pass. The aircraft was hurtling towards the ground.

'Switches on,' and a few seconds later, 'Pickling now.'

And then it happened.

3

Ejecting, Ejecting

The aircraft was plunging earthwards and at about 800 feet above the ground the major was about to fire off his last rocket. Suddenly the control stick motored back in one continuous movement uncommanded by the student, not slowly but not rapidly either; just fast enough to rotate the aircraft from a nose down attitude to nose up with an ever increasing high G load on the pilot. Sean in the back seat instinctively tried to push the stick forward, but he knew at once he was fighting against massive forces and it was impossible to shift it from the fully back position. He sensed immediately what had happened – a complete power control failure and an uncontrollable aircraft, just as Jack Spiers had briefed a few days before.

Sean quickly assessed the situation. The Phantom was now almost vertical and in danger of becoming inverted. Their altitude was about 900 feet above the ground. If they ejected with the aircraft upside down, the seat would almost certainly hit the ground before the parachute was fully deployed and they would be killed. A quick decision was vital. The major had come to the same conclusion.

'Out of control both hydraulic lights on. Ejecting, ejecting,' he shouted.

'Maidez, maidez, ejecting,' Sean shouted with his thumb on the transmit button alerting the range controller and his number two of his plight.

He knew he had to wait for the front seater to eject before pulling his ejection handle as otherwise if they both left simultaneously there was a chance that they would collide in mid-air. A powerful force of wind and dust debris hit him as the front canopy lifted off. A loud bang and a flash confirmed that the major had ejected. Sean immediately grabbed the yellow and black handle and pulled, keeping his head back and his back as straight as possible.

He remembered little except the blast of air and then unconsciousness. He awoke in a dazed state believing himself suspended in a parachute harness from the ceiling of a gymnasium, just as he had practised in training. In reality he was over the wilderness of central Florida. As consciousness returned, Sean began to remember what had happened. He looked down and saw trees, ponds and swamp coming up fast. He noticed that his flight suit was covered in blood and that his chin felt very sore. Alligators and snakes flashed through his mind, but there was no time to think or reflect on his perilous situation.

'Where was his student?' he wondered and hoped he hadn't come down into the fireball of the burning wreckage which he could see just below and to one side of him. Sean braced himself for the inevitable shock of landing, trying to adopt a proper parachute landing position as he had been taught those many years ago in training. He crashed through some low scrub, just missing some tall pine trees, finishing up in some soft swampy ground. He became unconscious again. He awoke in a daze feeling blood trickling down his chin and neck. He felt all over his body with his hands. No broken bones; only pain in his back, a sore chin and a lacerated tongue which hurt like hell. He had no idea how long he had been lying in the damp ground, the canopy of his red and white striped parachute draped around the surrounding bushes. Except for the distant crackling of fire, which he knew was his aircraft burning there was complete silence. He had landed in a swampy clearing surrounded by pine trees, from which long trails of Spanish moss shone white in the strong sunlight.

As he regained his strength and his senses sharpened he decided on action. No alligators, no snakes and Sean was relieved. He inflated his dinghy and retrieved the portable radio and smoke flares from his life jacket. Soon he heard the rhythmic pulsating notes of a helicopter in the distance. 'Good, they are looking for us,' he thought. He switched on his portable radio with its built-in location beacon which sent out signals that would be picked up by those in the rescue helicopter. At the same time he set off a smoke flare and was relieved to see the thick red smoke billowing skywards. Soon he would be out of all this. Sean tried to get up and walk but he felt a sharp pain at the base of his spine. 'Better not try to move too much. Might do more damage to my back.' He felt he should be looking for his student but knew that any such action would only complicate matters for his rescuers. Better to stay where he was in one place and rely on his location aids.

As he waited, he desperately hoped that no harm had come to the major. What a thing to happen so soon in his assignment with the USAF. Still at least it wasn't pilot error. The cause would soon be established when they found the vital pieces of evidence from the power control system. The noise of the helicopter got louder and soon it was overhead, the crewman looking out at him from the open side door. Sean knew it couldn't land where he was because there just wasn't enough room between the towering trees, and the ground was too soft to take the weight of the machine. He could hear rather than see it descend some distance away. Very soon a loud rustling noise through the bushes signalled the arrival of two men carrying a stretcher. A black sergeant spoke first.

'You'll soon be OK, sir. Are you hurt in any way? Can you move?'

'Just a sore back and chin,' Sean replied, making light of his injuries which in fact he suspected would be somewhat more serious. His thoughts suddenly switched to the social problems in America with the inner-city race riots and Martin Luther King's efforts to gain equality for the blacks. Here he was being rescued by one of those oppressed. Thank goodness there were few problems and no discrimination within the US military. Sean thought it would be hard for him to come to terms with such a situation. He thought of Northern Ireland and the problems that were brewing there because of discrimination and bigotry between two different religions. Why can't people settle their differences and learn to love and respect each other rather than ferment hatred and disharmony? We are all human beings sharing the same ultimate destiny on the same planet. Sean looked at this burly sergeant and knew he was just another of those warm friendly blacks whom he knew to be fine people with a good sense of humour and who had great loyalty for their Service and their country. He tried to get up but found it painful and the sergeant spoke to him firmly but gently.

'Don't move, sir, we will soon lift you onto the stretcher and carry you to the chopper. It's only a short distance away.'

'OK,' Sean replied, quite content to put himself in the hands of such competent professionals.

He was carried through the undergrowth with the sergeant shouting words of encouragement. Sean kept his hands clenched and squeezed hard to counter the pain in his back every time there was sharp movement of the stretcher up or down. He managed to keep silent because he knew the two were doing their best not to jostle him about too much. His mouth kept filling with blood from a lacerated tongue and his chin dripped blood all over his front. 'What a sight I must look,' he thought to himself. His tongue was really painful and he guessed a tooth had bitten into it during the ejection sequence or when he crashed through the bushes on landing. Never mind, from similar injuries he had received in boxing and rugby over the years he knew it would soon heal, given time. His back worried him more. A sharp pain in the lumbar region at the base made itself felt every time he moved, but he reassured himself by the fact that there was no paralysis or loss of leg movement anywhere. He knew that most ejection injuries were caused by the force of gravity (some 60 times) imposed on the body at the instant the seat cartridges fired. These propel the seat upwards with sufficient and necessary force to clear the aircraft's tail during high speed flight. The back injuries consist usually of crushed vertebra which heal up well with time. But he knew he was unlikely to fly again for three months or so.

After about ten minutes of rough going they came upon some more open woodlands and then a large clearing appeared. There was the rescue helicopter, its engines just ticking over with the rotor blades making a dull swishing noise as they rotated slowly in the humid air. Sean raised his head slightly and was relieved to see the major at the door smiling broadly and giving him a big thumbs up sign. 'Thank goodness he looks absolutely fine with no signs of injury. What a relief'. He felt himself relax, but his sense of responsibility soon surfaced and he thought of what might have happened. Had he carried out the correct actions? Could he have done anything better? Never mind, one aircraft destroyed but no serious injuries he hoped.

Sean was raised up gently onto the floor of the helicopter and as soon as he was secured safely he heard the increase in tempo of the engines, the fuselage vibrating and then lift off with a 'chop, chop, chop' noise of blades and a sound of roaring and whining as the main and tail rotors went to maximum power.

The major sat beside his outstretched instructor and said, 'Glad to see you, hope there's nothing serious.'

Sean, not wishing to comment said, 'How the hell are you, major?'

'Fine, no pain, no injuries but I was lucky. When I looked down from my parachute I saw the burning wreckage of the aircraft below. I was heading straight into it and only a few hundred feet above I pulled down on the rigging lines and just drifted to one side and past it. I could feel the heat from the flames.'

The major's face again split into a broad grin and Sean could see how relieved and happy he was.

The chopper's flight was smooth and after only about 30

minutes they landed at the helipad at the huge complex of MacDill Air Force Base Hospital.

The major walked beside Sean as he was carried up to the casualty ward. The characteristic antiseptic smell of hospitals was usually anathema to Sean. But this time, as an injured patient and not as a visitor, was different and he welcomed its embrace and its haven of cleanliness and efficiency. The major was shown to a side room off the main ward and Sean was wheeled away into a separate room some distance away. He knew they were being kept apart deliberately. This was the normal procedure to avoid any collusion or concocted story being made up.

As Sean lay flat on his back on the bed he wondered what would happen next. Had his parents back in England been informed of the accident? Would they have been told that he was basically well and only slightly injured? He didn't want them to learn about the crash from a Reuters report in a daily paper. He didn't have time to think for long about these matters as almost immediately Dr John Tucker, the squadron's flight surgeon, walked in.

'Well, that must have been a pretty hairy flight,' he said as he bent down to examine Sean's bruised and battered chin.

Sean acknowledged with a broad grin, glad to see a friendly face.

'Yes, I wouldn't like to do that again too often. Mind you, at least we know what caused the accident,' he added, trying to reassure himself that the inevitable enquiry would not last long.

God, he could do with a cup of tea and some biscuits. Don't these Americans ever put the kettle on?

Careful not to comment on the accident itself, the doctor noted the difficulty he was having with his speech and asked Sean to open his mouth wide.

Noting the deeply cut tongue he said, 'I'll just patch the chin up with stitches and then we will get you off to have your back X-rayed.'

With efficiency, speed and professionalism, the doctor

proceeded to give Sean a local injection in his chin, effectively anaesthetizing it.

As he used his circular needle to put in the stitches he said, 'That will soon heal but there is nothing I can do for the tongue. It will take a month or so before you recover its full use again and it will be sore.'

As he was wheeled down the long white corridors and onto the X-ray machine, Sean wondered whether there were any serious problems with his back. He knew that back injuries caused by ejection were common. They were caused by the seat cartridges firing and 'shooting' the pilot's seat skywards with enough force to clear the tail of the aircraft. The pilot's spinal column took a good deal of the shock and it was usual for compression fractures of the spinal vertebra to occur. These usually resulted in a sore back but eventually after several months they healed up with no long-term affect on mobility.

The X-ray machine whirred and clicked into action and soon Sean was back in his room, glad to be alone once more with his thoughts. It was an hour or since the accident and he felt hungry. He pressed the button beside the bedside table and soon he was enjoying steak, egg and chips, lots of tomato sauce and strong black coffee – just what he wanted.

A string of visitors came to wish him well. The squadron commander paid a more formal visit and reassured him that any problems, whatever they were, would soon be sorted out. He also told Sean that a unit inquiry had been convened and if he felt fit enough they would like to get a brief statement from him that evening. Sean welcomed the news and was eager to put his story in writing.

'The sooner we start the sooner it will be over,' he said to his boss.

A nurse came to the door with the portable phone and said that his mother was calling from England.

'Great,' Sean said, 'let me have it.'

He was surprised that she had heard so quickly and at the same time was relieved that he could give her facts rather than rumour. Thirty minutes later they were still talking.

Sean loved his mother and they got on well together. She, like him, had deep thoughts and had the intelligence to think out solutions to problems on her own, taking advice from others only when it suited her. His father was different altogether. A man who was difficult at times and prone to fits of depression and moodiness. Sean accepted this but never really had a close relationship with his father, who was often impersonal and uncaring, quite unlike his mother, who had a warm and generous nature. Sean often thought about the genes he must have inherited from them. 'Mostly good ones,' he mused. He put the phone down, glad to know that all was well at home. His mother had told him that one of his past girlfriends, Sarah, had seen a Reuters report in the evening papers about the crash and had phoned her asking for news. Sean made a mental note to drop her a line. He would like to see her again when he returned home in a year or so.

He had just got rid of the phone trolley when there she was at the door. Gayle looked dazzling in a blue linen sleeveless dress, hugging her figure and matching those eyes that Sean found so appealing and attractive. Her lightly tanned arms were bare and her shoulder-length hair was neatly rolled into a chignon. On her wrist she wore a chunky gold bracelet. Sean approved too of her perfume which wafted in through the door and which he recognized as Balmain's *Vent Vert.*

'Heard you had been in trouble,' she said with characteristic understatement. 'I had to come along to see how you were.'

'Oh, I'm OK. Had to jump out quickly after the controls failed. Something hit me on the way out and damaged my face. Hope you still like it?'

He grinned and realized he hadn't really meant to say those last words. Here he was lying in a hospital bed and looking up at someone he found very attractive physically and yet holding back on his emotions and inner feelings. What was this love that he was searching for? Will he ever find it? No he must not get involved – yet.

49

'You look fine to me,' she said, adding, 'you'll soon be out of here and back flying.'

'Yes,' he said 'but not for several months,' knowing that with back injuries, a three month ban on flying was automatic. 'Anyway,' he said, 'I will have a lot of spare time to see your vast and lovely country from ground level.'

Just at that moment a medical orderly came in and told Sean that the investigating team had arrived to take a statement. Gayle hesitated, knowing she had to go but not wanting to.

'OK, I'll go now. Take care, Sean.'

'See you soon and I'll take you out for that dinner we haven't had yet.'

Their eyes met and Sean felt that the relationship could so easily get out of control. In the months to come he knew he would try again to seek the companionship he longed for. She left, her high heels echoing down the corridor.

Sean recognized the leader of the three-man investigation team, a tall tough looking Texan called Ivor Downey. He was an instructor pilot on a rival squadron. His face was rugged and well-tanned and his dark hair was receding from his forehead. Sean guessed he was in his mid forties. Sean knew he would be fair and considerate and he remembered his good sense of humour and infectious laugh from late sessions in the bar.

'Well,' he said, looking straight into Sean's eyes, 'this is a good way to start your career in our Air Force. I suppose Martin Baker are giving you commission on each of their ejection seats you use.' He laughed and Sean was glad the ice was broken so early in the investigation. Ivor went on, 'This won't take long, all we want from you is a statement of fact as to what really happened. Don't forget the purpose of the investigation is not to obtain evidence for use in disciplinary action but is to determine all the factors relating to the accident. This is in the interest of accident prevention to avert any recurrence.'

Sean nodded his approval and after about 40 minutes he

had completed his statement which was also recorded on tape.

'We'll have that typed up for you to sign in an hour or so and then we will leave you alone for a few days. But you realize we may have some questions to ask you once we have assembled all the facts.'

Ivor looked pleased that there were no complications or contradictions so far.

It was mid-morning next day when Ivor returned with a big smile on his face.

'Thought you would like to know that we have found and recovered the hydraulic actuator in the control system. It was cracked just like all the others in the past and caused your controls to fail. Just like Jack Spiers told us all the other day – remember?'

Remember? Sean could hardly forget how he, like many others there, thought that it would never happen to him, but always to the other guy.

'Well, thanks for the news. I am mightily relieved. I suppose I will be able to see my student now?'

His voice indicated a question.

'Sure you can. We will fix that up, but I think the doctors will soon be letting you out in any case.'

They went on to discuss pleasantries for a short while. Sean hadn't slept well and was beginning to feel tired. He was quite pleased when a hospital doctor and his flight surgeon came in. Ivor made his departure with a wave of his hand.

'We'll be in touch with you again soon and then we can clear up some of the minor points.'

'See you,' Sean replied and turned his attention to the doctor.

The hospital doctor, a middle-aged, greying and some-what overweight man, dressed in clinical white and wearing a pair of half-moon spectacles, spoke first.

'Well, young man. You will be glad to know that we will be letting you out of here tomorrow, just as soon as we have fixed you with a removable back brace to keep your back straight and ease the pressure off your spine when you are walking. You will find that the pain will soon go in a few days, but just be careful. Do not bend unnecessarily and do not lift anything under any circumstances. Later this morning our orthopaedic carpenter, that's what we call him, will measure you up for the brace and will fit it to you tomorrow.'

'Thanks for all that, Doctor' and turning to the flight surgeon, Sean asked, 'When will I be able to get airborne again?'

'Well, you know ... it all depends ...' he started in his thick southern drawl. But Sean, knowing how long-winded he could be, interrupted him and cut him short.

'Come on, Doc, don't confuse the issue. Will it be more than the statutory three months, yes or no?'

'Well, no ...' Again he hesitated but seeing the pain in Sean's expression he continued, 'You should be back in the air by November, assuming your back heals in the normal way.'

'Good,' said Sean, 'can't wait to get back. I guess I will just have to be patient. I'll probably spend a few weeks travelling around and seeing your beautiful country from ground level.'

'Yes, good idea,' said the doctor, 'and don't forget to make use of all our military bases. You can stay very cheaply in our Bachelor Officer Quarters at any army, navy, marine or air force base.'

The back brace was fitted as expected and Sean found it quite comfortable. With it strapped on he could not bend his back and this gave him reassurance that he could move about without the chance of doing more damage. The next day he was allowed out of hospital and returned to the familiar surroundings of his room in the mess. It was hot as usual and Sean decided to spend just a few days recuperating by the open-air swimming pool. He had many visitors and he enjoyed socializing and their friendly talk and banter. He had been down to the squadron and with some statutory sick leave and some of his annual leave entitlement he decided to absent himself from the base for about five weeks.

When he first arrived in America he had made a decision that he would visit some of the sights of the country, probably in the autumn when it was cooler and the beautiful colours of nature were at their best. It would not be so now in high summer, but at least he thought he could take his time about it and enjoy a slower pace of travel. Normally he could only take about two weeks off at a time.

He invited Gayle out to a seafood restaurant in Tampa and they talked about the places he should visit on his forthcoming tour of 'The States'. She half-hinted that she could take time off work and would like to join him. He didn't pursue her offer, for offer he knew it to be, and changed the subject, making it plain that he wanted to travel alone. He realized he would not be comfortable with her for such a length of time. He welcomed companionship but this had to be with someone who shared his ideas, his love of nature and could converse at his level and most importantly someone who had great warmth and feeling. Again he pondered over this question, as he had done so many times before. Did such a person exist?

The day for his journey to start arrived in mid-August. His cases were packed. 'Damn,' he thought, 'why do I have to go bang in the middle of the holiday period? Still I can always change my mind and I will still find places for solitude and quiet beauty. I can walk and do my own thing whatever that turns out to be.'

He planned to stay a few days in New Orleans and drive up to St Louis, the home of McDonnell Douglas, and then across to Denver in Colorado. Another drive westwards to the Colorado River and the Grand Canyon. If time permitted he might visit Los Angeles and San Francisco, but he knew he could fly out to those places at any time on a cross-country exercise in his Phantom.

His back had already ceased to trouble him and his chin had healed up well, leaving just a small scar. Only his lacerated tongue gave him occasional problems, especially when eating. It was sore then but he remembered the doctor's words when he said it might take months to heal properly. He would just have to put up with it and be patient.

He had some 500 road miles to cover to get to New Orleans and, being used to early starts, he set off just before dawn, planning to arrive at dusk. It was dark and the roads were empty. Sean made good progress through places like Tarpon Springs and Crystal river. What evocative names, stirring the imagination and making the mind wonder what went on there and what sort of people lived there? 'I must visit them some time just to see,' he thought to himself. Across the Swannee River made famous in the negro spirituals of Stephen Foster. How often in his youth had he hummed 'Way down upon the Swannee River . . .'

And on through the flat pine-covered lands of Southern Alabama, past the metal plaques by the roadside marking the sites of battles long ago against the Seminole and Creek Indians and those of the American Civil War. How the Americans like to show off their history. 'Quite right too,' Sean thought; after all American history is relatively recent compared with that of Europeans. If the English tried to copy the American practice, the countryside would be covered with plaques. Across the Mobile River and through Mobile itself where great battleships of the war in the Pacific lie as huge monuments of the death and destruction of that time.

He passed the large colonial houses of the rich, when cotton was king and the poor blacks suffered in slavery. How these white mansions contrasted even now with the rusty tin-roofed shacks placed on brick pilings of the present day poor blacks. Sean stopped at one such shack as he went through Mississippi state. Outside was a large battered Chevrolet. A black man in his early thirties, obviously unemployed, sat on the wooden step. On his head a multi-coloured baseball cap and in his hands a guitar which he was strumming with obvious pleasure, his white teeth contrasting with his deep black face. The scene was made complete with a pile of neatly sawn logs on the wooden verandah. The scene was repeated almost exactly many more times in the miles that followed. Those colonial mansions with their beautiful gardens and tall trees were never far away, giving that contrast of the very rich and the very poor. How was it that here in this vibrant and affluent country in the late 1960s could such disparity exist? Did the cause and solution exist within the system of education, employment, religion, or what? Sean concerned himself with the problem, turning it over and over in his mind but he could not resolve it satisfactory. He conversed with the young black man about nothing in particular and was surprised by his level of knowledge and his obvious friendliness.

The sun was setting behind blue-grey clouds and the sky was coloured with shades of orange and yellow. As he passed through the seaside towns of Biloxi and Gulfport he knew his destination was only a few miles ahead. He booked into a motel and decided to rest before setting out to explore New Orleans the next day. It had been a long drive and he was weary.

The next day huge billowing white clouds of immense height heralded rain. The base of these clouds were deep black and their tops were anvil-shaped wisps of white set against the bright blue sky. Distant thunder could be heard and Sean wondered whether he should proceed into New Orleans itself. He was well-equipped with waterproofs, so why not, he said to himself. He walked through the streets of the city listening to the uplifting beat of traditional jazz being played by small bands in various cafés in the main streets and in the back alleys. He didn't care for the narrow streets overlooked by balustrades and iron railings. He felt claustrophobic and as torrential rain fell onto the dark streets, streams of water tumbled down off overflowing gutters and roofs. He made his way across an open square and took shelter in St Louis Cathedral built in 1794. Soon the sun came out and he paused for a while in a small park surrounded by purple bougainvillaea and aged palm trees with their thick trunks and fronds sprayed out at the top and swaying in the wind. He looked and wondered at the weathered green statue of Andrew Jackson, the seventh president of the USA, seated on a rearing horse that blended in well with the tranquillity and mellow colours of its surroundings. Andrew Jackson, he discovered, was a property developer and a large slave owner who in 1802 was elected Major-General of the Tennessee Militia. In 1814 he won national acclaim by defeating and destroying the Creek Indians at the battle of Horsehoe Bend in Alabama. In 1815 he went on to defeat the British themselves at the Battle of New Orleans. Hence his monument in the city.

Sean was always fascinated by history, but he found that the politics of the past was often too complex to understand and remember. He spent a few days in New Orleans and took a nostalgic and interesting journey up the Mississippi River in one of the relics of the past, an old paddle steamer.

And so on to Denver via Memphis, where he crossed the wide Mississippi; and St Louis the home of McDonnell Douglas. Denver was situated at the edge of the great mountains of Colorado, where Mount Elbert and Longs Peak topped 14,000 feet. This was also gold country where in the last century the mining of gold and gold prospecting made fortunes for many. On the other hand, many lost fortunes and their lives in gambling and the lawlessness of those times. Still dotted about were gold mines being prospected by hopeful old men, their piles of rusty tins outside wooden huts, indicating their poverty and eccentric lifestyle. Sean tried hiking up through the hills but the going was rough, the heat reflected off the bare rocks was intense and the distances seemed vast. He knew he had to be careful with his back and he decided that this was not the place to seek the solitude he yearned for.

He stayed in the recently built USAF Academy at Colorado Springs with its vast expanse of glass in the buildings and its magnificent multi-triangular-shaped chapel where many religions were worshipped under the same roof.

Wherever he went Sean found the friendship and warmth of the American people overwhelming. He found companionship with the pilots at the bases where he stayed and he was always sorry to say goodbye when he left, but he knew he had to press on with his journey.

Next stop after Denver was 400 miles away, across the mountains to the Grand Canyon National park and the Colorado River. Sean was always fascinated by the natural wonders of the world and he had seen many of them, from the Victoria Falls in Africa to the great glaciers of ice in Greenland and Baffin Island. However, the Grand Canyon exceeded all his expectations and he was amazed at the sight of it. Six miles wide in places and 6,000 feet deep, it had a unique power and majesty. During his exploration of some 200 of its nearly 300 mile length, he was able to just touch the surface of some of its unique and wonderful wildlife and botanic treasures.

The deep croaking of a pair of ravens echoed across the canyon walls and he was exhilarated to see them harass a lone red-tailed hawk as it twisted and turned to escape their attacks. He came across a tarantula climbing a vertical wall, its fat furry body seemingly oblivious to the scorching heat. He knew it was looking for beetles which it would kill with its venomous bite. As it bit, the spider would inject into its prey a dissolving fluid and would then suck up the resulting 'beetle broth'. How cruel is the world of nature, he thought. In places, particularly inaccessible to man, he could see through his powerful binoculars rock faces where permanent waterfalls provided an oasis of tropical and near tropical beauty. Hidden away here existed a micro-climate where exotic butterflies, humming birds and beautiful flowers lived and blossomed, seemingly forever. A six inch chuckwallah, that lizard-like creature whose ancestors saw the extinction of the dinosaurs, scuttled across the baking rocks. Sean soon found himself crossing the Little Colorado River and marvelled at its turquoise colour which it acquired from minerals scoured from the soil. This liquid turquoise was swept down deep gorges by floods and then was mixed with the brown of the main Colorado River.

Then on to Lake Mead, 110 miles long of blue water set

incongruously amidst the yellow brown Arizona Dessert. At its southern end Sean viewed with amazement the huge Hoover Dam, 700 feet high with its associated power lines draped over the surrounding landscape. Spill races at its base had been opened and huge jets of water spewed out to keep a good flow of water in the lower Colorado.

Las Vegas, nearby, was a spectacle he was quite happy to leave behind as he made his way across the desert to Salt Lake City, the home of the Mormon religion. On his way he visited the Valley of Fire, a large area of red sandstone which appeared like molten fire in the setting sun; nearby were petrified trees as hard as granite and thousands of years old and prehistoric inscriptions carved on the rock faces.

Sean decided not to visit Los Angeles or San Francisco. He was happy that he had seen many of the places he had set out to see and now he was glad to be on his way home via the mid-western states of Kentucky and Georgia.

He had been away just two weeks and he was pleased to be back in the familiar surroundings of the base and his room in the mess. He knew he had another two months before he could get back into the air again. He was given the job of Squadron Flight Safety Officer which meant looking into every aspect of flying with the objective of preventing accidents before they happened. He enjoyed the challenge and spent a good deal of time writing reports and investigating accidents to see if and how they could have been prevented. The weeks went by and Sean was getting restless. He needed to be back in the cockpit and to feel the rush of adrenaline and excitement of fast flight and danger. It was early November before the doctors gave him the all-clear to fly. His squadron commander, who had given him so much support and encouragement over the past three months, called him into his office.

'Well, Sean,' he said, 'the time has come for you to get airborne again. How about a three day cross-country to

California? Just about time enough for you to get the feel of the controls and get up to speed again.'

He leaned back in his chair and put his hands behind his head. Sean felt his eyes boring into him and, surprisingly, he felt a little uneasy in his presence. He knew him to be a kind and considerate officer who seldom lost his temper, but who at the same time expected his subordinates to match up to his own high standards of discipline and integrity.

Sean was about to reply when his commander suddenly leaned forward and said, 'Do you think that will be long enough for you to get your confidence back and be instructing again on your return?'

Sean, surprised that his superior would suggest that he had lost confidence replied quickly, 'I have never lost confidence, sir, and am very pleased and happy to fly off to the West Coast for three days or so. I feel sure that I will be fully fit and ready to take up my instructing duties on my return.'

'Good, fix up the details with the operations officer and have a good trip. See you when you get back.'

And that was it. He and another fairly experienced instructor set off the next day to fly over many of the scenes that he had just visited a month or so before on the ground. They flew across the USA, much of it at low level a few hundred feet above the ground where the country was sparsely inhabited, like the deserts of New Mexico, Utah and Arizona. Sean was exhilarated to see again the Grand Canyon, Lake Mead and the Valley of Fire. With this very different perspective, what evocative memories this close encounter brought back.

These three days of pure pleasure flying brought home to Sean what he had missed. Although his back was somewhat sore after each flight, he knew he could cope with any sortie in the flying syllabus, however demanding. What's more, he had proved to himself that he had not lost confidence in flying the Phantom.

So by December he was well back in the swing of instructing again. Ground attack with bombs, rockets and guns, air combat, air-to-air refuelling, instrument flying, cross-country flights; all these and much more made Sean a happy man again. The months went by quickly and he enjoyed his way of life with the Americans.

It was October the following year and a new course of students arrived to start their conversion onto the Phantom. Sean was given a young recently promoted captain, Bill Sheppard, who was previously a back-seater and was now upgraded to the front seat as pilot in command. He had just completed a tour flying and fighting in Vietnam and his experience proved invaluable to his fellow students, many of whom were new to the fast jet world. Sean liked this short, stocky and swarthy young man who had such a good sense of humour. His only drawback to Sean's mind was that he sometimes got over-excited, and swore profusely whenever things went wrong and he felt he could do better. Nevertheless, he had courage and a determination to succeed at all costs and he was easy to teach. He sailed through the initial conversion phase and was soon onto the more demanding close formation and formation take-offs.

It was on his first formation take-off that it happened. The day was cloudy, but hot and humid with just a hint of bad weather with dark lowering clouds out to the west. Sean had carefully briefed a two 'ship' aerobatic sortie which included a take-off in close formation. In the back seat behind Bill Sheppard he followed his student diligently as he completed all the checks of fuel, instruments, engine temperature and the many items necessary before the take-off commenced. The pair of Phantoms lined up either side of the runway with Sheppard's aircraft on the left-hand side in the number two position.

'Clear take-off,' the crisp clear voice of the controller came through over the radio.

The leader's head nodded forward and they were off. Sean felt the throttles go forward as he rested his hand gently on the duplicated pair of throttles in the back cockpit, ready to take over control if anything went wrong. He knew that take-off in formation was sometimes exciting with new students and he needed to be fully alert as they accelerated down the runway. He could see the jet nozzles of the lead aircraft closing as the power increased and hot air surged through the engine. The noise, even in the enclosed cockpit and under a cloth inner helmet and bone dome, was deafening. Suddenly the nozzles opened wide, a huge white-hot flame appeared with diamond-shaped shock waves in its midst. Instantaneously, a powerful roaring whine alerted Sean to the lighting up of the leader's afterburner. One hundred and eighty m.p.h. showed on the air speed indicator as they were lifting off the ground. So far Sheppard had done well – no need for any help from Sean, yet!

They were both now airborne and the wheels were being retracted. Sheppard had edged in a little too close for comfort, not allowing wing tip clearance between aircraft – dangerous, for if there was a sudden loss of power by the leader the number two would inevitably collide.

'Too close,' shouted Sean, but Sheppard had seen the danger and had moved the control stick to the left, so making the aircraft move out.

Two hundred feet off the ground and 280 m.p.h., Sean felt himself relax. His mental facilities and nerves had been at full stretch during the take-off, a chance to ease the concentration of mind and body. Nobody could keep up that intense pressure for long. Sean knew the next critical stage was coming out of afterburner at about 350 m.p.h. at 1,000 feet above the ground and as the leader shut off his burners, Sheppard allowed the aircraft to leap ahead, not anticipating enough the sudden reduction in power. Luckily, he had wing tip clearance and he soon recovered the situation by pulling the throttles back sharply.

'Steady there,' shouted Sean momentarily caught out by the sudden change of position brought about by his student's inexperience. 'Ease the throttles back slowly, don't make any sharp and sudden movements when in close formation unless safety is at stake.'

'OK,' Sheppard shouted back as the aircraft moved back into position.

He pushed the throttles forward again to maintain position, but there was no response, no response whatsoever as the aircraft slipped back and back. Sean had felt the throttles move forward and when there was no corresponding surge of power he knew immediately that they were in dire trouble.

'Both generator warning lights on,' shouted Sheppard. 'Hell, both engines have quit,' he added in an agonized voice.

'Hit the relight button,' yelled back Sean, trying desperately to remain calm in a situation rapidly getting out of control.

'I have,' came back the swift reply.

Sean pressed the transmit button.

'Maidez, Maidez . . .'

He shouted out the international and universal distress call, but stopped abruptly when he realized the radio was dead with both generators not working and producing no electrical power. 'No time to turn on the standby battery radio,' he thought. He hoped the situation could still be saved if the engines relit, but he knew that was a forlorn hope. Their speed was down to 200 m.p.h. and they were dropping fast to the sea below.

Sean's mind raced into overdrive. He had to think fast and make decisions quickly. A glance at the altimeter and he saw his height was now 600 feet. Only seconds left before they hit. He knew that even if the engines relit now it would take at least twenty seconds for them to wind up to full power. With horror he also noticed some yachts sailing on the sea below. He kicked the rudder to turn the nose away from the boats. Still no power and 400 feet . . .

'Ejecting, ejecting,' he shouted to his student, knowing that Sheppard would not delay once he heard him go.

Again that wind and noise and dust as the canopy blew off, the loud bang and sharp pain in his back as the cartridges fired and the seat shot up and away from the aircraft. The blast of air hit him but strangely he felt it wasn't so strong as before and then he realized of course that his airspeed was much lower this time. He felt a tumbling sensation and heard and felt the chute pop out and deploy as the automatic sequence operated. He looked up and saw the welcome sight of his parachute billowing out above him. He looked down and saw the aircraft hit the calm grey sea. A huge splash of white foam formed an ever-widening circle. It looked so unreal, a slow motion portrayal of an event Sean had hoped would never occur again. The yachts still sailed on as if nothing had happened and none looked as if they had been hit or damaged. He looked for Sheppard; there he was just up and to his left with a good chute deployed. No danger of falling into a fireball this time.

Only 100 feet or so above the water, although he knew height was deceptive in such a situation as this, only a few seconds and he would hit. He released his dinghy from his seat pack and watched it inflate automatically as it hit the water, but still attached to him by a long nylon cord. He splashed in shortly after and felt the sudden sensation of coldness and wet as the sea engulfed him. He found difficulty in releasing his parachute and as his head submerged below the surface fear and panic began to take over his mind, he couldn't get the release mechanism to work. He also knew that a wet parachute would soon drag him down through the water. The weight of the sodden parachute could even overcome the buoyancy of his inflated life jacket and he would drown. Sean felt himself fighting for air as he clawed his way to the surface over the rigging lines of the parachute. 'Don't get tangled up in them,' he thought to himself. Against all his training and self-discipline, he knew he was panicking and losing control of the situation.

'Hell, where were the release catches? They should be just on top of his shoulders. He felt all over and then his head broke the surface. He took a huge gulp of air before he was dragged down again by the now sodden chute and heavy metal attachments. 'Ah, there they are,' twisted back and over and behind his shoulder. 'Don't panic, feel under the metal collar and press. Thank God.'

He felt the dead weight and dragging of the chute disappear and he was free at last. He resurfaced and looked for his dinghy, dragged it in by the nylon cord and, gathering all his strength, put one hand over the narrow rear end and pushed down hard. He was about to scramble to the safety of this small one-man dinghy when the yacht appeared.

He heard him shout, 'Are you all right?' in a thin reedy voice.

The yachtsman was small and somewhat plump, wearing a pair of large dark glasses. He grabbed hold of the dinghy with Sean half in and half out and pulled it towards his yacht. Sean at the same time grabbed the side of the boat and clambered in. As soon as he was safely in he released the dinghy, which quickly trailed astern.

'Well this is exciting – never been in a race like it before. I'm in second place at the moment but it looks as if your plane beat us all into first place.'

The yachtsman looked truly amazed at the situation.

Sean looked at him, took a deep breath and in what he hoped was a calm, cultured and confident English voice said, 'Thank you so much for pulling me to safety. Just drop me off wherever is convenient and the chopper will come and pick me up.'

'Gee, a Limey. What's a Limey doing flying one of our planes?' he exclaimed in a surprised and excited manner.

'Take too long to explain,' shouted Sean over the noise of a rising wind which was whipping the grey water up into waves of green tinged foam.

The white sails of the yacht started to flap from side to side as his rescuer temporarily lost control of the steering. Other boats were now converging on the scene and in the distance Sean could hear the noise of the familiar chopper.

'Just drop me off by the jetty,' he said.

The man just grinned and asked him in a subdued and somewhat querulous manner, 'Are you sure you are OK?'

'Fine, fine,' replied Sean, wondering what was coming next.

'Good. Listen, I'm still second in the race at the moment and as you can see you are somewhat in the way. Do you mind getting back overboard and swimming back to your dinghy? Your lifejacket seems OK,' he added as an after-thought, seemingly to reassure himself that he wasn't asking for the impossible.

To say that Sean was taken aback was an understatement. He couldn't believe this. 'What a story to tell my children, if I ever have any,' he thought.

'OK, fine with me,' he said, ever the English gentleman wishing to be helpful.

So, not wishing to be troublesome, he climbed back into the choppy sea, which was dirty, with a hint of oil and chemicals, as are all waters leading to any major port in the world. He soon made up the distance to the dinghy 100 or so yards astern and without difficulty climbed aboard. He sorted himself out, clipped himself to the side with ready-made fasteners and said to himself, 'I'm not going to part with you again so easily.' He looked around him, really for the first time. He could see the sailing boats all seemingly serene and untroubled, without a care in the world. Everything looked so peaceful and as if nothing had really happened. He spotted Sheppard's dinghy, a spot of orange incongruous in all the tranquillity. 'Thank goodness he's OK,' he thought. No need to get out location aids as he could hear and see the helicopter fast approaching Bill Sheppard. Soon it would be his turn.

He began to gather his thoughts and for a second time he wondered how this could happen again so soon after the first. 'Will I be able to instruct again? Will they let me continue on the squadron or would they send me back home to the UK? Even if the worst never happened, will I ever find a student willing to fly with me again?

These thoughts soon faded as his senses became alerted to his immediate situation. The weather was beginning to deteriorate and a line squall of dark menacing clouds was appoaching from the west. Heavy rain could be seen over the low horizon and he could see it obliterating the trees and gleaming white buildings of the residential area just outside Tampa.

'Damn, damn,' he said to himself, 'heavy weather will hamper my rescue.'

A touch of nervousness entered his mind.

The helicopter came quickly and hovered above him, the downwash from its rotors easily overcoming any affect of nature's wind. Sean waited while the strop, a large canvas hoop with a metal weight attached, was lowered into the water beside him to dissipate any static electricity that might have built up inside it. Then the strop was manoeuvred by the helicopter's crewman into the dinghy itself. Sean grabbed it quickly, making sure to fend off the metal weight to prevent it smashing into his face. Only when he was safely installed with the strop around him did he give the thumbs up to the crewman. How many times had he practised this during training in the safe confines of an indoor swimming pool and also, more realistically, at sea? And now here he was for real. As he was winched up out of the sea he released himself from the dinghy. The noise was deafening and the sea sprayed up by the powerful downwash drenched him yet again. But soon he was at the chopper's door and the burly arms of the crewman dragged him inside. The door was closed and Sean was thankful for the reduction in noise and absence of wind and chill. He felt the chopper's nose go forward to gain speed as it turned to head for the base only a mile or so away.

Sean was pleased he was able to walk without difficulty as he got out of the helicopter. No sign of Sheppard, but he guessed he was already comfortably installed in one of the hospital rooms. He followed the white-coated medical order-lies to the ground floor lift, his flight suit dripping water all over the floor. He felt cold now and was glad when he was shown into a room and given some dry clothing and a pair of hospital pyjamas. He was advised to change and lie flat on the bed. There was Dr Tucker bang on cue and not a moment too late.

'Back so soon Sean,' he said laconically, laughing loudly at the same time.

'Hey, Doc, it's not funny. It could be serious this time because we don't know what caused the engines to quit.'

Now that he had time to think, Sean was worried about what had caused the accident. This was not going to be a straightforward investigation. What was now required was a detailed study of the events leading up to the engine failure and of the engine and fuel systems themselves. 'Oh well, may as well relax. I can't do anything about it,' he thought to himself, suddenly realizing that he was hungry and thirsty.

'Don't you Americans ever drink tea?' he said to the doctor. 'I could do with a cup of tea and some biscuits now.'

An orderly heard his remark and went off down the corridor. The doctor just grinned and started the examination of his patient.

A huge mug of coffee and a plate of biscuits was brought in by the orderly who remarked, 'Sorry, no tea at the moment, sir, but hope the coffee is OK.'

'That's fine. Many thanks,' replied Sean, not surprised that tea was not available.

Doctor Tucker completed his brief examination and said, 'Well not much damage this time, but we must send you for an X-ray of your back, just to be sure.'

'OK,' said Sean. 'There is a slight pain higher up than last time, but the previous injuries seem fine.'

'Well, subject to what the X-rays might show, you should be out of here tomorrow.'

'Thank you for that,' replied Sean.

Sean remembered to phone his parents to tell them what had happened and to assure them that he was uninjured. Then he was escorted off to the X-ray department. He was soon back in his room and an hour later an orthopaedic specialist arrived and told Sean that his back was in good shape, but there was another slight compression fracture higher up than before.

'Nothing to worry about,' he said, 'but you will be off flying for another three months.'

'Damn,' said Sean, 'what the hell am I going to do for another three months?'

The inquiry team didn't delay long in arriving and took a long and detailed statement from Sean. He tried to remember everything that had happened and was as helpful as he could be. They seemed satisfied but he knew it was just the beginning of a long process.

The next morning the reporter from the local *Tampa Times* came to see him for a short interview, having been cleared to do so by the Base Public Relations Officer. It was the same young man who had interviewed Sean twice before, once as the first Royal Air Force exchange officer to be stationed at the base and second after his first accident. Sean liked him. Despite his youthful appearance, casual dress and unfortunate acne covering his face, he had an infectious sense of humour and he wrote an honest article. On Sean's arrival the headline appeared 'English Jet Jockey Baffled by USAF Terms', referring to the different expressions used by RAF and USAF fighter pilots. Again, after the first accident the headline 'Language Didn't Matter,' referring to the fact that 'Eject, Eject' meant the same in both countries. The interview lasted about three-quarters of an hour and Sean was content with the proposed text of the newspaper article. Just as the reporter was leaving Gayle arrived.

'Well, you are making a habit of this aren't you?'

She laughed out her words. Sean took no offence, knowing what she meant and how she felt. His heart missed a beat as he took in her cool look and slim, beautiful figure. She was dressed in an elegant silk-lined suit of pale cream with matching blouse. She wore large earrings of tiny shells, each encircling a single pearl and these, together with her high cheek bones, accentuated her tanned complexion. He knew and felt himself succumbing to her countenance, charm and sheer loveliness.

'Come in and sit down and I'll get some more coffee,' he said with alacrity.

'OK,' she said, 'but I mustn't stay long as I know you must be keen to leave. I have an idea to put to you. You are going to be grounded for another three months aren't you?' Without waiting for a reply she went on, 'And you've seen America now, so you will be staying around here won't you?'

She had that look of hope and expectancy that Sean would agree to the idea that obviously excited her.

'Listen,' she went on, 'you know that Disneyland is coming to Florida some time in the next few years. Well, the property developers are out trying to make money and they are offering a three day free trip to a place called River Ranch Acres out near Orlando next to the projected site for Disneyland. Swimming, good accommodation, and horse riding through the wilderness, all for free. All we have to do is listen to their sales pitch for an afternoon. They will try to sell us land on which to build a home, but there is no obligation. How about coming with me? We can get single rooms,' she added quickly as an after thought.

Sean surprised at her obvious enthusiasm, warmed quickly to the thought of exploring central Florida on horseback and with such a companion. He had never ridden a horse but there was always a first time and he had an adventurous spirit. For a moment he hesitated as his mind reflected on the idea of single rooms, but he knew instinctively it would make no difference.

'OK. What a good idea. I would like to learn to ride and see another area of Florida.'

'Great,' she exclaimed excitedly. 'I'll fix it up and will be in touch when things have settled down for you. I know you will be busy with all the questions and the inquiry. That will take a few weeks or so. Anyway I will see you and keep in touch.'

She gave him a peck on the cheek and she was off, leaving

Sean suddenly alone with his thoughts once more. He missed her.

The days went by quickly. The inquiry team went about their work speedily and efficiently. They arranged for a salvage contractor to drag up as much of the aircraft as possible from the seabed and asked many questions of Sean and young Sheppard. Surprisingly, the two were only segregated for a few days before allowing them to confer together. The engines were quickly recovered but there were no immediate signs of why they both stopped so suddenly. Bird ingestion could have been a cause but neither pilot had seen or heard a bird strike and no bird remains were found in the engines. Sean remembered those occasions when he had experienced bird strikes before – especially when flying fast at low level a few hundred feet above the English countryside and over the mountains of Wales and Scotland. There was the thump, thump, thump of birds striking the fuselage. A quick check of the engines, instruments; jet pipe temperature, r.p.m. gauge, oil pressure all normal and within limits – no damage this time. It only needed one bird down the intake and the damage could be enormous and in a single engined aircraft like the Hunter, probable loss of the aircraft.

Eventually, after many weeks of deliberation the investigation found a mechanical fault which needed only a minor modification to put right. And that was it – many millions of dollars down the drain, to say nothing of the expense of the investigation and the cost of the salvage operation. No blame was attached to the crew, but there were inevitably a few observations made on pilot technique and servicing procedures. Sean was relieved, glad they had found a probable cause, even if it could not be diagnosed absolutely positively. And then he had a message that his squadron commander wanted to see him. Sean had wondered when this call would come. He had been expecting it for weeks. After a less than positive inquiry and after two major accidents was he going to be allowed to stay? He recalled his uneasiness when he was last in his boss's office. What was his future going to be now?

4

Bermuda Triangle

He knocked on the door. Sean felt nervous, he had not been sleeping well and his mind seemed preoccupied on what his future on the squadron might be. He even had doubts on whether he had a future here in America. 'Pull yourself together,' he said to himself, 'I must regain my confidence.'

'Come in,' he heard his boss shout and in he went.

As he entered, he noted the smile on the colonel's face and felt relaxed immediately when he rose from his chair with his arm outstretched in greeting.

'Well, come on in, Sean. We don't have many pilots who have done it twice in such a short time, but don't worry, we'll just have to see what's best for all of us in the situation we find ourselves. I've got an idea that I want to discuss with you. How do you feel yourself?'

Sean welcomed his boss's friendly approach. He knew now that he was genuinely trying to be helpful, there was now no need to be nervous and he knew he could speak frankly.

'Well, sir. I feel fit but know I won't be allowed to fly for a month or so yet, but I haven't lost any confidence. I am just anxious to get airborne again. But I must find something to do in the months ahead to keep me occupied.'

'Fine, I like your positive approach. With the experience you have gained since you have been with us, somewhat unique you will agree, I think we can put this to good use. How about becoming one of our small group of test pilots? You're familiar with what they do, as you know they are the first to fly an aircraft that has had major work done on it, like engine changes. They also take delivery of new aircraft direct from McDonnells and check it out and accept it for our Air Force. There will be a lot to learn about the test schedule itself and of course you will need to have a deeper knowledge of the aircraft's systems, but you have lots of time to study it and I know you would do the job well. What do you think?'

Sean felt and looked surprised. He was excited at the prospect and he showed it when he responded quickly with a smile on his face.

'That's just great, sir. What could be better. Just the challenge I need. How do you like that? You crash two of your ally's aircraft one after another and they reward you by making you a test pilot.' Then, hoping that he would still be an instructor, he added, 'Sir, I hope I will still be an instructor on the squadron.'

'Of course, Sean, your test flying duties will only take up part of your time and that mainly at weekends when the airspace is more readily available. I will still expect you to be a full time instructor.'

Sean knew that most of the test flights were conducted at the weekends and he was perfectly willing to give up his spare time to gain some exceptional experience; he felt his confidence, returning now that he knew the positive approach his boss had taken.

'Well, now I know what to do in the next few weeks. Thank you, sir, for the chance to improve my flying skills and for your confidence in me.'

'I'll go now and check in with the test flying department.' He almost added, 'and I won't be ejecting out of any more of your aircraft,' but thought better of it.

'Best of luck, Sean,' his boss held out his hand and grasped his firmly in his huge grip, 'and don't forget, my door is always open if you have any problem.'

'Thank you, sir,' and that was it.

A new job in test flying to add to his Instructor Pilot

duties. And a job that would set Sean off into one of the most extraordinary events of his whole life, leading to his ultimate destiny.

He returned to the squadron crew-room where the inevitable friendly banter of his colleagues kept him busy.

'I hear you came second in a yacht race,' said one, while another quipped, 'I understand you get ten per cent commission from Martin Baker ejection seats. No wonder you use them so often.' He took it all in his stride and even laughed at one student who said to another, 'Don't fly with the Limey – you might not come back.'

Sean made himself known at the small unit which housed that elite group of test pilots. He busied himself learning about his new role ready for the day he would be cleared to fly again.

Gayle phoned him about a week later.

'I've fixed up everything except the date – they want to know by tomorrow whether we want the first or second Monday to Wednesday in December.'

Sean, delighted to have the organization of such a trip done by somebody else, especially someone as efficient as Gayle, accepted readily.

'How about next Monday? I haven't anything on then and I can easily get the week off. I would prefer to keep the run up to Christmas free as I may go home to my parents for the festive season.'

'OK,' said Gayle. 'Take it that everything's arranged.' She paused for just a moment. 'My parents know that we are going and accept the situation,' she added almost as an afterthought. She knew the somewhat special relationship that Sean, a British officer in the USAF, had with her father, the Deputy Commander of the Base. She also knew she wanted to keep Sean forever. She had fallen in love with him. His seriousness, his physical strength, his presence and sense of humour, all these and much more gave her that sense of longing when he was not with her, and contentment and real happiness when he was with her. But she must not take advantage of her position to influence him to her side. Her love must be mutually shared and he must respond to her feelings.

'Well, that was that,' thought Sean as he chatted on casually to Gayle about nothing in particular. They agreed to travel in her car and she would pick him up from the Mess early the following Monday.

It was a typical Florida day in mid-winter. The sun shone from a brilliant blue sky with an intensity that hurt their eyes as they motored down the straight white road leading to Orlando. There had been a hint of frost that night and small fires had been lit at regular intervals amongst the orange groves. A thin haze of smoke lay over the flat countryside held down by an atmospheric inversion.

'You can smell the smoke,' yelled Sean over the noise of rushing air as they sped east in the open-topped Chevrolet.

He held in his hand the glossy brochure put out by the property developer and was examining the map showing the whereabouts of River Ranch Acres.

'Take the next turning on the left,' he said with authority and in the manner of someone who knew how to navigate and make decisions.

Gayle seemed very content and happy that for the moment someone else was in control of her destiny. She exuded charm and gaiety and simply sparkled in her light cotton dress of yellow and green. Her lemon-coloured earrings were matching and in complete harmony with her make-up. Sean was pensive. 'Goodness, she knows how to awaken a man's inner senses, she looks stunning,' he thought.

They drove up a long new white road constructed and carved through a wilderness of pines and low scrub. A huge sign of garish colours, so typical of those seeking attention, said, 'Welcome to River Ranch Acres, the Development of the Future.' On the sign was a huge mural of beautiful gardens with low-rise homes set amongst blue lakes and wide blue skies. This was what it was all about and what it was supposed to look like in a few years time.

They signed in at the reception and were met by a well-dressed young man in a dark blue suit and matching tie. His hair was dark and cut short with a perfect parting to it.

'Hi there,' he said, 'welcome to River Ranch Acres, *the* development of the future.'

He was the typical go-ahead salesman and he was not going to take no for an answer. Sean immediately disliked him from instinct rather than from anything he had said or yet done. His eyes were always looking around. 'Shifty' he thought.

'Have you come far? Let's see, Mr and Mrs . . . What name is it?'

He stopped when he saw Sean's obvious displeasure and Gayle's look that could maim, if not kill. Sean quietly interrupted.

'Gayle Cooper and Sean Foster,' he said in his best cultured English accent.

'Gee, all the way from England. You know I was in London not so long ago and met a guy called Watson. Yes, let me think, Frank . . . that was his name, Frank Watson. Ever meet him?'

He had heard all this before. Americans always reminisced about their visits to Britain and expected you to know all the people they met.

'No, I don't believe I did, but please could you show us our rooms.'

'OK. Here's a folder for each of you with a programme for your visit. You will find your rooms marked on the front of the envelope. Let's see. Numbers 33 and 34, just across there in the new annexe.'

He handed them their keys and pointed across to a long low building some hundred or so yards away, set amongst trees away from the car park.

'There will be a briefing in the big building just across the way there at 2 p.m. this afternoon, but before that we would like to welcome you to drinks here at noon just before lunch. I hope you enjoy your stay . . . both of you,' he added after a slight pause and looking directly at Sean.

75

As they walked to their rooms Sean noted the large outdoor swimming pool dazzling in the sunlight. Dotted around it were long lounge chairs with ample space between them.

'Only a few people here,' he said with obvious satisfaction.

'Yes, I think we can have a really lazy three days,' said Gayle in return.

He was glad she said that. Although he was looking forward to the horse-riding he was also looking forward to just relaxing in what was obviously a comfortable and quiet hideaway.

'My sentiments exactly,' he said and as they each approached numbers 33 and 34 he added, 'See you in a few minutes. Let's have a coffee and soak up the atmosphere before the programme starts at 12. Didn't think much of our host, did you?'

'No, I felt uncomfortable. He never looked you straight in the eye for any length of time. I wouldn't trust him. See you in a few minutes. Just knock on my door when you're ready.'

They both strolled around the complex before settling down beside the pool and enjoying coffee which they helped themselves to.

'It's all very new. They haven't had time to landscape a garden or plant nice shrubs and flowers. Still, I like the fountain and the lake with all the fish in it. Some of them are huge and I've never seen such a range of colours before. They must be Japanese koi carp.'

He looked at Gayle and saw her looking pensive and deep in thought.

'A penny for them,' he said. She quickly turned her head and gave him a questioning look. He went on, 'An English expression. What are you thinking about?'

'Oh, nothing really. I just wish we had more than three days together.'

He laughed and said, 'You know you would soon get fed up with my serious nature and I can be moody too.'

'Would I?' and before he could answer she said, 'Come on, time to join our hosts for drinks.'

76

They met their hosts, a hard bunch of young men and women whose only conversation revolved around the price of land and how it was about to escalate in the area around Orlando. Their only objective was to sell land and property quickly to suspecting and unsuspecting clients. Sean soon got bored and was glad when they were able to sit down to a light salad lunch in the large somewhat sparsely decorated, but nevertheless pleasant, dining room.

The briefing after lunch lasted two hours, with a short break for refreshments, and consisted of the hard sell. At the end each couple was allocated a particular salesman who would see them each day, show them around the development site and answer their questions. Sean had agreed with Gayle beforehand that they would show a modicum of interest until the last day, when they would say definitely that they were not buyers. They thought this would ensure that they were not asked to leave prematurely.

The evening came quickly. They met in the bar before dinner. Gayle was dressed in a ballerina length black taffeta skirt and cream silk blouse. 'She looks as alluring and elegant as ever,' thought Sean, 'not overdressed but just right.' He bought the champagne, pink, from California. They had a table set quietly in one corner of the dining room overlooking the lake with its water lilies, reed beds and koi carp and fountain. It was getting dark and the lake was lit with different coloured lights under the water around the edges. The colours of the fish showed up well in all their glory. Myriads of reflections played on the surface of the water dappled by the falling spray of the central fountain, itself lit up inside by different shades of azure and turquoise.

'Cheers,' said Sean and as their eyes and two glasses met he added, 'Isn't it beautiful. Let's hope I get the hang of this horse-riding we are trying out tomorrow morning.'

Gayle looked at him intently without saying a word. Her eyes moved horizontally to and fro as she looked into his as if to say, 'I love you'.

Instead, after what seemed like minutes but in fact were only a few seconds, she said, 'Cheers. Don't worry about tomorrow. You will do just fine and we will enjoy ourselves, I know. Now what shall we have?'

Each table had its own menu, a set one, and there was no waiter service because it was all free. Instead they had a buffet service. They walked up and joined a short queue and helped themselves to asparagus soup. They chatted about the prospects of making money from the property in the area and about the personalities on the base at MacDill.

Dinner was over quickly. Sean felt instinctively that they both knew what was to come. As they rose to leave he felt light-headed; the champagne had done its work. Gayle put her arm through his and they walked as one through the cool night over to their rooms in the annexe. He put his hand in his pocket for the key. She still clung to his arm and as he turned to kiss her she put her hands around his shoulder and pulled him hard to her. He knew he could not resist. He looked down at her deep blue eyes and gently pressed his lips to hers. Her response was fierce and swift. They quickly went inside and the door closed behind them. Sean knew that any resistance was impossible and he was completely hers. They made love, slowly at first, their bodies entwined, both feeling the affection and warmth for each other they so desperately needed. Their passion increased until it was all over in a burst of mutual ecstasy and they were left with their own thoughts.

As Sean lay beside her. He felt no sense of guilt and certainly no sorrow. He was happy that it had happened and, he realized, so was she. 'Was that real love?' he kept asking himself. 'Have I found the person who will keep me happy and satisfied for the rest of my life?' He was aware that in posing the question to himself he almost had the answer. Somewhere deep down within his consciousness reality prevailed and he knew that the attraction was physical and that true love still eluded him.

He wrestled with his conscience and decided that he would continue the relationship. 'Why not?' he mused. 'Perhaps we will both get hurt,' but he knew too that within the next eighteen months he would be away and back in the

UK. He hated himself for thinking in such a way. 'How selfish,' he thought.

The next day they rode through the wilderness of trees where huge spiders, six inches across, hung on large webs draped between the woodland paths, across swamps of lush vegetation and then dry areas of sandy soil where the grass was thin and the earth bare. The sun shone high in the sky and the cool winter breeze blew through their hair. The horses loved it and their riders loved it. Sean had quickly mastered the art of horse-riding in its simpler form. No fast gallops or jumping, just a comfortable canter on a docile older horse especially chosen for the novice.

They lazed beside the pool with long periods of contented silence between. They swam together in the sparkling water and Sean began to realize that this relationship was something new and exciting. 'Where would it all lead to?' he asked himself.

The day turned to evening, the sun fell down fast over the dark green pines with just a hint of pale orange. Evening turned to night and they made love again and again. Each had their own thoughts, but both shared a common passion.

The adventure and excitement of the past three days went so fast and soon the reckoning, packing up and the long drive back to reality and squadron life at the big Air Force Base at MacDill. On the drive back down the empty highway, Gayle was pensive and thoughtful and seemed preoccupied with some great problem. Sean tried to engage her in conversation.

'Well, that was some free offer wasn't it? Perhaps I should have invested in some land?'

She didn't answer right away, but after a short interval she perked up.

'Yes, I enjoyed it very much; but perhaps we went too far.' She smiled and then added, 'You know, we could always go back and then you could buy some land. Who knows, you might even have a property built and settle down there one day.'

She glanced at him for a brief instant but the road was

getting busier as they neared Tampa and she concentrated on her driving. He was quick to reply.

'Don't worry about the intimacy part. We did it and we enjoyed it. Let's be friends and not get hurt. As far as buying land – I wasn't serious and, anyway, I couldn't live in Florida – too hot and humid and far too artificial.' He saw the disappointment on her face and added quietly, 'I mean, I like the seasons, the changes in nature and in the country-side from winter to spring and from summer to autumn, here it doesn't change all that much. As far as artificial, I meant that to me the whole state has a materialistic feel to it – fast cars, speed boats, yachts, all affluence with little meaning . . .'

He stopped abruptly as he realized he had gone too far. He was digging himself deeper into a hole the more he spoke. Gayle drove on in silence through the busy streets of Tampa and onto the main north/south road called Dale Mabry leading to the base.

She dropped him off at the Mess and waited just long enough to collect his small holdall. He gave her a kiss on the cheek and said, 'Cheers.'

She gave him little more than a glance and replied, 'Bye for now, keep in touch.'

'Well,' he thought, 'the minds and moods of women. They take some beating, sometimes you just don't know where you are with them.'

The silence of his room hit him as he slumped down in the large leather lounge chair amply covered with soft dralon-covered cushions. Talk about an anti-climax. They were getting on so well, even made love, and suddenly she had changed. Was it something he had said or done? He looked at the antique bracket clock on top of his desk. He had picked it up for a song in a small back street shop in New Orleans. It was noon. This called for a drink and he poured himself a large gin and tonic with ice and lemon from the small fridge in the corner.

*

The days went by quickly. Sean decided to fly back to England and spend Christmas and the New Year with his parents. It was very much a family occasion in America as well as everywhere else and although he knew he would be invited to spend Christmas with one of his American hosts, it could never be the same as with his own family. His sister, Jane, would probably be there with her young family of two boys. He had always been close to his sister and he hadn't seen her for a year at least. Her husband was a fund manager with a City firm of unit trusts – he liked him too and found he shared his interests in world affairs and economics.

Sean felt the slight change in the pitch of the engine noise and then felt the almost imperceptible change in flying attitude of the Boeing 707 of TWA. The aircraft nose eased gently down and he knew they were in British airspace and descending from 33,000 feet into Gatwick. The flight from Tampa International had been uneventful and mostly over cloud. At about 28,000 feet Sean guessed from experience, the aircraft entered cloud and he knew then it would be cold, wet and miserable on the ground. He could see it was just that as the aircraft broke cloud at about 800 feet and the windows were streaming with the lashing rain. He looked down at the naked trees, the wet brown earth and green fields of his native Sussex. How different from Florida, but he liked it. There was always something of interest to see in the countryside, even in midwinter. He longed to walk in the Cuckmere Valley near his parents' home in a small village sheltering amongst the South Downs. His sister met him in the crowded arrival hall at Gatwick. There she was, her long auburn hair tied back and dressed casually in blue jeans, which accentuated her slim figure. She welcomed her brother with a huge embrace. Her two young boys stood aside in slight awe at the object of their mother's attention.

'Welcome back, Sean, after all your adventures. Good to see you again.' Before he could reply she looked down at the boys and said, 'Say hello to your uncle.'

81

'Hello, Uncle Sean,' they said in unison.

'Gosh it's good to be back in England and to see you all again,' was all he could think of to say as he shook hands with his two young nephews. 'Even the weather hasn't changed,' he said as he laughed, noting the dismal wet scene outside.

As they drove home they talked almost non-stop about family affairs. Sean was interested to hear that his father was thinking about taking early retirement from his work as an insurance consultant with a long established firm in London.

'I am glad to hear that,' he said. 'I know how he hates that journey up to town every day. But what's he going to do with himself once he gives it up?'

'Oh, he's taken up golf and you know how he liked his garden. He'll find plenty to do.'

They drove along the familiar roads and country lanes that he had known so well as a boy. How they were changing: more houses and more shops where there were once fields, traffic lights where at one time you just waited for the few vehicles to pass. Worst of all, he thought, was the huge increase in traffic as affluence spread down to the mass of population who could now afford to buy a car, two cars for some.

As they parked the car in front of the single garage, Sean was pleased to see the patch of winter heliotrope just coming into flower beside the hedge. This had always grown here and as a young boy he remembered how its large round leaves and vanilla-scented lilac flowers were always the first wild flower to bloom. His parents greeted him warmly and he quickly felt at home as he unpacked in the familiar surroundings of his small room at the back of the house overlooking the large rear garden with its vegetable patch at the bottom. How often he had dreamed dreams looking out at this scene in his youth. What would he do in his life? Where would he go? How long would he live for? Would he be rich or poor? These and many more questions he posed to himself as he grew up.

*

Christmas with all its festivites came and went. There were no family rows, not even little tensions that often blow up out of all proportion to become real problems. The detached but small house set back from the main road through the village had only three bedrooms and somehow accommodated them all, with the young boys excited at being able to sleep on the floor in sleeping bags. His sister left with her family after lunch on Boxing Day to return to London. Sean was sad to see her go, sad too that he had not gone for a long walk with her over the Downs. The weather had just been too bad and there really had been no time.

Still, perhaps he would phone his old friend Sarah who had been so anxious to hear how he was after his first accident. He had received a warm and friendly Christmas card from her and he had responded in kind. He was due to fly back on 2 January and if the weather improved he could take her out for a pub lunch and a walk. 'What a good idea,' he thought. But then, should he resurrect such a close friendship which previously ended in tears? He decided to call her. He dialled her number, a local call as she lived only a few miles away at Polegate. His apprehension rose as the dialling tone persisted for what seemed like minutes.

'Hello,' came a somewhat breathless reply. He recognized her soft Sussex accent.

'Sarah, it's Sean. Sean Foster,' he added unnecessarily, just to reassure himself that she would recognize his voice. 'Thank you for your card and for your good wishes. I have been back for Christmas with my parents and am flying back in a few days' time. How about meeting up? We could go for a walk over the Seven Sisters and I could treat you to a pub lunch at the Golden Galleon. The weather looks as if it will be clear blue tomorrow after all the rain.'

She hesitated for a few seconds and he felt his hopes of a reunion dashed.

'That sounds like a good idea. I am at a loose end tomorrow, so where shall we meet?'

His spirits rose. She sounded enthusiastic, just as she always was about most things.

83

'How about ten o'clock in the car park at Birling Gap? I'll bring some coffee and a rucksack.'

'That's fine,' she said. 'Sorry I took so long to answer the phone, I was upstairs ironing with the radio on, didn't hear it ring for a while. How are you anyway?' They chatted for a few minutes and then she said, 'See you tomorrow morning, ten o'clock at Birling Gap. Let me know if you change your mind because of weather or something.'

'I won't change my mind and I am confident the weather will be OK. See you at ten and then we can catch up on all our news. Bye for now.'

Sean woke just before dawn and, pulling back the curtains, he could see it was going to be a clear, crisp and dry day. As the sun rose he could see the white frost on the lawn and on the branches of the hazel bushes in the bottom hedge. What a wonderful day for walking beside the great white cliffs that make up the Seven Sisters. 'I wonder what we will see?' he thought.

By half past nine he had made up the coffee and packed his rucksack. He borrowed his parents' car and was down at Birling Gap ten minutes early. He waited, looking out at the cold grey sea still choppy from the Atlantic depression that had caused so much bad weather over Christmas, but now was well past and dissipating.

She arrived only five minutes late, which was good going for her. Sean remembered how exasperated he used to get when she was often as much as 30 minutes late for an appointment. He saw that her dress sense hadn't changed for the better either. Not the waterproofed anorak and sturdy walking boots for her. No, there she was in a woolly blue hat and matching pullover. On her feet she wore a lightweight pair of brogues, not exactly the right gear for the Downs in mid-winter.

'Hello,' he said, giving her a kiss on the cheek, 'long time no see.'

She smiled and squeezed his hand.

'Yes it does seem a long time, but really it was only two years ago since we said goodbye. I thought we wouldn't meet up again, but here we are. I am looking forward to the walk. What a lovely day.'

He was pleased to see her, even though he felt the romance they first shared could never be reactivated.

They walked up the unmade road to the little gate at the foot of the Downs at the beginning of the walk over the Seven Sisters, so called because, viewed from a southerly aspect, the South Downs end in seven dramatic chalk cliffs which rise to over 500 feet. The scalloped edges of the Seven Sisters undulate along the coast between Cuckmere Haven and Birling Gap. Years ago the chalk extended further seawards but the cliffs are continually being eroded as the sea pounds the chalk away. As they walked along the coastal path Sean pointed out to Sarah two large white sea-birds.

'Look at those two fulmar petrels. They have just come in from the deep Atlantic Ocean to find a mate and to lay their single egg on a cliff edge. They are relatively new to the Seven Sisters and seem to be spreading all around Britain's coasts, nobody really knows why.'

Sarah nodded but failed to follow up with any observations of her own. They walked on and over the Sisters; Went Hill Brow, Baily's Hill, Flagstaff Point, Brass Point, Rough Brow, Short Brow and Haven Brow. What evocative names and what tales they could tell of smugglers, shipwrecks, murders and just plain countrymen and lovers. They paused at Flagstaff Point and looked down at the patch of wet sand left by the receding tide. Sean pointed out the remains of an ancient ship whose ribs were sticking up out of the sand, clearly marking its size and shape.

'That was the *Coonatto* that floundered on those reefs out there at Flagstaff Point in about 1857. In one of the local museums you can see a picture of it loaded with bales of wool in Sydney Harbour just before it sailed for England and destruction. There are many such wrecks to be found along the coast here, an old submarine from the First World War and the remains of a barge and a large freighter.'

She seemed more interested now.

'How do you know all this?' she asked.

85

'Just picked up the information over the years from reading books on local history,' he replied.

'Were there many people drowned with the *Coonatto*? I mean, what happened to the bodies? Were they buried locally?' Before he could reply, she spotted a dead plant amongst the grass. 'What's this? Doesn't it look attractive! It's just like an everlasting flower, the kind one uses for flower arranging.'

'That's the remains of the carline thistle. Very prickly and it looks not much different than when it was in flower last August. You know it got its name as a commemoration of Charlemagne who made use of its medicinal properties by curing his army of the plague. As for those who inevitably drowned with the *Coonatto*, I don't know how many and have no idea if any are buried locally. Interesting question though.'

He raised his binoculars, which he always carried with him on walks, to view a small hawk flying low over the scrub beside the cliff edge.

'A kestrel. Pity I thought it might be a peregrine falcon, one of those beautiful and exciting birds that used to nest on the cliffs a few years back. Thanks to myxomatosis killing off the rabbits, its favourite diet, and pesticides like DDT getting into its food chain, the peregrine has disappeared from the local area.'

They came to Haven Brow overlooking the tranquil and secluded estuary of the Cuckmere where the little wandering river emptied itself over a shingle bank into the English Channel. A chill wind blew over the top of this first of the Sisters.

'Gosh, it's cold up here,' he said pulling, his quilted and weatherproof anorak top over his head. 'You know, on a calm day you can sit down undisturbed there on the beach and just hear the silence of the sea in this area of great tranquillity. Not many places you can do that around here nowadays. Very peaceful. You can recharge your batteries after a hectic week's work. Come on, let's get down into the valley, drink our coffee in a sheltered spot and then make our way over to the Golden Galleon for a spot of lunch. You can see it from here.'

It was midday as they walked up the steps to the entrance of the Golden Galleon. A roaring fire gave warmth and a friendly welcome as they made their way to the bar. A huge man with a black beard appeared around the door marked 'Private' as Sean ordered a white wine for Sarah and a special Cuckmere Beer for himself. He always liked the distinctive beers made here on the spot in the tiny brew-house by his friend, Adrian Edwards, the head brewer. A broad smile appeared on the big man's face as he recognized the RAF pilot.

'Hello, Sean,' he said in his marked Italian accent. 'Where have you been these last eighteen months or so, and what are you up to?'

'Stefano, nice to see you again. How's business – no doubt booming even in mid-winter? Hope the food's just as good.'

Sean always visited this hospitable place, which he knew had an efficient and friendly owner. He had known the owner, Stefano for many years and remembered as a boy the many times he had come for Sunday lunch with his parents.

Stefano took their order of home-made soup and shepherd's pie.

'You'll find the food is even better than when you last came and, yes, we are busy as always.'

He listen intently as Sean briefly brought him up to date with his exploits with the Americans. He laughed loudly when Sean told him how he came first in a yacht race.

'Well, that wouldn't happen to you in England would it?' He laughed again. 'I'll go and put your order through. Good to see you both. Take care and drop in when you return from America.'

He shook hands and Sean noticed the warmth and firmness of his grip. Sean enjoyed his meal with Sarah and chatted about old times and old friends and acquaintances. They were careful not to resurrect the closeness of their past friendship and the emotions that this had caused.

'Are you warm now?' Sean asked as they finished their coffee. Sarah nodded and he went on, 'I think we should leave now. There's a bus in ten minutes.'

They caught the bus back to East Dean, where it was only a short walk down to their cars at Birling Gap. As the bus wound its way up the hill he gazed over to his left at the young pine and beech trees that would eventually become a great forest. Perhaps when he retired he would come back to live in this lovely area and have time to really explore it. He wondered how Christmas had gone for Gayle back in Florida. Had she missed him? He wondered why he hadn't really thought of her much. Perhaps she wouldn't fit in and be happy in rural Sussex. His mind turned to the present and Sarah. She hadn't said much since they boarded the bus.

'What are you thinking?' he said, hoping to break the solemn mood.

'Not much really . . .' She hesitated, not sure whether to express her real feelings. She had enjoyed the walk and, although cold, she realized she had enjoyed Sean's company even more. 'Well,' she went on, 'I was just wondering how your last year with the American Air Force will go. Don't crash any more planes, will you?'

Sean sensed in the way she looked at him when she spoke that she still had deep emotions for him, emotions that he thought had been quenched when they parted those few years ago.

He laughed and said, 'No chance of that. They will keep a close eye on me from now on. I hope to continue to find life a challenge and enjoy it. I won't be sorry to be back though. I love Britain and its wonderful countryside and changing scenery and seasons. You don't get that in Florida you know, only sunshine.'

She nodded. They got off the bus at the small downland village of East Dean and walked to Birling Gap and their cars. It was late afternoon and clouds had rolled in from the sea with a freshening wind. They held hands as they walked the few yards to the old iron steps leading down to the beach. They both wanted to take a last look at the sea and the Seven Sisters. The wind was grey and cold and the gulls cried as they wheeled to and fro over the shingle of the shore. A pair of oystercatchers, those lovely black and white birds with long red beaks, looked forlornly out to sea contemplating this bleak scene. They seemed to match perfectly the ambience and feelings of the two lonely humans.

'Well, it's time to say goodbye,' Sean said. He held her lightly in his arms and gave her a gentle kiss on her lips. 'Keep in touch, we will always be good friends and I'll see you in about a year's time.' He paused and then added with more feeling than he really meant, 'Take care.'

She responded by pressing herself to him.

He noticed the tears in her eyes as she said, 'Goodbye. Yes, we'll keep in touch. You take care too.'

And she was gone. He watched her little blue Mini disappear up the road. Sean drove back home with mixed feelings, for he hadn't really meant to start up a relationship, just to remain friends, and feared that she was looking for much more.

Time flew by for Sean and soon he was back in a different world of Phantom fighters, noise and the comradeship of fellow pilots, far from the peace and tranquillity of the Cuckmere Valley. He threw himself into the job, anxious to learn more about the Phantom and its many complex systems.

The great day came and he was back in the air. A familiarisation flight first and then on to instructing. The course pattern was the same; conversion, formation, tactics, air combat and weapons training. He also flew two test flights with one of the test pilots before he was judged competent to test by himself.

Then came the day that was to change his whole life. It was late on a Sunday evening in February. They had planned to do the air test on the Saturday, but repeated engine faults had delayed the aircraft's readiness until midday on the Sunday. He had an experienced instructor, Bob Harding, as his back-seater and co-pilot. As they started up the engines Sean noticed that one of the generator warning lights kept flickering on and off; even as the engines came up to normal idling the light kept flickering. This was unacceptable on a normal flight, let alone a test flight after the aircraft had been dismantled and put together again during a major servicing. They shut down and Sean told the crew chief what was wrong. They set a deadline for 4 p.m., after which they would not accept the aircraft because regulations prevented test flights after sunset. They returned to the crewroom to await events. 3.00 p.m. came and went, then the phone rang and Sean picked up the receiver.

'Base Operations, Colonel Clarke speaking. Is that you, Sean?'

'Yes, sir. What's the problem?'

'Listen, it looks as if it will be touch and go whether the aircraft will be ready for your deadline of 4 o'clock. We are desperate to have it tested because we need the maximum number of aircraft for tomorrow morning's big exercise. I'll extend the landing time until after dusk if you are happy to do so. Use your own judgement.'

'Sir, if you order me to do so, I will do it,' Sean replied.

He knew the pressures that were obviously on Base Operations to ensure a maximum effort for the next day. At the same time he was pleased with the obvious faith that one of the senior officers had in his judgement and sense of responsibility. He felt proud.

The call came in at 4.45 p.m. from the crew chief.

'Your aircraft's ready, sir. Sorry about the delay but have a good flight.'

'Thanks, Chief. We're on our way out.'

Sean went out to the flight line office while his co-pilot went out once again to check around the external of the

90

aircraft. He looked at the servicing sheet and saw that the flickering generator light had been rectified with the words 'Number 1 generator light fixed – loose wire reconnected'. So that was it, he thought, just a loose wire which had not been properly connected the first time. 'Damn, now the last part of the test schedule will be in fading light and it will be dark by the time we land. Should be OK though, the weather is fine and, anyway, I was ordered to by Base Ops.' He persuaded himself that his judgement was sound and that this small deviation from the strict words of the regulations was justified and no risks were being taken.

They both went through the many additional and varied checks required of a test flight. They were meticulous, each cross-checking the other with the aid of specially prepared check-lists; radar built-in-tests, hydraulics, high speed engine ramp positions, electrical tests and so on and so on. They all had to be checked and tested. Their life depended on them and so did those who flew the aircraft afterwards.

They took off as the sun sank down towards the horizon of the sea over the Gulf of Mexico. All the initial flight tests went well. Slam checks on the engine and full power operation. Afterburner light up, engine relight operations, stall checks and slow speed flight characteristics. All were in normal operating limits. Sean called up the ground radio controller who was monitoring his position all the time.

'Pinetree, this is Chestnut. Request clearance for high speed run.'

The controller knew that the aircraft was now going to be put through a test run at up to twice the speed of sound at Mach 2. He also knew that this was potentially the most hazardous part of the test schedule and he had to direct the pilot into a specially cleared area over the sea to the south-west of the Florida peninsula.

'Chestnut from Pinetree. You are clear for high speed run on a heading of 180 degrees.'

'Chestnut, thank you. Commencing Mach run now.'

Sean could see they were off the coast just south-west of Tampa and he had some 200 miles of clear airspace in which to complete this exhilarating part of the test schedule. He could feel his body become tense and in the pit of his stomach a feeling of excitement that was difficult to describe but which sent a message to his brain, 'Watch out, there's danger around.'

'All OK in the back, Bob, check your oxygen and keep calling out your mach readings.'

'OK, Sean, everything's fine.'

And so the test began. Sean eased the control stick forward to gain speed and at the same time pushed the engine throttles forward and into full afterburner. Speed increased rapidly.

'Mach point nine,' shouted Bob from the rear seat.

The engine ramps, those solid sheets of metal in the intakes, designed to control the airflow into the engine at high speed, started to move. 'Good, they're OK,' Sean muttered to himself. His whole being was now tensed up and his nerves and muscles were wound up fully like a watch spring ready to react instantly to any sign of danger. They were now at 40,000 feet and he pulled the stick back to gain maximum altitude before he commenced a final fast descent and highest speed. He glanced to his left and far over to the west he could see in the evening darkness the thin white line of the ever breaking waves on that distant Atlantic shore. The aircraft buffeted slightly as it slipped through the shock wave created by the approach of the speed of sound.

'Mach One point one.'

Bob's voice was somewhat muted and lacked sparkle. For a moment Sean wondered whether all was well.

'OK, in the back?' he shouted as the ambient noise of high speed flight increased.

No response. He repeated the question.

'Fine,' was the somewhat low-key response.

They were now just above 50,000 feet. The sun was still visible on the horizon but Sean could see from the distant lights of Miami that darkness had already enveloped those on the ground.

Sean pushed the stick forward to gain a maximum speed

of Mach Two. He felt light-headed. Strange he thought and checked his oxygen flow. 'That's OK.' He noted the reading on his Machmeter, one point five and increasing fast.

'Bob, are you OK?' he asked as he remembered he hadn't heard from him awhile.

No response. He adjusted his rear-view mirror and was horrified to see the white top of his co-pilot's helmet. His head was slumped forward and he appeared unconscious. At the same time Sean noted that the lights on the ground were beginning to fade slowly at first and then they were gone altogether, as if a dark blind had been drawn across the earth. His light-headedness increased and he felt his whole body strangely listless and without vitality. He switched on the emergency oxygen and felt its cold flow on his lips and cheeks. He knew they were in dire trouble but he lacked urgency. As his anxiety and bewilderment increased, he tried to alert his controller on the ground but the radio was dead. Now in a dreamlike state, he noted that all the instruments seemed frozen, their needles seemingly locked solid and unmoving.

Suddenly, a white light appeared as if from nowhere. It was in front of them but how far away he could not judge. It got bigger and bigger until it engulfed them in its vastness and brightness. He could do nothing. He felt inert but vaguely knew the aircraft was plunging earthwards faster and faster. The light grew brighter and ahead he could see that they were proceeding down a huge tunnel with squared edges and dark lines down the sides projecting to infinity. Sean felt his powers of reasoning slip away. He was conscious, but for how long? A great sense of relief and happiness pervaded his awareness and he knew he was succumbing to some powerful unknown force. The great white light was all around him and he could do nothing. Deep in the recesses of his mind he was able with great effort and concentration to find some discernment of thought. 'This is impossible, impossible – after all I have been through.' His senses and flow of adrenalin for an instant made him feel fear and panic. By instinct he had already closed the throttles and he could tell that the engines were now at idle, but the aircraft was still descending with frightening rapidity. With a huge effort of will power he pulled back on the control stick and he could feel the aircraft respond. The all-enveloping light was dimming and the tunnel ahead was fading. The happiness and contentment that he had experienced that short time ago was now being replaced by reality and the adrenalin through his body was beginning to have an affect. His mind began to clear. 'Thank goodness,' he thought as he noted that the instruments were now working and he could see out at the lights of Miami, bright and clear. He switched on the internal lighting to full brightness and tried to rouse Bob in the back seat. But Bob had recovered.

'What happened?' he said. 'I lost consciousness and now have a real headache.'

'Thank God you are OK,' Sean said with great emotion and relief.

He told his co-pilot to select emergency oxygen but Bob confirmed he had already done this as soon as he had felt unwell. He knew that the situation was not due to a lack of oxygen. They were still at 30,000 feet and were now both fully alert. The strange and frightening symptoms had disappeared altogether.

'Chestnut, Chestnut, Pinetree calling.'

'Go ahead, Pinetree,' Sean replied.

'Have been trying to call you for about four minutes but unable to make contact. Everything OK?'

Sean made an instant decision.

'Affirmative, Pinetree. We had an electrical problem and lost our radio for a while but everything is OK now. Returning to base. Is the airspace around clear?'

He tried to make the question as casual as possible. Maybe the controller saw something on his radar, but he knew in his heart the answer even before the controller replied.

'All clear around you. Has been all evening. Steer zero one five for base.'

Sean turned onto the heading for home and began to tell

Bob all that had happened with a clarity and calmness that surprised him. He had heard of the mysterious and astonishing happenings in the so-called Bermuda Triangle. Most pilots had, especially those flying in these parts. They had just been on the edge of that area. He had never really believed in UFOs or the bizarre happenings in The Triangle, but now he was not so sure. In fact, he had felt an alien force had taken over his being and for awhile, at least three or four minutes based on Pinetree's account, he experienced an event between life and death itself. 'Is this how you feel as you die,' he thought, 'or perhaps I had a glimpse of the beginning of the next life for just an instant.' But certainty quickly took charge. 'Ridiculous,' he muttered to himself.

Bob could not help. He was as mystified as Sean and agreed that it would be difficult to explain what had happened. Would anybody believe them? Would they make fools of themselves? Sean wanted no more trouble. He had had enough already. They agreed a plan as they descended northwards towards the lights of Tampa and the Base.

The sun had set in a blaze of orange and pale pink reflecting off the calm waters of the Gulf of Mexico. It all looked so calm and peaceful as the runway lights appeared ahead. They landed as the last flickers of daylight disappeared in the west.

5

Toni Angelini

They landed and walked back to sign off the aircraft, each
with his own thoughts. Neither was happy with the decision
or story they had agreed upon. Sean particularly, having
been disciplined by the service to tell the truth at all times,
was concerned that he was afraid to reveal the details of this
awesome experience he had just come through. He knew
that Bob was dismayed and unnerved by his becoming
unconscious. Although he believed Sean's story, he still had
a suspicion that oxygen or lack of it had something to do
with their experience. This apprehension held despite the
fact that he knew the emergency oxygen flowed correctly at
the time, he was content to remain silent provided that Sean
wrote something about the need to check the oxygen system
in his report on the aircraft's serviceability after the air test.
Bob accepted Sean's notion that if he were to describe the
incident in all its astonishing and frightening detail, they
would both be held up to ridicule. Having crashed two
aircraft already, Sean would be on his way back home with a
big questionmark over his judgement, integrity and, indeed,
basic character. They both knew they would just not be
believed.

Sean was convinced that they had been involved in some
happening beyond comprehension and, indeed, something
out of this world. So he spoke to the crew chief at length,
amplifying his cryptic comments in the servicing record
book of 'Generator warning lights coming on intermittently,
leading to instrument failures' and 'Check oxygen system
especially the purity of the gas itself'. As he explained, both

his back-seater and himself felt a bit nauseous and light-headed, nothing serious, just worth a check. He also described how he activated the emergency oxygen system and therefore this needed to be refilled. He knew in his heart that nothing would be found wrong with the aircraft's system and that much time would be spent in their checking, but that could not be helped he thought to himself. Would they do any checking up of the real incident on the edge of the Bermuda Triangle if he reported it? He knew they wouldn't.

The young British fighter pilot would never be the same again. A deep thinker before, now his mind would forever be searching to discover the truth about man on this planet and what happens after death. He carried on much as before. He still relished the challenges and excitement of instructing on the squadron and he enjoyed the flow of adrenalin as his Phantom was engaged in combat with another; the sudden onset of G as he pulled ever harder to get behind his adversary, and again the sheer thrill of plunging earthwards at an ever increasing speed; the sudden firing of cannon at the square white target on the ground and the smell of cordite that somehow penetrated the cockpit and his tightly fitting face-mask.

After one such exciting sortie he met up with Bob, his co-conspirator on that portentous test flight of two months before. They were on their own in a quiet corner of the crew-room. They looked at each other and Bob opened the conversation.

'Did we make the right decision? I believed what you said implicitly, but, you know, I have often thought of what would have happened if we really had told the truth. Would we have opened up a can of worms and been made to look stupid, or would we have started a real investigation into the mysteries of the Bermuda Triangle?'

'Well, Bob, you know they found nothing wrong with the aircraft. They made a deep analysis of the oxygen and its systems and everything was OK. I knew that was your main worry. Even the electrical system was found to be faultless.

The aircraft has flown many times since, with only minor defects. They certainly wouldn't have believed my story and we would have looked foolish to say the least. So there you have it.'

Bob looked Sean straight in the eye as he slumped back into the leather armchair, his long well-manicured fingers clamped around a huge mug of coffee.

'Well I suppose you're right, Sean but, you know, I wonder what really was out there. What would have happened if you hadn't pulled us through? Still, I don't know how you did it, but thank God you did.' He paused for a moment. 'You haven't told anybody else, have you? Not even your . . .' He suddenly stopped. 'Sorry, of course you're not married. Almost forgot.'

Sean suddenly felt a pang of fear shoot through his body.

'You haven't told your wife or anybody have you?'

'No, no,' came back the instant reply, but Sean felt suddenly unsure of the whole situation. 'You know,' he said, 'once somebody else knows, everybody will know. The story is so sensational that everybody will be telling. We must keep it to ourselves at all costs. I have no idea what it was that happened. All I can say is that it did and it was something out of this world; almost an after-death experience, if ever there is such a thing. I almost expected the deep booming voice of God to make some profound statement as the white tunnel enveloped us. Maybe one day all will be revealed to everyone of us on this earth. In any event, I am not convinced that there is an afterlife.'

Bob leaned forward and said, 'You know I believe you, Sean, but having not seen what you saw, I am left without that deep conviction of life that you now have.'

'Well, whatever happens in the future, please don't tell anyone else, let's keep to our original agreement. I have completed another couple of test flights and, although I am apprehensive each time I start the Mach run, nothing has happened and I hope nothing ever will again.'

At that moment another two instructors joined them and they conversed about other every day events.

The months went by and Sean settled into an enjoyable routine. He continued to see Gayle and they made love frequently on secluded beaches by day and by night and when they went away at weekends, supposedly to see friends. They shared this social life of the squadron together – dinner dances, barbecues, those ordinary 'let your hair down parties' that friends found it so easy to put on at the last moment. They were seen so often together that tongues were beginning to wag. 'When will they announce their engagement?' Sean, of course, was well aware of what people thought and he was worried that he would be giving them the wrong impression. He tried hard to think that Gayle would make him a good wife, but he knew deep down that she could never be his true love and companion. He tried hard to convey this fact to her and he knew that she too felt within herself that this was not a true romance. Gayle herself had told him that the sex itself was great but it lacked the true feeling of love. He felt glad that she was open about it and that he did not have to pretend that he truly loved her. So they went on with the facade, knowing how it would end and at the same time enjoying it and enjoying the secret that only they themselves shared from the rest of their friends and acquaintances. How would they both feel when he finally departed in seven months' time? He hoped they would remain friends and stay in touch.

The next dramatic episode in his life started one weekend a few months before his return to England. He had just received notice of his next appointment, a staff job in a major headquarters, responsible for the introduction of the Phantom to the Royal Air Force. He was disappointed not to get a flying job, but he knew he had to take up a staff

99

appointment in order to further a balanced career – and he had notice of promotion that went with the assignment. He was pleased with that. He had told Gayle and she was pleased too. He had fixed up to go that following weekend to his favourite secluded beach near Sarasota where he had often been with Gayle. Sadly, she could not make it because the family were off to New York for a reunion with her grandparents – a visit which duty forbade her to miss. Reluctantly, Sean decided to go on his own.

It was hot and very humid as he drove down through St Petersburg and across the Sunshine Skyway Bridge. He felt as if he could drive the route blindfolded now, he had travelled the road so many times before. As he parked his car in the shade of a tall palm he noticed a shining new red Mustang a short distance away. Not many people visited this quiet stretch of the Gulf shore and he just wondered whose it was; he had not seen it before. Walking past the battered piece of tin where he and Gayle had encountered the black widow spider a year or so before, he wondered again about the incident that happened in the skies above him just 50 miles or so further south. His mind often turned the incident over and over again, trying to come to a conclusion on its true nature and meaning. Try as he might he could not fathom it out and his brain was left exhausted and devoid of ideas. He tried to block out the memory as profitless speculation, but his senses would not let go of it and he returned to it time and time again. He found a cool shady spot right near the waters edge and unravelled his beach bag. There was only a slight breeze and the low lapping sound of wavelets breaking on the wet sand and the rustle of the palm leaves was all that could be heard. Sean loved this tranquillity and peace of the place, such a contrast to the roar of engines on the hot white concrete of the squadron dispersal areas. He took out his roll of English newspapers and as he lay on his side on the rug he started to catch up on the weeks' news back at home.

Northern Ireland grabbed the headlines, as they had for the last several months: riots, burnt-out cars and houses, people injured, both police and civilians. Sean was truly distressed at what was happening there. He knew that there were two sides to every conflict, but why don't the politicians talk, talk and talk again to find a solution through consensus? Why give the hardliners on both sides the chance to create war on the streets? For war it was; there was no other word for it. Where would it all end? The British papers were full too of the war in Vietnam with an in-depth analysis of its origin and possible outcome. Unlike much of the American media which was generally hostile, the British press took a more balanced view. Sean again noticed how international the English papers were in their scope and coverage, whereas those in the USA were parochial in nature and, for instance, hardly ever gave much cover to the fighting in Northern Ireland.

As the sun rose higher in the sky and the temperature increased, he went in for his second swim of the day. The water was quite warm but still cool enough to give a welcome relief from the almost oppressive heat of the beach. When he returned to his rug he drank the cold white wine from a crystal glass and bit into a ham sandwich. What a life, he thought, as he lay back for a short snooze.

He heard him first, as the sound of a gentle splashing penetrated his senses dulled by the wine and heady atmosphere. He half-raised his head and then saw him. A tall lanky figure with blue bathing trunks, his hair was short and grey and he put him at about his mid-fifties. He was gently splashing water over himself in the shallows, his pale untanned and hairless body glistening in the sunlight. Sean looked over his shoulder and noticed the stranger's belongings neatly arranged some 50 yards away at the top of the beach, just where one of the paths from the road dipped down onto the sand.

As he looked at him the man waved and shouted, 'Hello.'

They were the only two people there and Sean was not too surprised at his apparent friendliness. Amercians were like that, always first to make an approach to the reserved foreigner, and Sean was obviously not American, with all those newspapers beside him. He picked one up but noticed the sun was now almost shining directly onto his previously shaded patch. He got up and then decided to join the stranger in the water. And so circumstance, or was it? took Sean onwards to his destiny.

'Hello, what a fine day,' he said as he splashed noisily into the calm sea and forgetting again that he was in Florida. He noticed the strangers' pointed chin and somewhat elongated ears. He looked unfit with a sallow anaemic complexion. He couldn't place his accent, which wasn't American but was possibly of European origin.

'Yes, it's great. Have only just arrived myself yesterday, came down from Washington. What brings an Englishman here? On holiday? By the way, Toni Angelini's my name.'

He put out his slim long hand and Sean took it and grasped it firmly. He was surprised at his weak handshake as he felt the stranger's piercing brown eyes command his whole attention. He wasn't uncomfortable, just slightly confused about his manner. He also noted how, like most Americans, he was very forthcoming. Sean was happy to respond in a like manner.

'No, I'm not on holiday. Actually, I live locally and am an exchange pilot with your Air Force. I am in the Royal Air Force and have only another couple of months here before I return to England.'

'Well, that's interesting. I have never met a fighter pilot before, face to face, I mean. I live a fairly unexciting life as a property developer, have come down here to see what's available and marketable. Where are you stationed?'

Sean hesitated. Of all the people he had met, Toni Angelini was one of the hardest to fathom. 'How did he know he was a fighter pilot?' He hadn't mentioned that he was. Just an exchange pilot was all he had said. 'Strange,' he thought. He doesn't really look like a property tycoon. He just didn't believe him.

'I am at MacDill Air Force Base just across the water and, yes, I am a fighter pilot.'

Sean looked straight into Toni's eyes as he made the final

102

remark, hoping to see some reaction, but he didn't flinch an eyelid. Predictably, he met the Englishman's stare with a penetrating gaze of his own.

'Yes, I guessed you must have come from that base over there. Noisy aircraft aren't they? Phantoms I suppose. Guess you are involved in that war of ours. What a terrible waste of our manpower, money and lives. We should never have got involved. Communism will eventually die on its own without having to fight it. People will see it for what it truly is: a dictatorship of the poor and oppressed. You know, if we just let South Vietnam go and concentrate on trading relations and commercial and cultural exchanges, then the people will eventually decide themselves which system is best for them. For instance, if McDonald's opened up hamburger stores there, even under the so-called government's control, then who knows how long it would be before a creeping form of capitalism got a hold on the economy? And no hot war involving napalm, guns and chemical sprays need have been fought. Again, the world's communications in the form of TV and computers are expanding so rapidly that soon we will all be interdependent one upon the other. You, of course, in joining the military are only doing your job and at present by flying with the United States Air Force you are helping to perpetuate the problem in South East Asia. The government here shouldn't interfere but should let the countries evolve themselves. Nothing personal against you, of course.'

Sean was amazed at this man's logic and broad thinking. Here was a person who thought as he did. Keen to prolong and deepen the conversation, he responded quickly.

'That's all very well, but what if some other power like China takes an active interest and tries to take over Vietnam?'

'Let them try. Like America, they will probably fail too,' he said.

'You think America will pull out. I don't think there's a chance,' said Sean.

'Yes, I agree, I just don't think the United States has the

will or motivation to carry on a war so far from home, just on the pretext of defeating Communism. What is Communism anyway? Most people here couldn't define it properly. Of course, you have your own problem in Northern Ireland. What do you think of that?'

Taken aback slightly by the swift change of subject, the Englishman, now on the defensive, sought to gain time by procrastination.

'Well, I'm only a fighter pilot and don't involve myself with politics. My main interest at home is natural history.'

'But you must have an opinion.'

Toni's eyes narrowed into black slits, his forehead became furrowed and Sean felt himself succumb to the inquisition of the stranger, whose eyes were now boring into him and demanding an answer.

'Yes, I have, but it's very simple.' He tried to parry his inquisitor and present a confidence he did not feel. 'You would probably disagree but, like every conflict in life, there is never one reason or any one solution. The sooner we can learn to look at history as a guide to past mistakes and not as a lesson on how to perpetuate nationalism, the better. We must eventually unite as one people on this planet or we will destroy ourselves. We must unite within Europe first and when we are all Europeans, the Irish problem simply fades away.' He could see Toni nodding his head, obviously in agreement. The inquisitional atmosphere had passed and he felt more comfortable. He went on confidently. 'We are all citizens of this planet. However old we are, we're here for only just a very short time and that time gets shorter as we grow older. What on earth are we doing in Northern Ireland, bombing, shooting and rioting against each other? All for what? Nationalism? All both sides are doing there is dividing the people into hatred and bitterness, with burnt homes, lost businesses and lost jobs. The longer it goes on, the longer it will take to resolve. Why can't both sides think, think and think again on how to be constructive, how to seek compromise with those with whom you disagree, how to love one another and how to build bridges to span the present hurt and hatred. I am sure that both sides can still perpetuate their proud history, not by marching to the sound of bombs and bullets, but by walking side by side with open hands of friendship and conciliation. How much better to build a safe place for their children and their children's children? I hope one day I will see a time when the wild and beautiful places of The Burren near Galway and the Glens of Antrim respond to the communion and happy laughter of all people of this planet. Perhaps one day, they and all of us, will be true citizens of this one world instead of citizens divided by bigotry and animosity. Perhaps in time all people will learn to talk to each other with a common language and love in their hearts. Utopia? I think not. I believe that if we have leaders with vision and courage we can get there.'

The warm gulf waters still lapped at their feet. A flock of pelicans, large ungainly birds, had found a shoal of fish just a short distance out to sea. They plunged headlong into the water with a loud splashing noise that interrupted the two people in their discussion.

Toni said nothing for a moment, deep in thought, then with authority and assuredness he declared, 'Well, that was very profound and I am glad to meet someone who thinks as I do. I too am a believer in a united world where all people have a sense of belonging one to another. You know, you huma . . .' he stopped abruptly, totally confused for a moment. He looked away and then splashed himself with water and went on. 'The human race has a long way to go before we get to your Utopia. You mentioned leaders with vision and courage. Where are they? I see nobody with the stature and authority necessary to bring it about.' He hesitated for a moment and then went on. 'Do you believe life exists on other planets?'

Sean was already surprised by Toni's reference to humans and his total confusion and obvious discomfort and now he talks about life elsewhere in the universe. Who is this man? Who does he represent and why has he met me here? Was it circumstantial or could it possible have been pre-arranged? A sense of fear passed over Sean, not a fear of immediate danger but more a sense of foreboding, a sense of apprehension and anxiety of what was coming next. Had someone told him of his recent experience in The Triangle? Was he checking up on him? Perhaps he was from The Pentagon or the CIA?

'Well, I don't know, haven't thought of it much. Astronomy is an interesting subject and I only wish I had time to study it. I'm certain there are other planets that are inhabited but I can't be sure that other civilizations have actually visited us until I meet them myself. Call me a believing sceptic.'

He laughed but underneath he felt very uncomfortable, uncertain where the conversation was leading.

Toni looked at him with a curious expression of bewilderment, or was it just plain disbelief.

'You haven't actually seen anything strange when flying way up there at high altitude?'

Sean felt the inquisitor was at it again.

'No, occasionally one sees things that at first are odd but are quickly explained as reflected lights from the instrument panel. Or once, when the moon rose in abnormal atmospheric light conditions and reflected off the sea and high cloud it looked like a huge bright saucer, but just for an instant.'

Now he felt that Toni really did know something.

'Interesting. Have you ever thought of leaving your Air Force and taking up another career?'

Another question out the blue. Sean was getting irritated. Perhaps he should break off the conversation and return to his newspapers. The sun was hot and he felt himself burning, even though he was still up to his waist in the cool Gulf waters.

'No, I'm quite happy with my present career and I love flying. Why do you ask?'

'Well, a young man like you with intelligence and energy is wasting himself in the military. You could make much more money working for me. I could give you a good job here in America.'

Sean hesitated for a moment. So that was it, a job offer. It had happened before. These Americans see our English accent as a powerful sales weapon in the cut-throat world of commerce. For a fleeting instant he thought of Gayle and her wish for him to stay in America. Would it work, a job here, a big house, lots of money and a beautiful wife? No it wouldn't work. He knew he loved England too much, its changing landscape and seasons, its gentle and kindly people and, above all, its rich natural environment; and anyway he enjoyed the flying and comradeship. He quickly dismissed the invitation.

'No thanks. Money is not everything. You can't buy happiness and I am happy in my job. I love it and I don't think I could live permanently in any country outside Britain. When, and if, I marry, then perhaps I will consider leaving the Royal Air Force and settling down in the countryside.'

Sean saw the disappointment in the American's face, if he truly was an American, but he bounced back.

'Don't be so hasty. Look, my house is just a minute's walk over there.' He pointed back across the beach and over the surrounding trees. 'Come on, have a Martini or, as I know you Englishmen like, a gin and tonic. I can give you some lunch too.'

'No, I've got my lunch here and I can't really leave my things unattended on the beach.'

Sean hoped that would be the end of it, but Toni persisted.

'Come on,' he said. 'Your belongings will be OK here. Nobody will steal them. I've seldom known anyone to visit the place, let alone pinch anything.'

The Englishman wavered. Toni intrigued him and he was curious to see his house. Maybe he would find out more about him. Wouldn't do any harm for just half an hour or so.

'OK then, just for a short while but I won't stay for lunch, thanks all the same.'

They both walked up the beach. A gentle off-shore breeze

had sprung up and it felt cool on their backs. Sean covered over his gear with the rug. 'Nothing much to pinch anyway,' he thought to himself. Toni gathered his few things together and they chatted on about politics and world affairs as they walked through the pine trees and across the road. He noticed that the red Mustang car was still there, obviously not Toni's, probably belonging to a visitor to one of the large houses or someone just out for a stroll.

The estate of low bungalows, all equally spaced and all looking exactly alike, was well hidden from view by a thicket of scrub and tall bushes. Toni guided Sean to one of the houses. They had all been newly built within the last year and as they walked up the white concrete drive he explained how this was one of the estates recently built by his property company.

'They all sold before completion,' he added.

Sean, wanting to believe him, noticed that at least two of the dwellings looked unoccupied. His doubts about his host increased as he entered the bungalow and observed the sparseness of the place: little furniture, no carpets on the bare wooden floors and only inexpensive drab curtains complemented the white Venetian blinds.

As if reading his mind Toni said, 'This is just a weekend retreat for me. When I get time I will organize some decent furniture and fittings, but it serves its purpose. I find it comfortable and quiet. Ice and lemon with your drink?'

He looked relaxed, which is more than Sean could say for himself. Surely someone who runs his own company involving houses could just snap a finger and get his own place properly and decently equipped and fitted out?

'Oh, both if you have them,' he replied.

As he sat down in a none too comfortable armchair that was obviously second-hand, he was handed a drink in an uncut and everyday glass. As he took the glass from Toni's outstretched hand he couldn't help but notice the strange thick blue line that ran from the inside of his wrist straight up the inside of his arm as far as he could see, and disappeared under the short-sleeved casual shirt he was wearing. The line was about half an inch thick and had blurred edges. 'Strange,' thought Sean, 'must be some sort of birthmark. Didn't notice it when we were on the beach.'

Toni sat down in the matching chair beside him.

'Cheers. Are you sure you won't even consider a job offer?'

'No, honestly, I don't want to leave the Royal Air Force and I love my country too much. My main interest is in flying and natural history. I would be bored by anything else, especially if it was in the field of commerce and business.'

'What's this love of natural history you keep mentioning? How did that start?'

'It must be in my genes. I have always been interested in the wild places, Scotland in particular and its romantic outer islands. Sub-oceanic islands they're called. My grandfather was a great walker of the hills and mountains of his native Sligo in Eire. He was also a poet. I must have got it from him.'

Sean detected a slight change in his friend's manner. He unexpectedly became more interested in his talk of wild places.

'Yes, but what about the natural history aspect, how long have you been interested in that?'

'Oh, since I was a young boy at school. I often won essay prizes when I wrote about birds and plants. With the money I received I bought more books on the subject and so increased my knowledge and affection for it. One of my objectives in life formed when I was about fifteen. That is to rediscover the Arctic bramble whose Latin name is *rubus arcticus*. There is a wonderful story about its first discovery and then its loss. I won't bore you with the details but a specimen of this beautiful and exotic flower can still be seen in the museum in Edinburgh. It was collected from its only known site Beinn a' Ghlo.'

Toni Angelini's face lit up in astonishment and incredulity as he quickly interrupted.

'Mountain of Mist,' he muttered to himself under his

breath and then sharply, with a slight menacing tone. 'Have you been to Beinn a' Ghlo?'

Sean was quite shocked at this sudden turn of events and noted that Toni was obviously familiar with the mountain, as how else would he know the true meaning of the Celtic name? He wanted to get back to the beach and his car and return to MacDill.

'No, not yet but I will one day. Why the sudden interest? How did you know about the relatively obscure mountain in the middle of Scotland?'

Toni, trying to recover his composure and sensing that his new friend wanted to leave, replied, 'Not interested really. Just surprised that you mentioned a mountain that I had read something about recently, but I just can't remember in what context. Let's talk about something else. We seemed to have set the world to rights and sorted out all its problems. How do you think mankind itself will evolve in the future? I wonder whether we as a race have stopped evolving physically. We seem to be totally in control of ourselves and with our knowledge of computers have almost stepped outside evolution altogether. What do you think, Sean?'

By now the Englishman was determined to get away. He was totally mystified and confused about Toni. 'Who is this man with such deep thoughts about mankind, who is lying about his background and seems to know more about me than he lets on?' he asked himself. He could tell when he mentioned Beinn a' Ghlo that he really became agitated and excited. 'I wonder why? What is behind it all? Something almost sinister seems to be involved?' His thoughts whirled about from one fantasy to another. He noticed that the blue line on Toni's arm grew darker when he became excited. Was it the blood in his veins that caused it? What did he know about his involvement in the Bermuda Triangle and who told him?' He had to leave promptly.

He gulped down his gin and tonic and said, with firmness in his voice, 'Many thanks for your hospitality, but I must be off. I've got an early start tomorrow, another test flight out into the Gulf.'

Toni smiled, the smile of somebody who knew everything there was to know about test flying Phantoms.

'I didn't know you were a test pilot too. Look, we have a lot of interesting things to talk about. I hope you will soon meet the girl you are looking for. I will be in touch with you again when you are in England.'

And with that he showed Sean out. At the door he held out his hand and with another weak handshake he said goodbye. Sean walked quickly back to the beach and collected up his belongings. Strange that he should make that parting remark about meeting the right girl. He had told him only briefly about his love life, not the details, just his aspirations for a loving, lifelong partner; and why should he be so insistent on seeing him again in England? He sensed a mystery of profoundness that was somehow connected with his recent encounter in the Bermuda Triangle.

He sped back to MacDill, back to the life he knew and could cope with. A life with excitement yes, but a life where everything was known and certain. Toni Angelini was anything but; an enigma and mystery surrounded him. Sean hoped he would just disappear from his life, but something deep down within him suggested otherwise.

Sean's last two months went quickly by. A few more sorties instructing students and that would be it. He would miss them all but that was service life. You moved on every other year or so. You learnt to say goodbye and look forward to new challenges and new friendships.

During the last week he met his replacement, a young flight lieutenant from a fighter squadron in Scotland. He knew him, of course; fighter pilots in the Royal Air Force were a fairly small bunch who all knew each other and considered themselves elite. He introduced him to everybody and showed him all he needed to know to get started. He would learn quickly. He had a wife and two young children, so in many ways his life would be different, more social and more routine in nature.

The Americans threw a series of parties for him to say goodbye. At one, the squadron's farewell, he was presented with a plaque of an ejection set handle and an inscription which gave the dates of his two accidents and the words 'Sixty yards at twelve o'clock', indicating the point of impact of the Phantom on the range, and 'Second in Tampa Bay yacht race'. When they made the presentation they all sang an irreverent song about 'One a day in Tampa Bay'. They would never let him forget and his name would always be known as 'the ten per cent Martin Baker man'. Gayle came to most of the parties with him, but they both knew that soon the inevitable parting would come. In their shared sorrow they became more morose and melancholy when on their own.

The day came when they had to say goodbye. Sean didn't want her to see him off at the airport where hundreds of other people would be there to see their grief. Instead they both agreed to part the evening before on a long walk across the sands of Honeymoon Island, just north of St Petersburg – an apt description of a beautiful place. It wasn't really an island though, Sean guessed it could have been once, hundreds of years ago, when the seas were higher. Now it was just a long stretch of sandy dunes that reached out to sea forming a causeway that linked the mainland to a large uninhabited island a mile or so offshore.

They had been there before of course, but during the day when it was a popular spot with many visitors. In the evening on a week day it would be less crowded and they both agreed that they could be themselves and cry their eyes out without disturbance by people. And so it was on a beautiful warm autumn evening they said goodbye.

She had brought dark sunglasses to hide her tears and as they walked along the seemingly endless shore with the low sound of waves lapping ceaselessly on the wet sand, she said, 'You know, Sean, I shall never forget these last eighteen months or so. We have got to know each other very well, we've had our ups and downs and our differences, but I really will miss you. I fell in love with you and for a long time

The scalloped edges of the Seven Sisters...   page 85

Firle Beacon stood out proudly...   page118

New Orleans - the weathered green statur of Andrew Jackson...   page 56

The huge vista of The Mountain of Mist appeared...   page 162

Mountain ash....with flame red leaves...
page 158

A huge cacophony....of thousands of sea
birds   page 173

The whole panorama of the north-west...   page 176

The attacks of these birds... page 179

The lonely shore with serenity and gentleness... page 180

I thought it would work out, but I know now that our differences and aspirations are just too great, no matter how hard we tried we would never overcome them and find a true happiness.'

Sean, almost beside himself with emotion and feeling, could only say, 'Yes, I will miss you too – terribly, but I guess time and distance will do their work and we will get over it and forget those intimate and lovely moments and go on to meet new people, new places, and, I suppose, more intimate moments. We just have to be realistic. I agree we would never reconcile my love of nature and the English country-side and your more cosmopolitan lifestyle and love of people, places and of course America.'

The sun was low on the horizon now. A large flock of gulls flew across its orange-red disc showing up as black specks, their raucous laughing and wailing calls giving a sense of disharmony to the occasion. The sun dipped down to the horizon of the sea and a colour of golden red spread across its surface. Night and darkness was not far away.

They made one last tight embrace, clutching each other for the warmth and companionship which somehow was about to elude them forever. The sun disappeared and they were left with a great sense of loss. They walked quickly to their separate cars, said one last goodbye and then drove away, each alone with their tears and only their thoughts to sustain them.

6

Shona

Sean said his farewells and his successor saw him off at the airport. He was bound for the UK via Washington where he was to have a short de-brief by the ambassador's air staff and then a flight back on a weekly RAF VC10 schedule.

It was mid December and their flight over the Atlantic was monotonous, a thick blanket of cloud had been beneath them all the way. England was again covered in stratus. At about 1,000 feet the VC10 broke out of a ragged cloud base and Sean could see the familiar green grass fields interspersed with the dark brown of ploughed land. In between were stark leafless lines of hedgerows. It was raining as usual and as they dropped lower he could see a tractor with white specks gathered behind like blossom falling off a tree; gulls foraging for worms turned up by the plough. The dark trees, naked from top to bottom, glistened with the moisture of several days' rain. 'God, how different from Florida,' he mused, but deep within him he knew the very bleakness he looked at had a beauty which touched his very soul. He could almost feel the spirit of the English countryside even at this time of mid-winter when most life was dormant and awaiting the warmth of spring as the planet tilted on its axis.

With a slight bump and a double squeal of rubber on hard tarmac, they landed. So many times he had to endure the tedious repetition of procedures at a large airport. Things were no different at an RAF transport base: arrival details, form filling, baggage collection, customs and then that loneliness when there is nobody there to meet you and you gather in a queue to get a bus to the station. A rail

114

journey to London and then another down to the south coast where he was making his base again with his parents. He had four weeks before his tour of duty started at the big headquarters at High Wycombe.

Christmas came and went. He spent a quiet time with his family enjoying the comforts of home and the familiarity and companionship of old friends. He saw Sarah frequently and they repeated the walk over the Seven Sisters. He made it quite clear that he did not want to get involved but was more than happy to see her as a walking companion and friend. They planned more trips up the Cuckmere Valley in the spring when the weather improved and Sean formed the idea of writing a natural history of the area. He knew then that his hours of work would now be more regular and that he would be able to plan his holidays in advance and he would have more time to pursue the hobbies he enjoyed. He also vowed to visit Scotland, climb its mountains and search for the Arctic bramble and visit the remoter islands of the Outer Hebrides; and his search for a wife, lover, friend and companion, all in one, might end in success, who knows?

Sean's work at High Wycombe was mundane and lacked the excitement he had always craved. He managed to get away on some routine staff jobs to Malaysia, Hong Kong and Australia that gave some semblance of adventure. Meanwhile, his main interest now centred on the weekends when he drove south to his beloved Sussex where he wandered the Downs and river valleys, sometimes on his own, sometimes with friends. He enjoyed the peace and tranquillity of the countryside which was full of interest for him.

He remembered one occasion particularly. It was mid June and he had just returned from living under canvas in the tropical forests of Eastern Malaysia where he had participated in a large tri-national exercise called Bersatu Padu. He had arranged to meet Sarah for a walk along a particularly interesting area of downland near the Cuckmere Valley.

They met at a country pub, The Plough and Harrow, in the little village of Litlington, where an ancient church, a tea garden and tall elm trees all epitomozed the typical English village that Sean knew and loved so well. No wonder those pilots in the Battle of Britain, and indeed all fighting men throughout the ages, were so well motivated to defend their country.

There she was, sitting in a corner of the low ceilinged lounge bar waiting for him with a glass of white wine in her hand.

'Cheers Sean, what are you having, a glass of wine? I got here early.'

'Yes, that will do nicely, good to see you and we have half decent weather to walk in.'

As she went to the bar to get his drink he noticed her slim figure, her long legs accentuated by tight blue jeans, and this time a pair of proper walking boots. 'Gosh she looks pretty and she seems happy too. She's obviously looking forward to the walk.' His mind wandered again over their past relationship and how he kept her at a distance, not wanting to get too close.

'Cheers,' she said as she returned. 'Let's enjoy our walk.'

They enjoyed a bowl of vegetable soup and sandwich but didn't linger. The sun came out and they set out on the ancient sunken trackway that climbed its way up to the top of the downs at Lullington. As they emerged from the trees that seemed to completely enfold the path in its lower reaches, Sean pointed out a deep and secluded valley off to their left.

'Look, Sarah that's Deep Dene, a coombe valley cut out by the glaciers of 15,000 years ago. It's a beautiful and lonely place, quite one of the most entrancing places of the South Downs. You know in the fifth and sixth centuries AD when the northern glaciers were still melting and the seas were rising, this country was invaded by the Saxon people from the low lying countries around Denmark. Their country was gradually being eroded by the sea and they were hungry for more land; so they arrived in small boats and pillaged the

116

little settlements along the Cuckmere Valley. The people probably fled and hid in Deep Dene which was then heavily wooded. It has an ancient history and that age-old carving in the chalk of the Long Man of Wilmington is just over the top there at the end of the valley.' Sarah seemed interested and listened intently as he went on enthusiastically, 'See those large banks on the side of the valley slope down there. Those are Celtic fields where the people three or four thousand years ago kept ploughing the same patch of ground to form a good depth of soil in which to cultivate their crops. As you can see, the soil here is very thin and unless this were done, little of substance could be grown, they are called lynchets which is a Saxon word meaning "little hill".'

As they neared the top, and the track became less steep their strides lengthened.

'Look down there amongst the dark green cornfield, a perfect circle. What caused that, Sean?'

Sean looked towards the point indicated by her outstretched arm, sure enough a perfect circle was transcribed in the dark green of the field of wheat. He had heard of the phenomenon of crop circles and they rested for a moment, sitting on the chalky bank as he tried to explain.

'That is known as a crop circle. Some people believe they are made by forces outside this world.'

He stopped abruptly as all the memories of his incident in the Bermuda Triangle and the mysterious Toni Angelini came flooding back. Sarah sensed his alarm and anxiety and placed her hand on his arm.

'What's the matter, Sean, you looked troubled?'

'No, no, nothing's the matter really. I have seen a video film taken at night over a field of ripened wheat showing strange coloured lights bobbing up and down at great speed and to great heights hundreds of feet in the air, and the next morning there was one of these circles where none existed the evening before. I was told that when a close examination was made of the stems of wheat the scientists discovered that the crop had all bent at the hard point on the stems called

117

the node or knuckle. No explanation could be given for this and certainly it is extraordinary that the stems would be bent at this point, the hardest place of all to bend a stalk of wheat. Even more amazing was that on further forensic examination of the bent stems it was found that at the point of bend the inside was all crystallized in the form of tiny pieces of mineral matter. All quite, quite mysterious. I just don't know what to believe myself but I am certainly not a sceptic; there are many strange forces in this world that we know little about.'

He turned and looked at Sarah and felt how much he would like to tell her of his own experiences but he knew he dare not. She was silent and they both looked down at the enigmatic and curious circle pattern and the cloud shadows sliding across the dark green field.

'Interesting,' was all she said as they continued their way to the top.

Soon they were looking at glorious views in all directions. To the south-west the ever-changing colours of Friston Forest stretched almost as far as the sparkling blue sea, and to the west, Firle Beacon stood out proudly as the tallest hill in the area. Around them were all the colours of early summer; pink and purple from the heathers of Lullington Heath and the yellow of the gorse which had its own alluring smell of coconut.

'Look over here,' he said as he led her off the path to a small pond tucked away amongst the surrounding bushes, 'This is Winchester's Pond, an ancient dew-pond of indeterminate age. If we sit quietly on the grass here we will see many of the birds and animals of the forest that come here to drink. Look, already there are yellow hammers and whitethroats around,' and he pointed over to the hawthorn hedges on the other side of the still waters.

Sarah was amazed and astonished to be shown this secret place hidden away from those that walk the well-trodden path nearby.

'I never knew of the existence of such a peaceful place. You can almost feel the spirit of the Downs here and the shepherds and sheep who once roamed the area and who made use of it. Wordsworth had a word for a place like this in his poem, written a few miles above Tintern Abbey, especially relevant after our discussion on crop circles

"and I have felt a presence that disturbs me with the joy of elevated thoughts; a sense sublime of something far more deeply interfused, whose dwelling place is the light of setting suns, and the round ocean and the living air and the blue sky, and in the mind of man a motion and a spirit that impels all thinking things, all objects of all thought, and rolls through all things . . ." I can't remember any more.'

She fell silent. They sat there each with their own thoughts on life and death and mysterious forces while the blue sky and scudding white clouds were reflected off the waters of the pond. Bullrushes formed tall fronds of green leaves around the edges and blue damsel flies danced over the surface, adding a magic quality to the place.

The contemplative mood and rapture was interrupted by the harsh calls of a pair of rooks which were mobbing a kestrel as it hovered nearby searching for a meal of mouse or mole. Sean jumped up to get a better view.

'Look at them chasing away that kestrel, why I don't know. I suppose they instinctively try to chase it away as of course it would be a threat to their own young, the noise they make will alert the intended victim and will also distract the bird as it concentrates on the kill.'

The kestrel was wheeling and diving as it tried to avoid the angry rooks and eventually flew off to hunt again elsewhere.

They walked on over the hills to a point overlooking the little village of Folkington. To their left was a low mound of obvious ancient origin.

'What's that?' asked Sarah.

'It's called Hunter's Burgh and I think it is an ancient burial place of Neolithic origin some 5,000 years old. The dead are laid out at one end, usually at the higher and wider side which faces east.' Sean pointed out the stark ruins of Hill Barn, whose flint walls stood out grotesquely amongst the beauty all around. 'What stories those ruins could tell of highwaymen, smugglers and just ordinary folk.'

Sarah just nodded, seemingly happy in herself, her companion and in the world in general.

In silence they traversed the ridgeline of this lovely stretch of downland. They felt a great sense of freedom and openness where the vast dome of the sky seemed limitless. The view stretched over ripening cornfields to the south and over woods and hedgerows to the High Weald in the north. Skylarks hung on fluttering wings pouring out their liquid song, and they both marvelled at their charm as they watched them gently descend to their nests in the deep long grass of early summer.

As they approached the easternmost ridge, Sean pointed out a village nestling in the wooded valley beneath them.

'That's Wannock. The name has an interesting origin. In old English the name appears as Weala Hnoc or nook of the foreigner. British tribes took refuge here when the Saxon raids were at their peak in the fifth century AD. The last of the British probably hid in Wannock Glen down there where there was water, wood and an excellent cover of trees. After the Saxons dominated and controlled the surrounding countryside these remaining British were known as foreigners.'

Sarah said nothing. She seemed annoyed and Sean noticed her periods of silence were getting longer. He knew she was moody at times and he had learnt to ignore it, but with the day as perfect as it could be he wondered what was really troubling her.

'What's wrong, Sarah, you seem very quiet?'

'Nothing, nothing,' she replied sharply. Sean stopped and looked into her eyes and saw they were filled with emotion. She turned away and burst into tears, her body shaking with great sobs. They sat down on a grassy bank. 'You know, Sean, the emotions of the past are catching up with me. I felt for you then and I feel for you now.'

Sean interrupted her flow of words.

He put his arm around her and said, 'It's no good Sarah.

We've been through all this before, we will always be good friends but . . .'

'I know, I know, but a day like this and I feel so close to you, but at times you are so distant. I learnt that poem of Wordsworth by heart because I know you liked it, but you didn't respond a while ago when I quoted it. I thought you might have said something.'

So that was it, Sean thought. She's still in love with me and I just can't respond and I don't really know why.

'There was no need to say anything. I loved it and you know I did.' He gave her a squeeze with his long arm still around her slender shoulder. 'But you know it's no good, I'm just not in love with you.'

Her sobs grew louder and deeper.

'You never will be, I know. Anyway, I can't keep pace with you, I can never compete with your intellect. You seem to know everything and I so little. I feel so inferior. Come on, I want to go home,' and with that she got up and started to walk quickly back the way they had come.

For a minute he let her go and then quickly caught up. The wind had got up and was blowing in their faces, but the sun, now dipping down to the far hills, still shone and sparkled off the distant sea. She dried her eyes on her sleeve and as he came abreast of her he tried to console her, his hand grabbing hers, but she would have none of it, she brushed him aside.

'No, it's no good Sean, you are right it would never work.' And with that they hurried back in silence.

A distant cuckoo called its plaintive note and Sean, wanting to break the tension said, 'That's late, they usually stop calling in May.'

She said nothing. They looked at each other and he held her in his arms, not too closely but tightly enough to show deep friendship.

They parted and as she left she said, 'Take care and keep in touch, Sean.'

'You likewise,' he said.

He remembered how he had watched her climb into her

little Mini and drive off down the leafy country lane. He took the long way back to his parents' home and stopped off at a car park on the side of the Downs overlooking the village of Alfriston and the escarpment leading off to Firle Beacon. As the sun set behind golden cirrus and sombre black nimbostratus clouds, indicating an approaching depression, he contemplated on his life to date. Not too bad, he thought. He had achieved a few things, a certain status as an officer in the Royal Air Force. But what was life really about? He had come close to death several times while flying, where but for a fraction of a second here or an inch there, he would have been sent into eternity. He wasn't particularly religious and attended church only occasionally, preferring to find his God in the silence and slow time of the hills and mountains. Nevertheless, he took an intelligent interest in religion and how its power affected people, their lives and their thinking. Not all that power had worked to the good of humanity as countries and nations fought each other in the name of their religion. It was all a mystery and an enigma which Sean tried to put into the back of his mind. But then his experience of the great white light, the tunnel and his total incapacity at the time kept returning to remind him that he knew there was a life beyond death. He shivered at the recollection of his meeting with Toni Angelini. Would he contact him again? He hoped not. As the sun disappeared behind the darkening clouds his mind turned to love and his absence of it. Would he ever meet the right person or should he just settle for someone he liked very much: like Sarah?

He remembered how he had returned from that weekend slightly depressed, not only because of those personal thoughts that affected him so deeply, but which had no solution, but also at the prospect of another dreary week sitting at a desk with a telephone continually ringing.

It was the weekend and he was spending it in the Officer's Mess, unusual for him but he had a backlog of work to catch up on. He was reading *the Sunday Times* magazine when an advertisement caught his eye. It was a full colour picture of the snow covered hills overlooking Loch Scavaig, Isle of Skye. Sitting serenely on the dazzling ultramarine water was a blue and white ship with a red funnel. 'Just like one of those McBrayne inter-island vessels I knew as a boy,' he thought. But on close inspection he could see that this was no normal boat that plied its trade between Scotland's west coast waters; this was a yacht that suggested style and luxury. He studied the caption and small print. '*HEBRIDEAN PRINCESS, THE ELEGANT WAY TO CRUISE THE SCOTTISH HIGHLANDS AND ISLANDS.* Cocooned in the sumptuous ambience of a grand country house hotel. Appreciate the finer things of life – comfort, *haute cuisine* and courteous, caring, yet unobtrusive service. Add a dash of magic! Now gliding majestically amongst the scenery of the West Coast of Scotland. Surrounded by undisturbed wildlife. Calling at fascinating and remote locations. An enchanting "away from it all" world of complete relaxation, with a touch of excitement – and a hint of exploration! You are in a timeless realm of the *Hebridean Princess. THE DREAM IS REALITY.*'

Sean was impressed and immediately sent off for the brochure. Here was a chance to partake in the thrill of a Scottish experience in great luxury. He realized it would be expensive and he also knew that he wouldn't normally choose this style of seeing his favourite country, preferring the experience of walking and hiking. 'What the hell,' he thought, 'and why not? I have saved up some money from my American tour and I may as well spend some of it.' The brochure came mid-week and Sean poured over it, marvelling at its high quality and presentation. Here were glorious pictures of many of the places he wanted to visit. He would book a cruise for sure next spring, but which one? There was a wide choice and all emanating from that delightful west coast port of Oban, all with evocative and descriptive names, Highland and Island Escape, Adrift in the Isles, Hidden Isles of the Hebrides and so on. Having carefully studied the itinerary of each he decided upon 'The Rugged

North West Highlands'. This would take him up the West Coast to Handa Island, visiting lovely lochs on the way. Since reading about it as a boy he had always wanted to visit this awe-inspiring island with its ancient history and remarkable bird life. He noted that the ship, after visiting Handa, sailed on to Tarbet in the Outer Hebrides.

He knew he could get leave just about any time he wanted as to some extent he was his own boss now. No more, the strict requirements of squadron life where a sudden emergency would see him flying off to some distant part of the world and having to cancel a holiday, even if expensive reservations had been made. Now if he booked a cruise he knew he would be able to go. He chose the departure date in the last week of May, a time of the year he knew from experience as being likely to produce reasonable weather. 'Good weather would make all the difference on a trip like this,' he mused. As he filled in the application form, the open brochure beside him, he noticed the reference to the single traveller being always in their thoughts. He wondered who he would meet at the captain's table. He decided on a single stateroom in the middle-price range called 'Sound of Arisaig'. He also decided to take his own car on board the ship at little extra cost, perhaps he would disembark at Ullapool and drive up north to the botanically rich area of Inchnadamph for the day. This was allowed for and according to the brochure he could rejoin the ship at Ullapool in the late afternoon.

Early in July he received a short note from Gayle. A very personal one.

My Dear Sean,

Well, it's happened. I have got engaged not to a dashing young fighter pilot but to an engineering officer in the USAF, the son of my parents' friends who I have known for many years. Is it love? We discussed it many times didn't we and never really came to any conclusions except that *we* probably would never really experience it. You know I did don't you? Anyway

I guess we will never meet again. I wish you well, and keep happy.

As always
With love,
Gayle.

P.S.

Getting married next month. It could have been us! Please destroy this letter. All the best and look after yourself.

Tears rolled down his face as he read it. He would destroy the letter but not now. Was he jealous? Should he have taken up the challenge and married her? 'Who knows?' he thought. His holiday on the *Hebridean Princess* became more important to him now and he couldn't wait for the time to pass.

He had nothing to do now but wait for next year. The confirmation of his booking soon arrived and life went on very much as usual. Weekends at home on the south coast or occasional visits to friends in other parts of the country. All very unexciting to Sean. Christmas and the New Year came and went. He saw Sarah of course several times and their platonic, if fairly close, relationship continued on an even keel. He told her all about the *Hebridean Princess* and his expectations of a holiday on it, but she expressed little if any real interest except to say she didn't like boats because they made her seasick. So that was it Sean thought, no wonder she wasn't interested.

May arrived and a huge high pressure area settled over the British Isles and Northern Europe. Sunshine and hot weather prevailed even over Scotland and its western coast and islands. 'I only hope it lasts until the end of the month,' he thought to himself. A sudden crisis arose in the office over a series of accidents that had occurred on one particular Royal Air Force station operating Phantom aircraft. This problem was partly his to resolve because of his responsibility for that aircraft. He was closely involved with the situation which revolved around whether the causes were pilot error or due to an aircraft defect. The latest accident, where both aircrew were killed, happened only the week before and a crisis meeting was being called for the middle of May at the Ministry of Defence in London to discuss the whole question. 'Damn, this would happen. I have to be on the boat at Oban by 4.00 p.m. on the 23rd May. I only hope this crisis doesn't prevent me going,' he said to himself. Sean was not exactly panicking but he was worried that this holiday, which he needed so much, was now in jeopardy. The meeting in London came and went with no real solution to hand, indeed nobody could agree on what was causing these accidents.

It was Wednesday and Sean was due to travel up to Scotland early on the Friday morning. There had been no more accidents and the general feeling was that the past few months had just been an upward blip on the Phantom accident rate and the problem or problems were probably due to a combination of unknown factors, including aircrew error. This had sometimes happened in the past and the troubles disappeared just as mysteriously as they had started.

He packed his cases into his red Volkswagen saloon on the Thursday evening, not forgetting to include his dinner jacket and bow-tie. The brochure had indicated that on 'Captain's Night' and two other nights each week 'gentlemen may wish to wear "black tie" although lounge suits were quite acceptable'.

It was cool at 3.00 a.m. when he set off on the long drive north. The first pale glow in the north-east sky indicated that dawn was fast approaching and soon the sun would be rising over the great moors of the Pennine Chain in central England. It was 7.30 a.m. when he arrived at the little town of Tebay near Kendal in Cumbria. This was his intended rest place for an hour or two as he knew of a small tributary of the River Lune where a track wound its way down beside it. Here, far from the noise of traffic, he could put his head back and doze if not sleep. A cup of coffee from his flask and some sandwiches and he would soon be ready for the second half of the drive to Glasgow and beyond, past majestic mountains and on to the west coast port of Oban. The sun was now quite high in the clear blue sky and curlews were calling with their wild cries of cur-lee, cur-lee echoing across low moorland fells. Large areas of bright golden yellow indicated the flowers of marsh marigold. 'What a glorious place,' he thought as his eyes closed and he nodded off into shallow sleep. He suddenly awoke to find himself surrounded by a herd of cows on their way from milking and being driven to their field by a somewhat dozy-looking boy with a stick and over-sized wellington boots. As soon as they were past he started up the car and headed back north. Through Glasgow and along the shores of Loch Lomond. What a contrast the green wooded islets of the loch and the purple mountain grandeur of Ben Lomond made with the concrete white tenement blocks of the city. People had to be housed but he wondered how long they would put up with this anonymous way of modern living dreamed up by those bureaucrats and architects of the 1960s. Better than the slums that existed before, or was it? At least in the slums there was a community spirit and neighbours knew and respected each other to some extent. Now neighbour didn't know neighbour and life was epitomized by the catch-phrases, 'Look after one's own' and 'I'm all right, Jack'.

Ben Cruachan appeared around a bend in the road with its typical cover of mist and Sean knew that his destination was near. Oban was beneath him, the lovely island of Kerrera just beyond, its green estate standing out from the sea sparkling in the afternoon sunshine. As he entered the town itself he could see the harbour and moored up against the quayside was the object of his long journey, the *Hebridean Princess*. Much smaller than he envisaged but quite majestic in its red, white and blue livery. A red canopy covered the walkway from the quay into the ship's reception area; above it the emblem of a blue and white crown on which is depicted the *Hebridean Princess* sailing on a calm sea. The car was soon driven on board the boat into the lower hold as

127

Sean was piped aboard by a Scottish piper dressed in full splendour. A glass of champagne was thrust into his hand by a tall dark-haired middle-aged man in naval uniform.

'Good afternoon, sir, I am Douglas Black, your ship's purser, Doug for short. I hope you will have an enjoyable voyage with us.'

Sean took the glass in his left hand and shook hands with the purser. He noted the smart appearance and firm handshake.

'Thank you, I am sure I will,' he replied. The purser smiled warmly and went on, 'I will be organizing many of the ship's events and if you have any problems or complaints please speak to me, I will sort them out promptly. My office is just over there,' and he pointed to an open blue door strategically placed by the entrance with a prominent notice-board, *D. G. BLACK – PURSER.* 'This lady will show you your room, your luggage should already be there.'

Sean warmed to this man, someone you could trust, who is friendly and approachable and someone who is efficient and gets things done quickly. He took another sip of champagne and observed its fine and persistent flavour, its rich and complex aromas of ripe fruit; one of the best he had ever tasted. 'Things are not done on the cheap on board this ship,' he reflected. As he followed his guide to his room, she pointed out the relevant parts of the ship, the Tiree Lounge with its elegant 'old-world' fireplace, wide hearth and oak-beamed lintel; the library with well-stocked shelves and conservatory giving wonderful views out of its wide windows. The exquisiteness and graceful furnishings throughout accorded the ship a degree of luxury and extravagance that Sean felt could not be bettered anywhere. Given good weather, and the portents looked good, this holiday could be one he would never forget. The 'Sound of Arisaig' was as perfect and luxurious as he had come to expect in his short tour of the ship. The room was spacious, with twin opening portholes and featuring a large Victorian-style bathroom whose walls and floor were tiled in real marble. The furnishings were of very elegant fabrics with a baronial feel and there was ample wardrobe space with interior lighting. A dressing table, TV, trouser press and comfortable single bed completed the excellent décor. Sean was impressed to see his luggage at the foot of the bed. 'How did they get those up so quickly, I didn't even see them go?' he thought. On the dressing table was a large envelope. He opened it to find a welcoming letter and details of the ship's programme. In the evening there was a pre-dinner drink in the Tiree lounge for all those that wished to attend. 'Good, I shall meet most of my fellow guests there and no doubt some of the crew,' he said to himself.

The appointed hour had arrived and Sean, suitably dressed in a dark suit, made his way up to the lounge. He paused in one of the smaller recesses and looked out again at Kerrera Island, its colours of deep green and brown subtly different to when he had viewed it some three hours before. Small white gulls sped across the sky to harry a buzzard that was circling lazily over the distant shore, looking no doubt for a young rabbit on which to feed. Other guests were beginning to emerge and he observed that most were elderly, over 60 for the most part and generally accompanied. As he entered the lounge he was greeted by the captain and a steward presented him with an assorted tray of drinks. He chose an orange juice as he shook hands and replied almost automatically, 'Yes, thank you, I know I will enjoy the cruise.' He was again pleasantly surprised at the enthusiasm and friendliness of the ship's officers and crew who introduced themselves to their guests.

He was discussing the weather prospects for the week to come and the vagaries of the Scottish climate with the purser when he first noticed her. Across on the other side of the crowded room she stood alone, a drink in her hand, and looking somewhat ill at ease, until a young officer stepped over and introduced her to a middle-aged couple, intent seemingly on trying to meet everyone at the same time. She was soon submerged in a large group of people all making small talk and finding out as much as they could about each other. Sean noticed her powder blue dress and matching stole. She wore little make-up and he couldn't really call her beautiful, but nevertheless he thought he saw a great warmth in her face, highlighted by the natural curls of her auburn hair. For just a moment their eyes met, but she quickly looked away. He wondered if she was alone, but despite his initial impression he doubted it. She looked in her early thirties and he couldn't believe she would have come unaccompanied on such a cruise as this.

'The high pressure is holding and certainly tomorrow will be another glorious day.' The purser brought Sean back to the present. He had been miles away, his mind distracted by the young lady he had just seen.

'Uh, sorry, yes, what were you saying?' He tried to gather his thoughts together.

'I was just saying that the sun will be shining again tomorrow, you want that don't you? We all do.'

Douglas was trying to be polite to this young guest, who obviously was not enjoying the small talk amongst a lot of strangers. 'He seemed distracted by something,' he thought to himself.

'Yes, of course I want that. I hope to be able to get a lot of colour slides of this lovely country of yours.' He was slightly irritated that he had been caught out not appearing to be interested in what his host was saying. Trying to make amends he went on, 'You know, Doug, you did say that was what you wanted to be called didn't you?' His host nodded quickly. 'I have a great interest in natural history and I really have a long held desire to land on Handa Island. What are the chances?'

'None whatsoever, I am afraid, the only landing site is on the south east sheltered side where there really isn't a suitable anchorage for us. But we will sail close by the great cliffs on the north side to see the huge colonies of guillemots, razorbills and puffins that are there, they really are an amazing sight. How did you get interested in Handa? Most people have never heard of it?'

'I've always been interested in the west coast of Scotland and the remoter islands of the Hebrides and beyond, even as a small boy. I have many books about them and the more I read the more I want to learn about them and the people that lived there in the past, and of course I now have a great urge to see them at first hand. I've flown over some of them at low level as part of my job in the Royal Air Force.'

'You're a pilot then. How interesting, we're often buzzed, if that's the right expression, by some of your colleagues as they fly low over the sea. I am sure they are looking for targets like the *Hebridean Princess* on which to practise mock attacks. Are they?'

He laughed in a gentle friendly way.

'We have strict rules on that sort of thing and they certainly wouldn't be deliberately attacking.'

Sean knew from Doug's expression that he didn't believe him, but what else could he say? He had to defend the integrity of the Royal Air Force and although he realized that the occasional tearaway did break the rules and carry out unauthorized low level attacks, most kept strictly to the guidelines and did not unnecessarily frighten or harass the public.

'That's reassuring, but I'm sure you'll see what I mean. If the weather stays fine we will see some of your friends visiting us. I'm glad to learn of your great interest in our islands, they are indeed beautiful and some say romantic'.

And then the captain interrupted and introduced another couple to them.

'And this is my purser, Douglas Black. Mr and Mrs Noble from Newcastle-upon-Tyne,' and turning to Sean, 'I'm sorry, I've forgotten . . .' The English pilot helped him out 'Sean, Sean Foster, nice to meet you,' and with that he knew the small talk would start again.

'Where are you from . . . oh that's interesting . . . never been there myself . . . the weather should be fine' and so on and so on . . .' How he hated it, but still sometimes you met some interesting people. Pity though, he was just getting to know, and like, Doug Black. The captain, a middle-aged man with a greying, neatly trimmed beard and spectacles, turned again to Sean.

'Mr Foster, I should have known who you were because you're on my table tonight, a pilot in the Royal Air Force I believe and on your own.'

It wasn't so much a question as a statement of fact. 'He has done his homework,' Sean thought. 'I wonder who else is with us on the captain's table this evening.' He would soon find out.

'Yes that's right, not married yet, haven't met the right person.'

He wanted to make his position clear right from the outset, no point in waiting for those questions politely and innocently put, but with an underlying element of probing, trying to elicit information about one's own private life. Some people are quite adept at it and can ask the most personal questions and get away with it without batting an eyelid or causing embarrassment.

'Good, we'll be going in to dinner shortly. I'll just round up our other three guests, we don't want the whole crowd going in at the same time as it puts a strain on the restaurant staff.' He turned to a young officer and said, 'Please would you gather up Miss Warren and Major and Mrs Piper and bring them over? We'll be going in to dinner shortly'.

'Yes, sir, right away,' and he was off across the room to find the guests.

'How long have you been in the Royal Air Force, Sean?'

He was quick to adopt the informal approach.

'Ever since I left school, always wanted to be a pilot, the excitement appeals to me. Unfortunately, I am on a ground tour at the moment doing staff work. How about you, captain, what made you join this company?'

'Please call me Ian, Ian McCloud. I started ...' He was interrupted by the arrival of the other three guests. 'Ah welcome, let me introduce you. Joan and Bob Piper, that's right isn't it? This is Sean Foster, a pilot in the Royal Air

Force. You will have something in common, both being in the services.'

They shook hands and Sean realized that Bob, he remembered the major bit, was at least 60 and must have been retired for a few years. And then the big moment. He couldn't believe it as he saw her being escorted across the room to the captain who had obviously met her earlier.

'Shona Warren, may I introduce Sean Foster.'

This time their eyes met at close range and Sean was captivated by their brightness and their colour, a sapphire blue of immense depth and intensity. He detected sadness too as she said · 'Hello' in a soft accent of the Scottish borders. Her hand too was soft and gentle and seemed to epitomize the rest of her personality, or at least that was his first impression. The preliminaries over, they strolled through to the elegance and luxury of the Columba Restaurant.

The meal was sumptuous, an assiette of smoked Scottish seafood, followed by pheasant consommé, homemade ravioli with crayfish essence, white peach sorbet; and then the main dish of prime Scottish beef, wild mushrooms and a pink peppercorn sauce. A passion fruit dessert and the finest cheeses completed a feast of great pleasure and palate. Throughout, conversation was easy and relaxed. Shona sat opposite him with the captain in the middle and he was able to catch her attention from time to time. He gathered that she was a legal secretary from a small village to the north of Glasgow, not far from Loch Lomond. She liked walking and poetry and read books on history. He would have to get to know her better. It was so difficult when three other strangers were present and he was expected to make polite dialogue with all of them. He liked her and wanted a chance to talk to her on a one to one basis.

Luck was with him and after they had tried the cheeseboard and there was a lull in the conversation, the captain said, 'You may not all be with me tomorrow night as we do rotate the passengers to other tables. Please be free to have coffee in one of the lounges. The ship is just starting its engines and will be under way in a minute. You may wish to watch the scenery pass by as we depart Oban.'

Now's my chance he thought and said to Shona, 'Will you join me for coffee? We could go up to the Tiree Lounge.'

He was quick off the mark, too quick perhaps. Would she reject the offer?

She hesitated and then said, 'Yes, that would be nice,' and turned to the major and his wife and said, 'Will you join us?'

They politely declined but indicated they may come up later. 'Hope not, they seem a decent couple and I hope they take the hint to leave us alone,' he said to himself.

They sat down in a quiet corner of the lounge. The sun was setting and a glow of pale orange rays shone down from behind wisps of grey stratus clouds and sparkled off the sea. They could see the lights of Oban flickering on as twilight and growing darkness enveloped the mainland they were fast leaving behind. The *Hebridean Princess* headed on towards Loch Sunart, past Maiden Island and through the Sound of Mull under the great mountains now growing darker by the minute as the sun finally vanished.

'Beautiful isn't it?' he said, to open the conversation.

'Yes it is, I love the west coast and these islands. What brings you here on such a cruise?'

He looked at her as she sat comfortably in the large armchair opposite him, only a low mahogany coffee table between them. She looked so attractive and for the first time he could really look into those deep blue eyes that promised so much.

'Probably, like you, I just wanted a break from a busy life and I too have always loved the Western Isles and their romantic history. Have flown over them many times but never thought I would see them like this. Lucky I saw the advertisement in *The SundayTimes*.'

She looked at him for a moment as if to say something, but then turned her head to look intently out of the window. Their coffee and chocolates were brought to them unobtrusively by a uniformed steward.

'White or black, madam?' he asked.

'White please.'

'Can I get you anything else?' He looked at both of them in turn but they shook their heads in unison. As he departed she looked Sean straight in the eyes and said 'Are you married? I mean you're alone on the boat aren't you?'

Sean was surprised at her directness, but he was glad as he liked candidness and at least the preliminaries were now at an end.

'No never married. Haven't found the right person,' he was tempted to add the word 'yet' but thought better of it. 'How about you?'

She hesitated, and looking wistfully again out of the window almost whispered, 'Look there's Ben More, I would love to climb that.' She hesitated again and he said nothing. 'No I am alone, I nearly got married last year but it all fell through as he decided it wouldn't work. He left the town and I have never seen or heard from him again.'

Her voice became hesitant and Sean could see the moisture in her eyes.

'Never mind. You'll meet somebody else soon.' He leaned over and touched her knee and she put her hand over his for just a moment and then they both withdrew, the moment of intimacy passed.

'Do you want to talk about it? It will do you good you know,' he said, trying to comfort her.

'No, no, not just now. It's my problem and I'll get over it. It's the reason I came here. The trouble is both my parents are dead and I have no brothers or sisters and, although one can talk one's problems over with friends, it's not the same is it? Have you a family?'

'Yes, both my parents are alive and I have a married sister.' He went on to tell her his life story, not in detail but just enough to keep her interested, and she responded by telling him about her family, how her father, a local headmaster, died some ten years ago of a heart attack when she was only twenty, and how her mother died of cancer only three years ago. She was left with a small family house just

135

outside Glasgow and some money, so she was fairly comfortable. She had a good job in a city law firm.

'You know, Sean, I was absolutely bereft after my mother died, but my religion and my love of the countryside, the mountains, birds and flowers, kept me sane. I used to go for long hikes through the hills. And then I met Ian. I was vulnerable . . . oh let's talk about something else. What are you interested in?'

Sean knew then that this was going to be the start of something very important in his life. He had already half fallen in love with her but he was aware of how easily he, and indeed most men, can fall in love, however you define the word. Her mention of the mountains, birds and flowers, well that was a fascinating coincidence of great significance to him. He had not mentioned his great love of nature, philosophy and the mysteries of life itself. Here was his great chance and he opened out about it all. She didn't interrupt, didn't say a word, but he could see she was captivated by all that he said.

After five minutes she just said, 'Well, we have a lot in common, haven't we?' and again those blue eyes looked straight into his and held him captive for what seemed ages but in reality was only a few seconds.

'Yes, we have, but look at the time, it's half past eleven. Listen, don't answer now but what do you think if I was to fix up a table for two for the rest of the cruise? Otherwise we could be seated anywhere tomorrow. If you want to change your mind we can always go back to square one.'

She laughed, a gentle soft laughter which was instantaneous and so obviously genuine.

'I don't have to wait to answer, just fix it up and let's see what happens.'

She got up, touched him gently on the shoulder with her slender warm hand.

'See you in the morning, breakfast about nine o'clock?'

'That will be great, nine o'clock, see you then.'

And then she had gone and he was once more alone. He

looked around and the big lounge was empty. He had hardly noticed that the ship was now quiet and had anchored close by the island of Carna in Loch Sunart. It was not completely dark and a full moon bathed the bare rocks on the shore in a silvery light. He took a stroll on deck to assemble his thoughts on what he now knew was a momentous moment in his life. He liked Shona and he had the feeling that she liked him. He must behave as naturally as possible so that she would see him as he really was. There must be no mistake this time as she had already gone through a difficult and traumatic period. He found himself already protective towards her and he knew deep down inside him that his fondness and warmth could too quickly turn to wild passion. As he leaned over the rail he heard the sound of a splash and he saw just a few yards away the fluorescence of disturbed water sparkling in the moonlight. A salmon, he wondered, or perhaps an otter? He went down to his stateroom with a peace of mind and contentment he had seldom felt before.

He awoke with the dull noise of the engines as the ship once more got under way. He looked at his watch on the bedside table and was astonished to see it was 8.30 a.m. 'Goodness, I must hurry,' he thought. Service life had made him a quick mover and soon he was dressed in casual trousers and open-necked shirt. He made his way up to breakfast and there she was, delightfully dressed in a pair of stone-coloured slacks and a shirt of periwinkle blue. Her make-up was natural looking, a little mascara and a touch of pale pink lipstick. 'All that was needed,' he thought.

'Good morning, Sean, hope you slept well.'

She sounded cheerful and her smile said it all. She was very happy.

'Very well. You look great this morning.'

Quick as a flash she said, 'What you mean is, I didn't look good last night.' She laughed and then added, 'Don't forget to get us a table for this evening and let's share a bottle of wine. What do you think?'

'What a good idea.'

He liked her directness as he sensed a person who was decisive and knew what she wanted and usually got it.

Breakfast was a delight and they chatted easily about themselves and the places they were passing. As they left the Sound of Mull behind, Shona pointed out the slope of Ben Hiant dropping down to the sea shaped like a nose and named Maclean's Nose on maps of the area, and Mingary Castle with its history and legends. The day passed quickly and the sun shone again out of a deep blue sky. They had seen the prominent lighthouse at Ardnamurchan Point, the most westerly tip of the British mainland, and they looked at the beauty of the white sands of Sanna bay. They said little as they took morning coffee on the upper boat deck. The scenery was breathtaking and the island of Rum swept into view as they entered the Sound of Sleat separating the mainland from the Isle of Skye. Volcanic Rum with its tall mountains of dark grey rock, shades of purple heather on its slopes interspersed with light brown moor grass and patches of green alder and birch.

'Beautiful, isn't it?' Sean said as he glanced at Shona.

She was quiet and looking wistfully out over the blue sea, slightly choppy with flecks of little white waves seemingly alive as they tumbled to and fro in the freshening west wind.

'Yes, wasn't Rum the home of the white-tailed sea eagle that last bred on Skye in 1916? Quick, look out there at the porpoises.'

She pointed out to an area just to the left of the ship's course and some 200 yards ahead. Sure enough, Sean could see a large school of those marine mammals as they leaped from the waters crossing and recrossing the ship's path at incredible speed.

'Wonderful, just wonderful,' was all he could say.

The evening came and they sat down to dinner at a table for two that Sean had specially chosen in a quiet corner of the restaurant. The meal was sumptuous, as they had come to expect, and during a lull in the conversation he could see her eyes moisten as she turned away to avert his attention.

'What's the matter Shona?' he said with a softness and sympathy that surprised him.

'Oh nothing . . .' She hesitated. 'Well, you know, Ian . . .' She didn't complete the sentence but went quickly on. 'All that's past now but I'll never forget him.' A small tear trickled slowly down her face and she made no attempt to wipe it away. 'And now I meet you and in a few days you'll be gone and I will be once more alone in the daily routine of commuting in and out of a great city which I hate.'

'Who says I'll be gone? I hope we'll see more of each other. Look, let's not talk about it now. In a couple of days we arrive at Ullapool where they give us a whole day to ourselves. I have a car aboard and we can offload it and drive up north to Inchnadamph, a wonderful place for rare flowers. What do you think?'

She dabbed her eyes, smiled and said, 'Yes, I'd like that.'

The next morning he glanced out of the porthole as the ship slowly sailed its way out of Loch Duich. A great grey and white house stood beside the loch and caught his attention. Large lawns, soft in the morning dew, swept down to the edge of the water whose reflections accentuated the purple, brown and green of the hills behind. Around the house grew large fine trees and the whole scene seemed to come alive with the splashes of white, red and yellow from numerous rhododendron shrubs that dominated the garden. The sun shone brightly yet again and Sean looked forward to another great day on the *Hebridean Princess.*

The days passed quickly and the young couple gradually became more and more comfortable with each other. The low granite buildings of Ullapool appeared almost as an anachronism amongst the loneliness of Loch Broom and the hills of Wester Ross. Sean's car was put ashore and they drove off together up to the limestone outcrop at Inchnadamph. The narrow road north was empty and they both fell silent as the great mountains, lochs and small lochans sped by with colours and a grandeur that kept them spellbound. Magical names like Stac Polly, Quinag, Canisp, Suilven and Cul Mor; all mountains made up of Torridonian sandstones some one thousand million years old, stood out like fairly castles of childhood tales.

They ate their packed lunch of smoked salmon and egg and cress sandwiches under the great massif of Ben More Assynt. They had spent an hour finding rare plants and Sean was delighted to discover that his new friend had a good deal of botanical knowledge and was able to show him the delight of mountain avens and Norwegian sandwort. As they sat amongst the limestone boulders with the River Traligill tumbling and splashing below them Sean spotted something.

'Look at the dipper,' he whispered, 'down by that little waterfall.'

She looked with her pair of lightweight binoculars.

'Yes, I've got it. Look at it bobbing and bouncing up and down. Lovely.'

It suddenly took off downstream, flying swiftly and purposefully without swerving from its straight course. With all this tranquillity Sean felt he could safely probe the personal problem that seemed to possess her.

'Shona, do you want to tell me about Ian? Maybe I can help.'

She was quiet for a moment, ignoring his question.

'You remember those lovely cliffs and the seabirds around Handa. I was enchanted by them. I would love to visit that island some day as I'm sure the whole place has a history and a story to tell.'

She absolutely doesn't want to talk about it at present he thought to himself and, remembering his own hopes and ideals as the ship passed the great cliffs of Handa ony two days before, replied, 'Yes, Handa is one of the more important bird sanctuaries up here in Scotland. Like you, I would like to visit it some time. Perhaps on our way back we could ask at the hotel back there how one could get on the island. They should know and Handa is only some twenty miles north of here. Would you come with me to Handa?'

He hardly dared ask the question. He had only known her for four days or so. What if she says no and he was rebuffed?

He needn't have worried and her response was quick and positive.

'Yes, that would be nice sometime.'

He saw the dipper again, flying up river on its characteristic straight path. 'I wish my course in life was as straight as that,' he mused. And then, as he poured hot tea out of a large flask and into the plastic cup, the memories of that evening over Florida came flooding back. The great white light and his near death experience, or was it? What really caused it and who was Toni Angelini? He started to perspire as he realized that perhaps it could happen again some time, conceivably even here in this remote highland glen, where the white limestone rocks and the huge peaks, capped now in cloud, made him feel detached from reality and not for the first time he sensed the irrelevance of life.

'What's the matter?'

She surprised herself at her sensitivity in perceiving his uneasiness. She was getting to know him and she felt good about it.

'Nothing, nothing really.' He would never tell anyone about that part of his life. He pulled himself together and got up quickly. 'It's getting cold and it looks like a weather front coming. Look at all that high cloud approaching from the west. We must get going, we've got to be back at Ullapool to get the car on board by four o'clock. Remind me to call in at the hotel to ask about Handa.'

They packed up their rucksacks and retraced their steps back down the magnificent glen, where only the golden eagle and the red deer stags held sway. At the hotel Sean discovered that Handa was managed by the Royal Society for the Protection of Birds (RSPB) and they would give permits to people with the right credentials to visit. There was a fisherman from the small harbour of Tarbet nearby who would land them on the island for a small fee.

'That seems easy. I'm a member of the RSPB and I'll write for a permit to visit. How about next year?'

She nodded her agreement.

Two hours later and they were back on board taking tea

together in the library. The ship got under way and they looked out and saw the purple hills and dark crags of the vast empty region of An Teallach and Beinn Dearg Mor sliding by. They passed a small tug boat bustling with aerials anchored incongruously in the waters of Loch Broom. Sean noted its blue funnel with a broad red stripe on it, together with an emblazoned hammer and sickle. 'A Soviet intelligence gathering ship ostensibly made out to be a fishing trawler,' he thought to himself. 'I wonder what its doing up here?' The cold war was at its height and Sean knew that Soviet vessels were everywhere, trying to gather information on naval movement, especially of submarines.

'Only two more days of the cruise left, Shona. I think we've had the best of the weather, tomorrow will be cloudy by the look of it.'

He glanced at Shona and she looked at him. They both realized that soon it would be time to say goodbye.

'Yes, and soon we'll be back in Oban,' she said wistfully, sadness showing in her face.

As they knew would happen, the two days were soon over. They had seen the 'blue hills' of Harris and they had a day ashore on North Uist where they visited the bird sanctuary at Balranaid. Here was a harsh crofting landscape surrounded by a rocky shoreline with large dune beaches. There were areas of marsh and loch, interspersed with flower-strewn coastal grasslands called 'machair' after their Gaelic name. They heard corncrakes, their characterisitc penetrating and persistent call 'crex, crex' resounding over the wilderness of bog and marsh, and they saw rare phalaropes and terns. They passed by the island of Eriskay where Bonnie Prince Charles set foot on Scottish soil for the first time in 1745, with hopes of winning back the throne for his father, the son of James II. Shona explained how the pink flower of sea bindweed growing profusely in Prince's Bay was said to have sprung from seeds dropped by the prince himself.

The last evening on their way back to Oban was spent anchored in Loch Scavaig under the Cuillin Hills of Skye. It

142

was a beauteous evening, calm and still, the blue sky merging subtly and unobtrusively with the huge circle of rock ridges that made up the Cuillins. Small wisps of white cloud, puffed up in places like cotton wool, clung to the slopes of the nearer hills. The atmosphere was mystical and enchanting. They each knew it was their last evening together for a while and they had found a quiet place on the top deck where they were alone. Each had a glass of champagne in their hands as they leaned over the rail looking at the sight before them; the blue sea, the white sand of a nearby beach, a thin line of green machair behind and then the majestic mountains of blue and purple shades. The captain, sensing the place and the occasion, had Mendelssohn's *Scotch Symphony* playing softly over the loud speakers, the music blending perfectly with the landscape. Sean put his arms around her and she turned, her face looking radiant and her eyes matching the colour of the sea. He kissed her lightly on the lips and she responded with a deep passion, full of emotion. They said nothing, but he kept his arm around her shoulders.

He saw them first as small specks low on the horizon to the south-west and knew exactly what they were. Two Buccaneer aircraft from a nearby base were approaching at high speed. He realized that they would soon be above them, the roar and thunder of their engines only a second behind. He squeezed her hard as the deafening noise hit and the ambience of the occasion was lost forever.

'Noisy things,' she said as she laughed.

The next day they said goodbye, promising each other to write and keep in touch by phone. They agreed to meet on a long weekend early in October when they would walk across the hills of Braemar and see the colours of autumn in the Highlands.

The office was not the same again. It was high summer and the beech woods of Buckinghamshire gave shade around the headquarters building. He was bored and frustrated that

143

Shona was so far away amongst the mountains of his favourite country. They kept in touch and her weekly letters were warm and full of interest. He remembered he was gazing out of the window on a Friday morning, thinking of what she was planning to do for the weekend, when the phone rang. He picked it up, another call about those damned shelters he thought.

'Squadron Leader Foster.'

'Hello, Sean?' The voice sounded distant. 'Is that you, Sean?'

'Yes.'

'Thank goodness, I've got to see you right away, urgently.'

He recognized the agitated and nervous voice of Toni Angelini.

7

Braemar

Sean was angry and he felt a pang of fear flash through his body. The very sound of Angelini's voice revived those memories on a Florida beach which he thought he had left behind some years ago. He was tempted just to put the phone down, but he realized he could not get away, he had to answer.

'Yes, Sean speaking. Listen, Mr Angelini, I don't want to know, I am not interested in what's happened, not interested at all.'

He tried to sound calm, but even his hand trembled.

'You must see me.' Angelini would not be put off. 'We are aware of your incident, you know.'

Now he was really afraid. How did he know, who told him and who the hell is he?' Angelini kept on talking.

'Look, meet me tomorrow 2.00 p.m. sharp. I've got to see you, I'll be by the information desk at Gatwick. You'll recognize me.'

He muttered something about Roswell Air Force Base. Sean knew about that story, anyone interested in UFOs knew it. It was just a weather balloon and the media had hyped it up as something more sinister: aliens. He found himself agreeing to see him.

'Yes, OK. Fourteen hundred hours, I'll be there tomorrow.'

He replaced the receiver very slowly, glad at last to be free from that voice. 'Damn, damn, why have I agreed? What is it all about?' he mumbled to himself, angry again that fear had gripped him and he was losing control of his ability to

145

think rationally. This was not the sudden fear of the cockpit and fast moving air combat. He could cope with that and had been trained to do so. No, this was a much deeper terror of the unknown. He had experienced it before since leaving America. There had been times when foreboding and apprehension had built up inside him, to the extent that for a day or so he found it extremely difficult to cope with life. He could not eat as anxiety clutched at the pit of his stomach. Somehow he had always managed to overcome his fright by believing it would finally go away as time passed and the incident became a more distant memory. His holiday on the *Hebridean Princess* and his meeting with Shona had almost convinced him that a new life lay ahead and now this man, Angelini, comes back to haunt him.

The next morning, after a sleepless night, he set off for Gatwick. The roads were fairly quiet as it was a wet dismal day and people were content to remain at home rather than venture out. As he neared the terminal his fears grew stronger. Why not just turn back, or press on to his home by the coast and his parents, only an hour or so away? That would be the easy course he thought, but deep within him he knew he had to conclude his meeting with Toni Angelini. He must find out what he knew about the Bermuda Triangle incident. Somehow he felt that this strange man knew the answer to the mystery and he would learn more about this unknown dimension to his life.

He parked his car halfway up in the huge concrete parking complex and made his way to the main terminal and the information desk. He was an hour early and didn't really expect to see Toni waiting for him. He wasn't, so he crossed over to the small bar that sold just about anything for the hungry and thirsty traveller. He ordered a sandwich and a gin and tonic and bought a *Daily Telegraph* to read while he waited. He tried to absorb what was on the front page: riots in Londonderry, the Soviets still probing the UK air defences with Bear bombers off the north coast of Scotland and the Americans still fighting and losing an unpopular war in Vietnam. 'Would conflict never end?' he thought to himself, but couldn't really absorb the detail. His mind was too preoccupied with what he knew would be a momentous meeting. The airport was quite busy with people of many nationalities, different shapes and sizes; dressed, some casually, some formally and just a few in the exotic costume of a far-off country; all milling around waiting, waiting and waiting. Sean wondered what was going on in each person's mind; nothing as great as the upheaval and trauma that seemed to be occupying his whole being. He would give anything to swap with one of those carefree holidaymakers off to their island in the sun without a worry in the world. Life was not like that and he had to confront reality. He put his paper down and then he saw him. Tony Angelini had just arrived in the main hall and was making his way across to the information desk. He hadn't changed much, still tall and lanky, but with just the hint of more weight about his middle. Sean got up and walked towards him and as he got closer he noticed the expensive tailoring of his light blue suit. His hair was much greyer and thinner on the top and he still looked pale and anaemic.

'Hello, Toni, I got here early and have been waiting for you,' he said.

Toni half turned and looked Sean straight in the eye as he held out his hand.

'Nice to see you again,' he said in a friendly but somewhat excited manner. 'We have a lot to talk about, let's find a quiet corner.' He looked around but there seemed nowhere where their conversation would not be overheard. He looked again at the Englishman. 'Where's your car? You came by car, didn't you?'

'Yes, of course, it's parked up in the multi-storey car park. We could talk there if you wish.'

He felt those piercing brown eyes striking fear into him again. How he hated those eyes. He quickly finished off his drink.

'Yea, OK, let's go, lead the way,' and they strode off back through the corridors and up the lift into the dark, dank and somewhat smelly confines of the concrete cavern that made up the modern car park, their feet echoing around the walls as they made their way to the small red Volkswagen.

They sat in the front seats. Toni got out a little silver oblong box that shone with a diffused metallic light. He swung it around through 360 degrees and then, seemingly satisfied, quickly put it back in the inside pocket of his suit.

'What's that for?' Sean said apprehensively, 'Checking for a tape-recorder or something?'

He had seen nothing like this before. The colour and its metallic glow was unnerving.

'Damn it, it's nothing, forget it. Just listen very carefully and only interrupt to answer my questions.' Angelini was clearly excited and not in the mood for argument or discussion. He was totally in command and Sean could only obey. 'Have your circumstances changed in any way?'

'Listen, who are you, who do you represent and what. . .?'

He got no further.

'Sean, please don't interrupt. We know all about your experience. Your life could all change, so just listen and answer. Now, have your circumstances altered. Have you found that girl you have always been looking for? Perhaps you're married now?'

Somehow Sean felt Toni knew the answers to his own questions.

'No, just the same. You know where I work because you phoned me there.'

He hesitated and then told him about Shona and how he now knew she was the one he had been looking for all his life. He really hadn't meant to bring her into the story, but something about Toni's manner told him that he must tell all about his personal life; this man was just in complete command and he had to be obeyed. He seemed to be interested in Shona, who she was and their feelings for each other. He answered with a frankness and honesty that surprised him and then Toni planted his bombshell.

'Now this will seem unbelievable to you, but it's true. We have talked in the past about solving the world's problems, about violence, about hatred, about how the people of this

148

planet should learn to live at peace one with another and I have listened to your ideas on the evolution of a world government. Well, what you are about to hear is true and you will see how it has a direct bearing on this earth and its citizens.' Toni explained in detail and at some length, how 'black holes' existed in the universe where galaxies combined to form another dimension, a dimension in which everything was one and one was everything. Gravity here was almost infinite and time itself did not exist. It was to these places of a single dimension that all earthly life would return; after death when time itself was without meaning. He went on to talk about many things ending up with what he wanted of Sean. 'We need your help, which will involve your trust, understanding and above all, your courage.'

Sean didn't interrupt. He was spellbound. He couldn't believe what he was hearing; about life itself, about the happenings on North Rona, that island that had always been in his thoughts since boyhood, and on Beinn a' Ghlo, Mountain of Mist. Toni Angelini left him with a mission, a mission impossible, or was it? He could easily do it but what would happen to him or anybody else that might be with him, and he thought of Shona, that beautiful girl whom he loved. Who was Angelini? He was not forthcoming and it was no good asking him. He knew he was someone of great importance with a strange and earth-shattering purpose. Could he be from the American government? If not, from where? Whom did he report to? Why, oh why, did I get involved in all this? He had to take everything Toni told him on trust. He could ask no questions and certainly Toni did not reveal how he knew about his own experience with the unknown. Somehow Sean believed that all that had been revealed was true, totally true, and he had to carry out the task given to him.

Toni left with a brief farewell and Sean was alone in the dimly lit car park. Nobody had seen them and now he was left with a huge task. He recalled the words of the poem that Sarah had recited on the Downs above Lullington '. . . and I have felt a presence that disturbs me . . . a motion and a spirit, that impels all thinking things, all objects of all thought, and rolls through all things.'

How apt he thought as he started the car and headed for the warmth and certainty of his home and his parents on the south coast.

Sean spent the weekend quietly with occasional walks alone over the Seven Sisters, where he sat for hours looking out to sea watching the lobster boats and their fishermen hauling up lines of pots from the rocky seabed. He thought of nothing else except his mission, as outlined by Toni, and how it would affect his life and his aspirations towards Shona. He started to plan in his mind the expeditions to the places he would have to visit. He had already agreed to go with Shona to the mountains around Braemar in October. Next, he would visit Handa the following May, and in July he would visit North Rona, and shortly after the ultimate visit to Beinn a' Ghlo, the Mountain of Mist, ostensibly to find the Arctic bramble, but in reality to carry out the assignment he had been given by the mysterious Toni Angelini. The timescale had been left for him to decide, provided the visits to North Rona and the mountain were completed within two years. It was clear to Sean that he had been chosen because of his knowledge of science and aircraft, his intelligence and, above all, his adventurous spirit and his love of nature which gave him the ideal pretext to visit remote places. He still wondered why Toni was so interested in his marital status and love life. Sean had naturally told his parents about his new-found friend in Scotland, but he was careful not to divulge his intense feelings for her. His mother had asked a lot of questions and he knew that she had realized the truth of their relationship. He had told them that he was going up to Scotland to see her again, but of course they knew nothing of the change of direction his life was taking and the different, dangerous circumstances that had now occurred. They had noticed that he seemed preoccupied and pensive over the weekend, but they put it down to his new relationship and perhaps a work-related problem.

He returned to his office, a very perplexed and worried young man. Nothing would be the same again until his task was complete. His work became routine and he knew he was not putting his whole mind to the problems of the Royal Air Force; his boss had already spoken to him in his office and asked if anything was worrying him. He denied that anything was wrong and was not wholly surprised that his lack of motivation and interest had been noticed. Somehow he did enough to please and he had a good staff and was able to delegate. He kept in regular touch with Shona and was looking forward to October and their planned trip to Braemar. He could not, nor would he ever, tell her about Toni Angelini and the task that he had given him. He knew she would find it difficult to believe and his credibility would suffer a severe, if not fatal, blow. No, he must stick to Toni's command, to tell nobody.

Although he was able to speak on the phone to Shona, he always looked forward to her letters which were warm and friendly, until one morning in September, a month before their next meeting, he felt a change in her tone.

My Dear Sean,

Just a quick line to say I have booked two single rooms in a small hotel called The Dell. It looks nice from the brochure and I am sure we will both like it. I think it best if we meet there as it will save you coming up to Glasgow. You know I am worried about where this friendship will all lead. We are two different people with different backgrounds, you with your public school upbringing, and officer status, and me from a local school with a narrow and quite parochial outlook. Then there is Ian, whom you know I find difficult to put behind me, but you will never understand about that.

Anyway, I look forward to seeing you again and learning more from you about life and nature.

Warm regards,
Shona.

151

He was taken aback. He was hoping to collect her from her house near Glasgow and driving up the 90 miles to Braemar together in one car. Maybe she was concerned about this new man encroaching on her territory and the reaction of her neighbours and friends, or perhaps she wanted to keep him at a distance until such a time that she could forget forever her previous lover. 'Never mind, I mustn't rush it, this relationship must work out,' he thought. He replied immediately, with warmth and sincerity and surprised himself with his candidness.

... How can you expect me to understand unless you tell me about your past friend. I hope when we are together again you will feel able to unburden yourself and tell me about your past and present relationships. You know deep down that I will understand. You are just afraid that you will be hurt again, but you needn't worry. As far as our backgrounds are concerned, I disagree that they are different, and anyway what does it matter provided we appreciate each other's company and share the joys of the things we do together?

He concluded his letter after much deliberation, 'Warmest regards, yours forever, Sean.' He hoped and expected that the tone of his letter would help her to be more forthcoming in her relationship with him. He would know shortly.

September passed quickly and he soon found himself on the road north to Scotland. He rested at his usual spot and as the sun rose over the purple clad hills he heard the call 'zee-zee-zee' of a peregrine falcon. There it was flying low and fast, its head tilting from side to side as it searched for prey. Suddenly it swept high into the heavens, soaring upwards, ever upwards, until it was just a tiny speck in the pink dawn sky. Sean kept sight of it until the falcon saw what it was looking for and plunged downwards rapidly onto an unwary pigeon. A small bunch of white feathers falling gently to earth and fluttering sideways in a light breeze marked the point of impact. 'What a sight to see,' he thought to himself.

The hotel was in a quiet back street of the town. The atmosphere was damp after recent rains and Sean could smell the sharp tang of the tall pine trees that surrounded the little garden at the front. She had seen him arrive and met him at the steps. 'She looks as lovely as ever,' he thought as he saw her.

'Hello, Sean, nice to see you again,' and she kissed him lightly on the cheek and clasped his hand briefly in hers as she led him to the reception. 'It's a family run hotel and very nice,' she said as an elderly lady with a round friendly face appeared.

'You must be Mr Foster,' she said in a broad Scottish accent. 'I see you've met your friend, Miss Warren;' again that warm smile. 'I'm Betty McIntyre and I hope you will be happy here. Let me show you your room.' Sean followed her with Shona just behind. 'Here you are, number seven.'

He said thank you as he took a quick glance around: two twin beds, a dressing table, built-in cupboard and a large window overlooking a long back garden with green lawn, flower beds and his favourite mountain ash trees in autumn colours. A wash basin and mirror stood in the corner.

'Do tell me if there's anything you want. Miss Warren knows where everything is in the hotel. Oh, I forgot to mention that there's a small library in the lounge with books on Scotland and its history. Do use it if you will. You may need to as I am afraid the weather forecast is not too great,' and with that she was off down the stairs leaving them alone.

'What number's your room?' he asked.

'Next to yours, number eight,' she replied.

'Great, what sort of journey did you have?'

He was glad that they were together again.

'Oh fine. I had a good drive up; but you must be tired and hungry after such a long way. Let's go down to the bar. We can get a sandwich or something while we decide what we are going to do.'

'OK, but give me ten minutes to unpack and tidy up. I'll see you in the bar shortly.

He squeezed her hand and she looked up at him, those deep blue eyes again. He kissed her, their lips meeting in ecstasy and in a passion of lost time. It seemed ages before they parted and for a time he was in a dream, deluding himself that all his problems were melting away with the pleasure of love. Reality soon intervened.

'See you in a few minutes,' she said as she broke away and then was gone.

They talked in the bar over a glass of wine and a light lunch, catching up on all their happenings. He was careful not to touch on her private life, waiting for her to tell him all, as he knew she would sometime. He tried to keep his mind off his own inward turmoil, but, try as he might, it was always near the surface of his mind. 'North Rona and Beinn a' Ghlo; what was really happening there and was Toni telling the truth?'

They decided to walk around the little town of Braemar. Drizzle had settled in for the day and the surrounding hills and trees were covered in a low mist. After a short while they both agreed that, despite its attractiveness and neatness, Braemar was essentially a place for tourists seeking the feel of the great mountains without having to make the effort to walk them. There were many shops selling the usual garish plates, white heather and other cheap items with a Highland flavour. Shona stopped at an obviously expensive clothes shop.

'Look at these, Sean, you would look just right in one of those,' and she pointed to some multi-coloured, thick sweaters made out of Shetland wool. 'I wouldn't mind one of those ones over there, let's go in,' and with that she led the way, the door opening with the characteristic sound of a bell.

Half an hour later they both had their sweaters chosen and accepted by each other, Sean a cream cable-knit and Shona, a round-necked navy blue one.

They returned to the hotel and studied a map of the local

area. They decided that, weather allowing, they would walk up and around Glen Quoich to the west of Braemar. The evening passed quickly and dinner was an informal affair, a family atmosphere providing a welcome change for Sean from the formality of an officer's mess. Wholesome food of mulligatawny soup followed by roast beef and vegetables was served up by a young and overweight Scottish lass. They sat in the lounge looking out at the wet lawn and dripping wet trees while they drank their coffee. A solitary blackbird pecked for worms in the grass as dusk turned into darkness and enveloped the garden in gloom.

'Doesn't look good for tomorrow,' he said. 'Better put our waterproofs in the rucksacks'.

'Always the pessimist.' She laughed and his somewhat melancholy mood was boosted by her obvious cheerfulness. 'You know,' she said, 'you don't know the Scottish weather. It can change in a very short time and tomorrow could be glorious. Anyway, you look tired and you must be after such a long drive. Time for bed, we've got the whole day tomorrow to talk.' He tried to protest, but it was no use. 'I'm tired even if you aren't, which I don't believe. See you at breakfast, eight o'clock or eight thirty?'

'Eight thirty,' he said as she got up to leave.

He sat for a while alone. The hotel was small, only about eight bedrooms he guessed, and it was quiet, only one other couple were at dinner. They were elderly and had little to say to anyone, let alone each other. They seemed unhappy, Sean thought, probably from London and unused to the Highlands when the weather is bad and low cloud obscures any prospect of a view. They had retired to bed early and he was now left alone in the lounge with his thoughts. The waitress came to clear up the coffee cups.

'Will that be all, Sir, or can I get you a drink from the bar?' she said with the soft lilt of a lowland Scot.

'No thank you, I'm off to bed now,' he said, his musings about what tomorrow would bring, interrupted.

The clouds had lifted and the rain had ceased as they headed off after breakfast in Sean's car for Glen Quoich along the minor road that ran westwards out of Braemar and through the woods on the south side of the River Dee.

'While I was waiting for you yesterday I was reading up about Braemar in one of the books in the lounge. Did you know the town has an ancient and long-standing lineage with royalty? In the misty days of the eleventh century King Canmore of Scotland, who killed McBeth in 1057, often hunted here and indeed the Braemar Highland gathering originates from a foot race that King Canmore began as a prelude to establishing some kind of communication system . . . are you listening?' she asked sharply as Sean was trying to overtake a slow moving milk van on the twisting road.

'Yes, of course I am. I'm always interested in history, you know that. I'm trying to take it all in as well as concentrating on the road. Go on.'

He was a bit irritated by her remark.

'Sorry,' she said meekly, and went on, 'Well, the King promised a purse of gold and a suit of armour to the first man who could reach the top of Creag Choinnich, that's the hill that rises just to the east of the town. You could see it from the hotel this morning when the clouds lifted. The name of the hill, literally Kenneth's Crag, comes from the very first king of Scotland, Kenneth Macalpin, who ruled in the ninth century. No wonder the present royal family has such an interest in the area. Of course, Queen Victoria and Prince Albert bought Balmoral Castle nearby in the 1850s.'

They had reached the bridge over the Dee at the Linn of Dee.

'That's very interesting, I'm so glad that you are as fascinated with history as I am. How about music?'

They had passed Mar Lodge and Sean was looking for a place to park.

'Love most of it, except pop music and most operas . . . but I like the popular parts like Verdi's Chorus of the Hebrew Slaves. Again, this conjures up for me history and what it was like for those people in Egypt thousands of years ago.'

He parked the car in a small gravel lay-by and they

removed their rucksacks from the back seat. He was glad she was in a talkative mood. 'Hopefully,' he thought, 'she might unburden herself from her personal problems, particularly with regard to her relationship with Ian, past or maybe still present.' Suddenly he felt anxious. Perhaps she still loves Ian. Apprehension and nervousness now began to surface in his mind. Perhaps she still sees him despite her suggestions to the contrary. He must find out the truth.

They walked up through the ancient pine forests, the swollen River Quoich roaring over its ancient bed of rocks. Great drops of water descended in showers from overhead branches of pine and birch.

'Look over there across the bridge,' as she pointed to a ruined old cottage made up of grey granite block walls with gaps for windows, the panes of glass having long disappeared. The old roof timbered crossbeams were still in place but only a few slates still clung on precariously to their battens. 'That must be Queen Victoria's old tea house where she often came up to have afternoon tea. What wonderful surroundings. Betty McIntyre from the hotel told me about it. Isn't this fascinating?'

They walked on and Shona pointed out The Devil's Pot, a huge bowl scooped out of the rock beside the raging river.

'Gosh, look ... look there you can see how its being made,' and she ran down the side of the bank to an overhang just above the great bowl.

The river was running high with great splashes of white water cascading over the huge boulders. Frequently a surge of water hurled itself over a high ledge and fell into the bowl itself. There were some round stones inside and these swished round and round the interior of 'the pot' itself, and over the passage of time had enlarged it and made it perfectly smooth, like that of a potter's vessel.

'Magic,' was all he said, glad that he was being taught and shown so much by his new-found friend.

A red squirrel bounced along just in front of them.

It had not seen them and Sean gently grabbed her arm

and said, 'Shsh, keep quite still,' he held her a while and she seemed to enjoy their closeness.

The squirrel scratched around in the mossy soil beneath the trees, its reddish-brown coat distinguishing it from the commoner grey squirrel. Away it went, sprightly scampering up the nearest tree as it heard their slight movement. Up, up it went, dodging behind the trunk and then peeping curiously round uttering a 'vut vut' in anger at the disturbers of its peace.

'Lovely,' he said. 'I have never seen a red one before. The grey is very common in the south,' and he reluctantly let her arm go.

They continued up the valley, climbing ever higher until it seemed they would soon enter into the mist of grey stratus cloud that still clung to the higher hills around.

'I have never seen such autumn colours before. They are much more vivid here than in the south. Look at that mountain ash,' and he pointed to a small thirty foot tree appearing on fire, with flame-red leaves already beginning to fall onto the ground and into the river. Around it were aspens with their leaves all shades of green and vivid yellow. A kaleidoscope of ever-changing colours met them at each turn of the path. Always the raging river was not far away where cataracts of plunging waters cascade over chasms and rocks with a dreadful impetuosity.

Shona was quiet, acknowledging occasionally the beauty all around, but he thought, seemingly preoccupied with deep thoughts of her own. They had walked for nearly two hours and had headed up a small track leading up the mountain side. The river had been left far below and only the barking of red deer stags disturbed the peace and tranquillity of the surrounding hills. A patch of blue sky appeared and Shona pointed to a small lochan a short way ahead in a deep valley.

'Let's stop beside the water there and have our lunch. It will be sheltered from the wind,' she said.

'Good idea,' agreed Sean.

As they unpacked their lunch, made up by the hotel, and

sat down on one of the many flat topped boulders strewn around, he decided to take the bull by the horns and tackle her head on.

'Now what's troubling you? You've been very quiet and I know something's on your mind.'

He waited for her answer as he bit into the fresh wholemeal brown roll filled with cheese and tomato. He glanced at her face as she sat down beside him and saw her eyes full of tears.

'It's so lovely here,' she started, hesitated for a moment, and then went on, 'you know, Sean, I've had a very traumatic experience. This man came into my life and we fell in love. I was naïve and believed all he said. Recently divorced with no children, that's what he said, and I still don't know the truth.'

Her lips quivered and he put his arm around her. She let her head fall on his shoulder, her hair brushing his neck, sending a sensation of deep affection quivering down his spine. She cried and the tears fell down the side of her face.

'I gave him my all, more than you can ever imagine.' She looked up into his face. 'You know what I mean?'

He nodded and then added, 'Where is he now?' hoping that she would tell him more about the person that came between them.

'I wish I knew. He just left one day saying he would see me again in a few days. He had a flat in Glasgow which I visited often, said he owned it and worked in one of the large insurance companies that had offices in the city centre. Well, he never did contact me again and that was over a year ago. Of course I tried phoning his flat, but the phone had been cut off. I even contacted the company he said he worked for, but they had never heard of him. So there you are – naïve I suppose, but I can't get him out of my mind. I still love him,' and with that her whole body shook with sobs of intense emotion.

He waited until her sobbing had ceased and then said gently, 'You will get over him. Time is the great healer and

159

all this will pass. However painful the hurt, you will forget and a new life will begin, believe me.'

He squeezed her once more.

'Thank you,' was all she said as she wiped away her tears on the sleeve of her sweater.

The sun at last emerged from behind the thinning cloud. They were both quiet for a moment, looking at the reflections of the reeds seemingly etched forever on the dark and limpid waters of the lochan.

'I suppose you've experienced the same yourself at some time.' She looked at him with a warmth he had not observed before.

'Well, yes and no. It happened once or twice before but I know now, even if I didn't then, that it was not real love,' and his mind turned for a moment to Sarah.

He realized he hadn't heard from her for ages, so much had happened to him since he last saw her.

They ate their lunch and then resumed their walk across the hills and then down the valley of the River Dee to where he had parked his car.

That evening, over dinner, Sean decided that he must attempt to visit the mountain that was seldom from his thoughts since that last encounter with Toni Angelini: Beinn a' Ghlo. He had studied the map and discovered that by taking the main road south they could approach the remote mountain by way of a track up a long winding glen. He told Shona about his long held quest to search for the Arctic bramble and she seemed very interested. 'It was supposedly found in the late eighteenth century and again in 1841 around Beinn a' Ghlo. It is a lovely plant with bright red petals. Most botanists think it is now extinct, but I believe it could still be found somewhere on the mountain's slopes. Anyway, it's a beautiful place to visit, I have flown over it but have never seen it from the ground before. How about a visit to the area tomorrow, just to see what it's like. It will be a long walk but if the weather is reasonable then we should enjoy it. We won't find the bramble of course since it flowers in late June. What do you think?'

160

'Yes, let's go. I'm sure we will see something new and the weather looks a bit more settled now.'

They sat in the lounge until quite late, looking through the variety of books, many obviously belonging to the family owners of the hotel. Sean found one on the geology and origins of Scottish mountains and was deeply engrossed when she came up to him and said she was off to bed.

A light kiss on his lips and then, 'I need time,' she paused, 'time to adjust to that new life you mentioned.'

She squeezed his arm and left.

Sean put down the book, his emotions running high. He thought about tomorrow and The Mountain of Mist. The old fears and trepidation came back to haunt him and he knew he would have a sleepless night.

They set off early and parked in a lay-by beside the main road to Pitlochry. A blanket of stratus cloud covered the hills but Sean could tell that as the sun's heat got to work it would soon break up and give a reasonably fine day. They started their long hike up the glen that led through the mountains and up to Loch Loch under the mountain.

They said little to each other as they walked up the gravel road used by so many Highlanders in days gone past. Small crofts still dotted the hillside, smoke from their peat fires swirling out of the chimney, showing that they were occupied. Sean knew that there would be many more dwellings further up the glen that would be just ruins, with piles of granite boulders and moss-covered, crumbling walls marking the sites where people lived before the Highland clearances of over a hundred years before.

The colours of autumn were all about them, like the day before. Yellow aspen, orange and green birch and the vivid gold and deep red of the rowan trees dominated the river valley. The moorland had that special hue, seen only at this time of the year in the Highlands, of pale purple and delicate shades of brown and light red. The silence and tranquillity of the scene was broken now and again by the echoing roars of rutting stags across the glen.

'Look, there they are, over there just above that crag.'

He pointed with his outstretched arm, sorry in a way to intrude his voice on such a peaceful scene.

'There must be twenty or thirty of them,' she whispered as she held binoculars to her eyes. 'They must be the hinds and amongst them is the dominant stag roaring and warning other potential challengers to keep away.'

'Yes, I am sure you're right. I've read a bit about the red deer and it is at this time of the year that the stags start to come down from the high ground where they have been most of the summer. Then an individual gathers up a herd of hinds which he claims for his own. He tries to keep his hinds together on ground over which he can easily run, just as a collie does with sheep. Occasionally another stag will try to interfere and then there could be a fight, but such fights are not common, I gather, as it's not in the interest of the species for heavy fighting amongst the males in which one might be killed and the other exhausted.'

They sat down and watched the herd of deer for a while as they crossed the moor on the far side of the river.

'I'm enjoying this,' was all she said.

The stag, having made his point, fell silent and all that could be heard was the sound of the river, its waters bouncing and breaking into great splashes of white as it tumbled over the rocks in the valley just below them.

It was well past midday when on climbing a small rise, the huge vista of The Mountain of Mist appeared before them. True to its name, the tops were hidden in wreaths of cloud that tumbled down the side like a great white blanket. This was Shona's first sight of the mountain.

'It's beautiful, just as you described when you first told me about it. We're not going to get to the top today because of the time and weather, but I am looking forward to next July when we can come again and search for the Arctic bramble.'

'I'm glad you like it,' he said, but he suddenly had a pang of fear and he was glad he did not plan to climb to the top that day. 'We have lost a few aircraft in the past around here,' he added.

She quickly took up the point.

162

'Why, what happened?'

'Nobody knows really,' he hedged, wishing he had never raised the subject. 'When you're flying fast at low level in the mountains you have to be very careful if there's low cloud around. One mistake and it's too late. I guess they all just made a mistake.'

He tried to sound convincing and was glad when she didn't pursue the subject. He knew that next year he could discover the truth about the mountain, a truth that Toni Angelini had more than hinted at.

They sat down to eat their lunch, viewing the splendour of mountain, moor and river that surrounded them with an atmosphere of permanence and slow time. 'Was this really a mysterious place as Toni had indicated?' he thought to himself, 'with all this beauty and symmetry'. He found the story difficult to accept. He shuddered involuntarily and tried to hide his growing fear and apprehension.

'Time to go,' he said, putting away the large tea flask and gathering his things together.

Shona didn't make a move immediately but just sat there awhile. The clouds had partially lifted revealing deep glacial coombes and valleys strewn with large boulders and rocky crags.

'Pity, it seems a shame to leave such a place. Can't wait to climb it next year,' and with that she got up and they began to walk slowly back to their car.

A flock of redwings, with their white eye-stripes and chestnut-red flanks, flew past heralding the approach of winter weather. Shona pointed out the blue flowers of scabious, harebells and milkwort, their colours standing out clearly amongst the gentle green of the grassy bank beside the road.

The next few days were cloudy with constant drizzle and they were content to pass the time reading and exploring short walks in the forests near their hotel.

The time came to say goodbye and as they parted she held him tightly and he felt the warmth and softness of her body.

'I can't wait to see you again. I shall miss you more than you can imagine . . .'

She paused, waiting for his reaction.

'I know, I will miss you too . . .' she interrupted, 'but Sean, I need time, perhaps more time than you will let me have.'

'No, you can have as much time as you like. I understand and I will wait, forever if necessary. I love you, you know that, don't you?'

'Oh Sean . . .'

She gave him a long loving hug and kissed him.

He felt alone again as she drove off, the gravel of the hotel car park making a discordant scraping noise under the tyres.

8

Handa

New Year 1974 came and went. Sean's relationship with Shona developed and matured. He had almost gone up to her home for the New Year celebrations but they both agreed that perhaps their planned holiday together alone on Handa and the north-west of Scotland would finally prove the depth and extent of the feelings they each shared one for the other. Then and only then would she feel free to let him enter and share her life and friends in an open and honest manner.

Sean had obtained the necessary permission from the RSPB to spend three days on Handa the following May. They had given him details of a boatman who would arrange the trip from Tarbet, a small isolated community just north of Scourie in Sutherland, to the island itself. They were advised to take their own food, matches and other essentials for their short stay. In asking about Handa he had also taken the opportunity to seek information on North Rona which he planned to visit in July. He had obtained a pamphlet on the island's history. This contained a good deal of information and explained how for generations men of Ness in the Outer Hebrides sailed each year to a storm lashed granite rock called Sula Sgheir near North Rona to carry out the culling of young gannets. These sea birds once formed the staple diet of the people who lived on the islands some 200 years before; they were also used as a source of oil for cooking and lighting. In July and August ten men from Ness, under the leadership of a man they call The Gaffer, still make the journey to the isolated rock and are allowed to kill 2,000 young birds for food. The pamphlet went on, 'The birds are killed swiftly with a special fowling stick which has a spring-loaded jaw designed to throttle them and break their necks simultaneously. They are then decapitated, plucked, singed and then salted in a make-shift factory. At Port of Ness they sell for £13 a brace and the meat is said to taste something like kipper. It is regarded as a delicacy and is now exported to the Continent.'

He managed to get a contact in Port of Ness who could arrange for a landing on North Rona by one of the trawlers engaged in the culling of gannets. Sean had phoned this contact, a Mr Hamish McEvoy, who turned out to be the owner of a trawler, who provisionally booked them a trip at the end of July for three days.

'This is just tremendous,' he thought, 'things are moving fast; Handa in May which will allow me to prepare for the more difficult challenge of North Rona in July. At the same time I will really get to know Shona and she will have the chance of deciding on her own future with or without me.'

He did not have any access to Toni Angelini, but he had assumed that contact would be made early in 1974. Sure enough, in March he phoned him from a hotel in London.

'What plans have you made to get to North Rona?' he said, his voice sharp and conveying a sense of urgency and importance.

Sean outlined the details of his visit and he seemed satisfied.

'Who are you going with?'

'Shona, of course.'

'Is that the girl you told me about before, from Glasgow?'

'Yes.'

He didn't want to enlarge.

'I need to know more about her and your relationship with her.'

'Why?' was all he said.

Sean was determined to hold his ground this time and did not want to involve her.

He sensed Sean's stubbornness and directness and, surprisingly, didn't pursue the question. His parting words brought to him the enormity of his task and its meaning and importance.

'Don't forget to collect up any pieces that could come from these craft, especially metallic objects. You know what to look for. I will let you know when you get back after your visit how to get them to us,' and he was gone.

Sean became alarmed. 'Who did he mean by "us"?' He recalled Toni's original description of UFOs, what they were and what they were doing. He remembered his story of what Neil Armstrong had seen on the other side of that crater on the Moon and his dramatic account to NASA's Mission Control. The public had never been told of this, nor had the tapes ever been released. He also remembered vividly Toni's account of how the astronaut, Gordon Cooper, had seen UFOs way back in the 1950s well before the advent of modern military jets with which they are now sometimes confused. Again his explanation of crop circles; why such a high radiation level was present, why the grain was magnetically charged, how the genetic alteration of the grain stalks was made and how the precise layout of each individual stalk into perfect geometrical patterns was constructed. Sean believed that one day all these and many other mysteries would be common knowledge, and their reasons understood.

His plans were complete. Shona was to pick him up from Glasgow Airport and then they would motor up to Scourie, spend the night in a bed and breakfast and then land on the island the next morning. They would take enough food and bottled drinking water for three days.

It was a truly awful day when he arrived at Glasgow, rain was teeming down and a strong wind was blowing. On the approach to land he had seen nothing of the magnificent hills and lochs that surround the city to the north and west. He was glad to see Shona waiting for him at the baggage reclaim and he was happier still when they had left the people and the clamour of noise behind in the airport buildings and were alone together in the privacy of her car.

There they were able to talk and catch up on each other's news and just enjoy each other's company again.

'What a day to arrive in my favourite country,' he joked.

'Well, never mind, it will clear up and anyway we will be travelling all day. Did you bring everything needed to light a fire? You agreed to be in charge of that, remember?'

'Don't worry, I've got everything except the wood which I am told we will find all around the shoreline. What about the food? What do we need to get? I'm happy with a few tins of baked beans and sausages.'

He remembered how they had allocated their individual responsibilities and she seemed happy, and indeed eager, to be looking after the provisioning of food and water.

'I've brought the basics, but I thought we would stop by at a supermarket just to see what else we might need. Here's the list I made. Everything ticked, I've got.'

He looked down the list as she drove out of the car park, the windscreen wipers going at full speed to cope with the torrential downpour.

'All I can see to add are some spare batteries for the torch, my two tins of beans and some chocolate. I'm addicted to that, you know.'

'Your teeth will fall out if you eat too much. I had to give up sweets and chocolate because of the damage they were doing to mine. My dentist frightened me,' she grinned, 'but I still eat them occasionally.'

They drove up past what should have been the beautiful shores and wooded hills around Loch Lomond, but which were now enshrouded in mist and low cloud. And all the time the incessant rain, rain and yet more rain.

'No sign of it stopping yet,' he said in a gloomy voice.

'Always the pessimist. I know it will be fine when we get on Handa tomorrow. Cheer up for goodness' sake or you'll have us both down in the dumps,'

'You're right. You know I need somebody like you to criticize me and make me realize my faults.'

He turned to look at her, but her face stared straight

ahead as she concentrated on the road in front. He continued looking, admiring her strong features and delicately shaped and slightly up-turned nose. Her hair was longer this time and fell over her ears with long curls. 'I wish I could see those eyes,' he thought.

'What are you staring at?' she exclaimed in a somewhat abrasive manner.

'Just admiring your beauty.'

She laughed and if there was a slight tension between them it was soon overcome as for a few seconds she rested her hand on his knee.

They arrived at Fort William where they stocked up at a supermarket and had a late lunch in a roadside café. It was still raining.

'Are you sure you don't want me to drive?' he asked.

'No, honestly, I prefer to drive and I know the car. We'll be at Scourie by six,' she replied.

They reached Ullapool at a quarter past five.

'Hasn't changed much since we were here last year,' he chuckled as they drove up the grey and unappealing main street.

'Much wetter though,' was all she said.

She had been very quiet during the long journey but he felt she was more happy and relaxed within herself.

'You must be very tired.'

'Yes, I am a bit, look forward to a good night's sleep and then beautiful Handa tomorrow.'

She glanced at him and their eyes met fleetingly. Somehow he detected a real depth of feeling in that look, an intensity of emotion that he sensed was affection and even love. 'I hope I was able to convey the same message to her,' he mused.

As they came over the hill the wide expanse of the Atlantic came into view and a few scattered white houses on the bleak hillside marked the little northern settlement of Scourie. Sean's experienced eye detected a slight lightening of the sky on the far horizon.

169

'The rain has eased a little, I think I can see a clearance on its way.'

'Told you so,' she said. 'Here, look at this. It's the address of the bed and breakfast I have booked. It shouldn't be difficult to find,' and she thrust a piece of paper at him as she braked hard down a steep hairpin bend.

Scourie was nothing more than a scattering of small houses, a petrol station, hotel and an assortment of small shops. They soon found their home for the night, a new modern house set on the side of a rocky slope, just outside the village. A steep gravel drive led up to the front door. They were made welcome by the friendly Scottish owners, unpacked, had dinner in the local hotel and by ten o'clock were ready to retire to their single rooms.

Sean took one last look outside and, as if to apologize for the dismal day, a few rays of the setting sun flickered through the leaden clouds which had just begun to break up over the sea towards the west and the Outer Hebrides. He was satisfied that tomorrow would not be quite so bad.

He was wrong. It was raining yet again as they set off for Tarbet where they had made arrangements for Johnnie, the local boatman, to transport them to Handa, a mile or so off the mainland. The road to Tarbet was no more than a dirt track with large potholes and a grassy ridge down the centre.

'Watch out for the holes. We don't want the sump of your car ripped off now that we have come so far,' he said.

Shona muttered something unintelligible. She was concentrating hard and both missed the glorious scenery all around. It seemed ages, before on rounding a bend, they looked down on Tarbet or, to be more exact, the two houses that made up the tiny hamlet.

As the car rattled and bumped over the uneven track in its descent to the little harbour, Sean commented excitedly, 'There's Johnnie just getting the boat ready.'

'Yes, I see him, but we're not there yet and I don't like this road or its affect on my car.'

She seemed a little worried and annoyed.

170

A fine soft drizzle had set in and the dark mass of Handa could just be seen occasionally disappearing and then reappearing in the gloom.

The car was parked near the old stone jetty and as they donned their waterproofs, Johnnie, a strapping young lad of about 22, came up and introduced himself.

'Sure, you must be Sean and Shona, hope the weather improves for your three days on Handa. Here, let me help you load up the boat,' and with that he busied himself carrying the assortment of bottles, plastic bags and boxes to the small eighteen foot boat with an outboard engine on the back.

Shore birds of many kinds picked over the seaweed of the falling tide on the rock-strewn beach, their piping calls giving atmosphere and aura to a place of great tranquillity.

The sea was calm for the most part and just the deep but gentle roll of the Atlantic was felt as they left the shelter of the little islets protecting the harbour. To their left they could see huge waterfalls, large tails of white plunging down over the dark black cliffs made of gneiss, one of the oldest rocks in the world. They sat in silence as the boat carved its way over the silent sea towards the dark mass of Handa.

'You'll be going to see the birds no doot,' Johnnie broke the silence with his broad Highland accent. 'You'll see the eider ducks over there, they're nesting on those little islets,' and he pointed to some large skerries tipped with green grass and yellow tinged moss.

It was still drizzling as the boat approached a sheltered sandy bay on the south east side of the island. Johnnie cut the engine and the boat slid up the gently shelving beach with a soft crunching noise. They leapt out into the shallow water, oblivious to their soaking feet. 'We're going to get wet anyway on this visit by the look of things,' Sean thought to himself. Johnnie helped them offload their food and belongings and stacked them up on the sand above the high-tide mark.

As Sean looked for his wallet to pay him, Johnnie shouted above the engine noise, 'Pay me when I get you back safely;

ten o'clock here on Thursday, three days from now. Enjoy yourselves,' and with that he put the engine to full power and he was off.

'Thanks,' yelled Sean, watching the boat as it hurtled through the waves towards distant Tarbet.

Suddenly they were alone on the beach, their possessions around them. He looked at her and they both laughed together.

'This is wonderful,' Shona said as she threw back her head, her wet hair clinging to the sides of her face.

They embraced and kissed, the warm soft drizzle forming small rivulets down the back of their necks.

'Come on,' he said, 'let's get our things under cover up there at the bothy.'

'OK, don't spoil it,' she replied and she clung to him for a few more seconds.

They carried their things up the steep grassy slope to the old shepherd's hut. The windows had recently been renovated with glass panes and the old wooden hut had been given a coat of green paint.

'The RSPB have obviously been looking after the place,' he said, with obvious pleasure.

'Yes, look they've even put an old carpet on the floor. We'll be comfortable enough here,' she said as she unrolled her sleeping bag on the floor beside the window.

They looked around. A long table with a bench stood on one side and on the other a huge open fireplace lay with blackened pieces of old driftwood showing the remains of a fire lit not too many weeks before. A piece of flat driftwood was hung from a nail above the fireplace, on its surface was burnt the words 'Old Dan' and a series of dates starting '13.4.30' and ending '13.4.44'. Obviously Old Dan was the shepherd who visited the island to tend his flock every year between 1930 and 1944, and this was his diary which each year he burnt onto the same piece of wood when he slept in the bothy.

They had a snack lunch and as the clouds lifted and the drizzle stopped they decided to walk up the well-worn path to the huge cliffs on the west side. On the way Sean pointed out the remains of the ruined village.

'Sixty people lived in these old croft houses and down there, where those dark lines show up just above the beach, are the fields where they grew their food crops of oats, barley and potatoes. They are called lazy beds. The potato blight struck in the 1840s and the starving people were evacuated to Nova Scotia in Canada by the Duke of Sutherland. He then proceeded to stock the island with sheep.'

'How do you know all this?' she asked.

'From a book I have had since a small boy about the history of the remote Scottish islands,' he replied.

They walked in silence, their path either side covered with purple heather and dotted every now and again with the delicate pink and white flowers of the heath spotted orchid. Shona saw it first.

'Shsh . . .' she whispered and pointed to a spot only a yard to their left. 'A red grouse. Isn't it tame?'

Its bold red comb above its eye stood out well against its dark chestnut body. It walked quickly away a short distance and then flew off strongly with a characteristic call of 'kouk-ok-ok-ok-ok' and then glided back down to cover a 100 yards or so away.

They heard them well before they arrived; a huge cacophony of sound of thousands and thousands of sea birds. As they neared the cliff edge, Great Stack appeared, its layers of compressed sandstone forming a stack nearly 300 feet high, with ledges teeming with nesting birds, their excrement forming large white splashes down the grey and black cliffs. Guillemots, their cries of 'arr, arr, arr' echoing around the great cliffs, jostled for room on the narrow ledges and competed for space with other birds like razorbills, kittiwakes and puffins.

In this dank, dripping place all was hustle and bustle and on Handa only the puffins seemed to have the time to stand and stare. Here on the edge of the cliff tops they stood guard over the entrances to their nesting burrows. The two of them sat in awe as they watched this great spectacle of nature. Those loveliest of sea birds, fulmars, which spend most of their life out in the mid-ocean, hovered and danced on the wind sweeping over the cliff tops.

'What a most magnificent sight,' Sean was quite emotional. 'All those birds, different species as well, all seemingly living at peace with each other in the most adverse of circumstances. Imagine what it must be like for them in a westerly gale and driving rain.'

'Wish the human race could learn to live peacefully in the same way,' added Shona. 'I'm cold. Let's walk on round the island.'

The rain came on more heavily as they hurried round the western side.

'Can't even see the mainland now, but I bet on a good day the surrounding mountains are a wonderful sight. Look at those seals on the rocks over there. Good place for otters too, but I doubt if we will see one.'

'Yes, it's all lovely, on a sunny day, but at the moment all I want to do is get that fire going in the bothy.'

She was determined to get back to what was home for the next few days.

They ran for the shelter of the hut as it emerged through the rain. As the door closed behind them they each looked at each other, their boots sodden from the sea as much as the wet grass, and their hair soaking and covering their faces in wet strands of black and auburn. They laughed at the sight of each other.

'I'll go and find some dry wood somewhere and get the fire going and you put the things away and rustle up some food. Lucky we still have some sandwiches, eh!' he said.

'Yes, sir, and where do I put the things, sir?' she asked laughingly.

Soon they were sitting on their sleeping bags in front of a roaring fire. Sean had found some dry wood which the previous visitors had placed under a sheet of corrugated iron at the back. 'How thoughtful of them,' he acknowledged to himself.

174

He told her more about the island, about how the people lived and how many hundreds of years ago they elected their own parliament and appointed the oldest widow on the island to be their queen.

'So they had quite an effective and regulated system of government. Where were they buried?' She asked the question out of curiosity rather than real interest. She couldn't stand graveyards and seldom visited those of her parents in the local churchyard.

'I'll show you tomorrow. There are a number of grave-stones just near the site of the old chapel over there,' and he pointed vaguely in the direction of the landing beach. 'There is an interesting story of how the local mainland people used to bury their dead on the island to avoid the wolves which often dug up the shallow graves near Scourie. The last wolf was killed in Scotland in 1743, so presumably the practice ceased after that.'

She listened, fascinated at the tales he related on the history of Scottish islands and amazed at the knowledge he had accumulated since boyhood.

As evening came, the skies cleared suddenly, as it so often does in Scotland, and the sun, now low on the horizon, shone with a brilliance that amazed them both.

'It's going to be a fine day tomorrow, so let's get some rest so that we can really explore and make the most of the day. It won't get dark much before midnight, the sun won't set until about eleven o'clock up here. I'm going to have a quick wash in that stream outside.'

And with that he grabbed some soap and a towel and went outside.

He awoke early with sun streaming through the window. His watch showed half past four. She was still asleep, her head buried beneath the cover of the blue sleeping bag. He lay awake, his mind racing with the many things that occupied his thoughts. 'She loves me, I am sure of it. She seems so happy and the kiss she gave me before she went to sleep on her side of the room said it all.' And then Toni

Angelini and the UFOs. 'What would they find on North Rona? probably nothing but seals and birds.' He hoped that would be the case, but somehow he had his doubts.

He heard her turn and as he looked towards her she opened her eyes.

Disbelief registered for a moment and then she said, 'Goodness, it took me a moment to realize where I am. Good morning, Sean, or should I say sir?' she laughed. How he liked to see her so happy.

'What time is it?' she asked.

'Five thirty and a beautiful, beautiful day. I've been awake since four thirty, tried not to wake you as I got the fire going again so we can have something hot for breakfast.

By 7.00 a.m. They were ready to explore and the sun was already high enough to give warmth with the promise of much more to come.

'It's going to be hot later,' he said as they climbed up the hill behind the bothy to explore the small group of lochans that were indicated on the map.

As they reached the top the whole panorama of the north-west lay spread around them. To the east were the massive tops of Foinaven and Arkle streaked with white quartzite and to the south the smooth-shaped tops of Quinag, Canisp and Suilven. Little black islets stood out amongst the deep blue of the sea, ever-pounding waves surrounding them with flecks of white. Eleven miles to the south, the Old Man of Stoer stood out as a pinnacle of towering rock against the horizon, separated from the mainland by a short stretch of sea. Much closer and just below them lay a remote island lochan reflecting in its waters the blue sky and small white cumulous clouds that had begun to develop.

'Look, there, a red-throated diver,' he whispered quietly to Shona.

They both raised their binoculars in unison. There, with its long dark neck lying snake-like and motionless on the water, was the diver. For a short while it lay there and then, having obviously seen them, it flew off, its long neck stretched out in front.

176

'If you look carefully near that dark rock just to the left you will see that diver's mate sitting on its nest,' said Sean.

'You've got such good eyesight,' she said as she moved her head slightly. 'Yes, I've got it, she's hidden away amongst those reeds. I don't think we should disturb her. Let's move on to the next lochan and then explore the beach below the old village.'

They avoided the nest site of the diver and trekked over the thick clumps of heather and moor grass towards another small freshwater lochan. Here they sat for a moment, watching a pair of mallard duck on the far side gently swimming to and fro looking for food. The flowers of the bogbean plant stuck up through the water like little white stars, their shadows falling on the limpid black waters. Occasionally a light breath of air swept across its surface and then it seemed to come to life and sparkled in the bright sunlight.

'Another magical place,' said Shona as they looked across the lochan and over the hillside to the sea.

In the distance, little sandy beaches and small white houses, just specks on the mainland, gave a hint of civilization; but to the two in their remoteness, that civilization seemed far away, illusory and almost non-existent.

They said little as they walked hand in hand across the open moor and down to the dunes of sand and machair beside the southern shoreline. They came across a deep hollow in the dunes strewn with shells of many shapes and sizes, and Sean explained its significance.

'This is an ancient waste tip of Neolithic man some 5,000 years ago. It's where they threw away the bones of animals and fish and sea shells that they had eaten. Let's have a closer look.'

They scratched away amongst the bones and shells and found a sharp pointed piece of bone about five inches long and only a quarter of an inch wide. A round hole had been neatly carved at one end, and the other had a sharpened point.

'A bone needle,' he exclaimed with delight. 'To think

they used this for so many purposes those thousands of years ago, really remarkable and what a find.'

'Let's look for more,' she replied enthusiastically, and they continued searching, but they found little more of significance.

'I'm hot,' he said, 'let's go and sit up on the machair and have something to eat'.

She agreed readily. It was midday and the sun's warmth had brought out the insects. Bees hummed over white daisies, pink cranesbills and blue speedwells, just some of the mass of flowers that adorned the soft green carpet of grass. They ate in silence just soaking up the sunshine and atmosphere.

He put his arm around her, she turned her head and they kissed, a long passionate kiss of tenderness and warmth.

'She's got over her Ian at last,' he thought, their heads still touching as they looked out to the distant blue hills of Harris on the horizon.

The air was surprisingly calm and only a slight offshore breeze rustled the duneland grass. He gently ran his fingers through her hair as they listened to the silence of the seas from the far off Hebrides.

She caressed his thigh with her hand and without turning she said simply, 'I will love you forever, Sean.'

He knew then, if he didn't before, that here was the chemistry he had sought after for so long, here was true love.

'I love you too, so very much,' he replied quietly.

They clung to each other passionately and neither could stop themselves. They made love amidst the beauty of the machair with a desire and intensity that neither had experienced before. Later they lay back on the grass and watched the small clouds slide across the sky.

'You know,' he said, 'this could have happened anywhere; but here, well this is just heaven on earth, a magic moment in time, where time marks the birth of life itself and death when it departs. Between lies happiness and unhappiness, ecstasy and torment, excitement and boredom; all feelings that must inevitably be found together; one cannot exist without the other and each is dependent one on the other. We have just experienced the first of each of these.'

Shona paused for a moment and then said, 'That was profound,' at the same time thinking 'What else can I say? I've never met a man like this before, I love him so much.'

Above them a pair of snipe started their courtship drumming as they dived down from high in the sky, the wind vibrating through their feathers.

The days passed idyllically and their happiness was complete. They watched the terns, those swallows of the sea, as they began to mate and lay their eggs on the rocky shoreline.

'Difficult to believe they've just flown some 10,000 miles from Antarctica,' Sean remarked.

'Amazing,' she replied.

They found the nests of the great skua and the Arctic skua, their eggs well-hidden and camouflaged amongst the grasses on the hillsides. They endured the attacks of these birds as they tried to drive them away from their territory by diving down from a great height, calling harshly and hitting them on the head with their feet, an unnerving experience which they found difficult to cope with.

They felt completely at home and at peace with the island and accepted completely its mood of silence and slow time. They ate when they felt like it and made love frequently. On the last morning Sean woke up at 5.30. Dawn had long since passed as he looked out of the window. A light frost had withered the grass outside and the great grey peak of Foinaven had been covered overnight by a light coating of snow, looking like icing sugar. The sun was already up above the mountains, its warmth beginning to cause small wisps of vapour to rise from the ground. 'What a morning for a swim,' he thought to himself, 'and the chance to wash myself.'

He grabbed a towel and soap and as he opened the door Shona raised her head and said sleepily, 'What's the time?'

'Five thirty,' he said and she turned over and went back to sleep.

He slipped out quietly and made his way bare-foot

through the grass and reeds. A snipe flew off just ahead of him with a harsh call 'scarp', and zig-zagged its way skywards. The beach looked pure and sparkling, 'inviting' he thought as he hurried onwards down the steep bank, it was calm and still and his only doubts were about the coldness of the water. He stripped off in the sun, his nakedness in keeping with the peace and tranquillity of the place. He walked slowly down the beach to where the waves, hardly waves, just little wavelets, were lapping the lonely shore with serenity and gentleness. He need not have feared the water for the Gulf Stream had kept its temperature up and, although cold, it was not unbearable as he gently eased himself into its embrace. A good splash and rub with soap and it was over. He felt a warm glow over all his body and he emerged and ran up to his towel and pile of clothes.

A flock of oystercatchers and gulls flew past, their shrill calls echoing across the sand to the cliffs and mountains of the mainland. As he strolled up to the hut he looked all around him at the landscape bathed in the ever shortening shadows of the rising sun.

As he entered she raised her head and said, 'Where have you been?'

'Just for a swim and a wash,' he answered with a grin.

'You must be quite mad, quite, quite mad, at five thirty in the morning. What am I letting myself in for?'

The tone in her voice showed how surprised she was.

'You don't know what you missed, an experience never to be forgotten,' was all he said, not trying to answer her question.

He sat down at the table and pulled out a heavy leather bound notebook which they found when they first arrived. It was used by visitors to record what they had seen during their stay on the Island. He thought it important to mark their short visit and wrote:

One of life's great experiences. A place where one's soul and very being are affected by its sheer beauty, tranquillity and peace. A place made even more wonderful by the motion and harmony of the seabirds whose vast numbers are an example to man and show how we could get on one with another even under great stress. The environment on the immense cliffs is often adverse to the birds, yet they still manage to live together in peace. Sit on the beach at dawn as the sun climbs up over the great hills and listen to the waves as they make a gentle lapping on the lonely shore. Hear the drumming of the snipe, the calling of the cuckoo bird and see the orchids, so delicate with their multi-coloured flowers and dark-spotted leaves. Take away with you the atmosphere, mood and spirit of this island and let them give strength and sustenance as you leave to face the problems and pressures of all this unintelligible world.

He signed it Shona and Sean, May 1974.

He went outside to take a final look at the mountains and across the sunlit ocean to the Outer Hebrides, and wondered what lay ahead in a few months when they visit North Rona and Beinn a' Ghlo. They had come so far now in their knowledge of each other and their shared thoughts. Should he tell her about Toni and the strange craft from outer space? He dare not. He hoped that perhaps it would all go away when he reported back that nothing happened and he had found nothing.

The rest was mundane. The boat came and picked them up and soon they were on the road back south. His evening flight had been pre-booked and he was due back at the office the following day. She saw him off at the airport and said, 'Can't wait until July. We've had some useful experience of an island, but North Rona will be our *ultima Thule* and much more demanding. Take care, I love you and always will.'

They kissed amongst the throng of people at the departure gate and he couldn't help but compare it to the solitude of Handa.

181

'I love you too and take care.' As practical as ever he added, 'Don't forget I will get the tent and cooking things. You look after the food,' and he left with a heart heavy with emotion, and his mind worried about what the future held.

9

Ultima Thule

He had returned to the office physically tired after the long journey, but exhilarated in mind and body that at last he knew he had found what he had been seeking all his life; a person with whom he could share everything, a person he could trust and love and one who felt the same for him. No more the doubts and sorrows of parting, and no more making love in the knowledge that it was physical desire rather than true and lasting affection.

They were in touch constantly on the phone and their weekly letters contained much to sustain and nourish their love in their physical absence from each other. He ended one letter with a PS:

I have bought you a ring with eye-matching sapphires, and I shall give it to you when we reach your *ultima Thule.*
All my love again,
Sean.

She was ecstatic in her reply with a letter ending, 'and the blue will also match the wide sky and boundless sea which we will share until eternity. My love for ever, Shona.

He had half-expected a call from Toni checking to confirm his plans for North Rona and the mountain, but none came. 'Anyway,' he thought, 'I can do nothing more. He knows the approximate dates I am going and he said he or his agent will contact me after I return.'

The day came and he flew up to Glasgow to be met by a

joyful Shona. They embraced and checked all the items they would need for their three days on the island while waiting for their connecting flight to Stornoway, the capital of the Outer Hebrides. They took off 30 minutes late and soon entered a layer of low stratus cloud that stretched far off into the Atlantic and hid the glorious views of western Scotland. The aircraft, an old propeller-driven Vickers Viscount, was only half-full and they sat together at the back on their own. Sean noticed that she had had her hair cut short. He liked it as it made the features of her face stand out and he told her so.

She smiled and said, 'I'm glad you noticed. Nobody has ever told me about my features before, not even . . .' and she stopped abruptly. 'Why, oh why, was I about to say Ian? I thought I had forgotten him,' she said to herself. She turned to look at Sean and he smiled, a smile that was full of compassion and love for her. He clutched her hand tightly, their fingers intertwined.

'Don't worry, he'll crop up from time to time, but it won't be long before you've forgotten him completely. Have I told you about the history of North Rona, your *ultima Thule* as you call it? What an apt description.'

'No, you haven't. I know a little bit as I went to our local library last month, but the only book they had was one on the Hebrides; North Rona was only mentioned briefly.'

'The known history of the island dates back to the eight or ninth century when legend tells of a certain monk, St Ronan, coming to Lewis to preach and teach people about Christianity. He was a young man full of zeal, but he found the people impossible to teach because they were always quarrelling amongst themselves; the men fought and the women shrieked at each other. He prayed to be taken away from the place, and his prayer was answered. A large whale appeared in a storm; then an angel appeared and commanded St Ronan to mount on the whale's back and so he was carried to the island we now know as North Rona. Here he found the island inhabited by monstrous hairy animals with round red eyes that when confronted, slid off the sloping beach making deep scratches in the rocks with their huge claws. He is supposed to have built the chapel which is still to be found there today and is called St Ronan's.'

He looked at her, very conscious that their hands were still tightly interlocked.

'Still want to go?' he asked as the stewardess brought them coffee.

'Of course, I can't wait to see the seals, or are they hairy monsters?' she said laughingly.

'Well,' he went on, 'that legend is still spoken of today and it has been passed down from the people of Rona itself to their descendants. The island was inhabited up to the late seventeenth century by up to 60 people consisting of five or six families; they lived in stone houses built into the ground and grew crops of potatoes, barley and oats. They had sheep and cows and of course they caught fish and seabirds to help them vary their meagre diet. It was a plague of rats, possibly from a passing ship, that saw their demise. In about 1680 these rats ate through their store of grain, and when next visited all the people were found to be dead. Some years later new colonists landed, but when their men folk all drowned in a boat at sea, the ancient race of people was finally extinguished. Since then and until about 1885, only a few families of shepherds have lived there for any length of time. The final inhabitants were two shepherds who died in February 1885 and their gravestone can still be read in the ancient burial ground. Quite a story really. They must have been very hardy, as no doubt we shall see. I love the brief description of them by someone who visited in about 1549: "They have an agreeable and hospitable temper for all strangers." Considering the island lies some 50 miles north-west of Cape Wrath I am surprised that they had any visitors from strangers.'

The note of the engines changed and the plane started its gentle descent through the cloud.

'Looks pretty dismal down there,' she said as the bleak landscape of northern Lewis came into view. Rain was sweeping over the hills from leaden grey skies.

'Never mind, it will probably improve,' he said without much conviction.

They landed and were soon installed in a comfortable bed and breakfast just on the outskirts of the town. The next day brought a clearance in the weather as they set off in a taxi for the Port of Ness and their trawler, *The Corona*, that would take them to their island. There it was, a modern ship with a radar aerial on top of the wheelhouse and large winches with nets neatly stacked around them. They unloaded the taxi on the quayside.

'I'm looking for a Hamish McLean, the skipper.' Sean said to a man arranging some ropes on the fore deck.

'Och, I be him. You must be Sean and Shona,' and he leapt down and shook them warmly by the hands.

He was a short stocky man about fifty with a grey beard and receding hair. He helped them stow their belongings on the deck, his large weather-beaten hands and muscular arms making short work of the task.

'Make yourselves at home here,' he said as he showed them briefly round the ship. 'We sail in about two hours time and it will take us about five hours to get to Rona. A big anticyclone is coming in from the west so the weather should improve all the time; more importantly, the sea should be calm so we should be able to land you OK. We'll then be gone to Sula Sgeir to collect gugas, young gannets to you. Hopefully, we'll remember to come back and collect you three days later.'

He laughed, a deep laugh of real joyousness. They both took to this man and felt safe in his hands.

Sean was quick to retort, 'Well you won't get your money until we are safely back at Ness,' and they both laughed and shook hands to seal the bargain.

Sixty pounds cash was what Sean had agreed to pay the skipper and he thought that was a fair price for the responsibility of landing and taking them off again from such a remote spot.

'What are you looking for on the island?' Hamish asked,

his face clearly showing that he felt they must both be mad to leave the luxuries of civlization and visit such a place.

Shona answered 'Oh, we like to feel the remoteness and see its plants and wildlife.'

Sean added, 'I want to make a detailed list of the plant life and to count the grey seal population if I can.'

He needed to hide the real purpose of his visit and to give no inkling that he was other than a naturalist intent on studying its magnificence.

'Well, you both be careful. The rocks and cliffs are dangerous places.' He looked at them both with a fatherly eye and added, 'mysterious things happen on these islands, look what happened on the Flannans. Och now, I mustn't be alarming you, I have work to do before we sail. Help yourself to coffee in the galley,' and with that he was off.

Shona looked at Sean and said, 'I like him, what did he mean about the Flannans?'

Sean shuddered and felt that fear and dread in the pit of his stomach again, a fear growing stronger as he got nearer to his search on North Rona.

'As you know the Flannans are a group of small islands some 25 miles west of Lewis. A lighthouse was built there in 1898 and only a year later a passing ship, *The Archer* as I remember, noticed that the Flannans' light was out. A signal was sent to the shore station and a ship, already preparing to pay a Christmas visit to the keepers, got under way. The crew landed and found an uncanny silence in the light house, the clock had stopped ticking, a meal lay uneaten on the table and all around was neatness and cleanliness. The beds had been made but the lamp in the lamp-room was cold. The last entry in the log was on 0900 hours on 15 December 1899, no sign could be found of the three missing keepers. Many explanations have been offered about their disappearance, but all have been discounted. Even an account of a storm and the possibility of a huge wave brought about by the shape of the rocks near the landing and engulfing them, does not stand up as a plausible

187

explanation. The riddle remains, a haunting, unexorcized cloud hovering over the rocks of the Flannans.' He looked at her. She seemed mesmerized. 'Don't worry, it won't happen to us,' he said fervently, hoping that it wouldn't.

As *The Corona* sailed out of the port of Ness the winds were light north-easterly as a large high pressure area settled over Ireland. They headed north north-east and soon the Butt of Lewis lighthouse was left astern. Despite the light wind the Atlantic swell was there as ever, the small boat rising and falling with the rhythm of the waves, occasionally broken when the bow hit hard into one out of sequence. The boat crew got on with their job with little fuss and the only noise was the gentle throbbing of the diesel engines. Sean and Shona stood close to each other looking out at the horizon, never near but always far. The day was one of those timeless endless days when conversation was unnecessary. They said little, just the odd remark and touched each other when one or other wanted their presence to be felt. She saw it first.

'Look, land,' she shouted and pointed to a tiny speck on the horizon which kept appearing and then disappearing. Sean quickly saw it too.

'Well done, that must be Toa Rona, the three hundred and fifty five-foot hill on the eastern side of the island. Soon we should see the hump of another hill on the island appear, the Paps of Rona as they are called.'

Soon Sula Sgeir appeared to the westward and Sean was quick to explain, 'That's Rona's companion rock with its huge colony of gannets where the boat is bound, and where the men will cull the young gannets and bring them back for export to our Continental friends.'

'This is wonderful,' she said, 'and it looks calm enough for us to land. Look, there's the village,' and she pointed to a dark heap on the hillside looking incongruous against the green of the surrounding vegetation.

Sean said nothing for a while. There was no need, it was a magical moment for him which held elation and at the same time a deep foreboding. Within a short time the whole island appeared and took colour, slate grey and brown cliffs with a green sloping back. A band of white surf played where land met sea, indicating the ever-present Atlantic waves which were never still. To the north was a long low peninsula of broken rock and storm beaches, called Fianuis. The blue sea sparkled in the sunlight as the ship set anchor just to the south-east of Fianuis and the crew prepared for their landing. A small inflatable took them to the south side of the little hill where a small creek flowed over the rocks into the sea. They landed easily and their provisions were man-handled onto dry land.

'Will be back for you in three days. Enjoy it,' yelled Hamish across the water.

The Corona sailed away and they were alone. Everything was new, pink thrift and yellow buttercups gave colour to the green grasses and Arctic terns flew past with lazy undulating flight. A graceful fulmar greeted them with an aerial display, swooping and hovering in the breeze.

He had in his pocket the ring he had chosen for her. He clasped her hands and pulled her towards him. She was waiting for this moment. They looked each into the other's eyes, the majesty of their surroundings making the perfectness complete.

'Will you marry me, Shona?'

'Of course I will, my darling Sean.' Slowly he slipped the ring on her finger. She held it up for them both to see as tears rolled down her cheeks. Gone were all her doubts and past sorrows. 'This is perfect,' she whispered and then kissed him, a long lingering kiss of feeling and warmth.

The sea around them was intensely blue and small white clouds had begun to form in the wide sky.

'Let's collect up our things and take them over to that old dry wall over there.' He tried to control the deep emotion he felt and pointed to a line of stones that were obviously man-made and stretched across the peninsula. 'We should be able to pitch our tent beside the wall. We should be sheltered there too.'

Thirty minutes later they had the tent up and their few

provisions stored under cover. They sat on a boulder and drank from the flask of tea they had made up on the boat, all around them the never silent sea and a limitless horizon. She broke the stillness of their solitude first.

'How frail I feel and of so little consequence here on this small island so far from anywhere.'

'Yes, quite awesome really, especially if you consider its history and the people who lived here for a thousand years or more,' he replied, but his mind was elsewhere. 'Come on, let's go up over the ridge to the ruins of the old village.'

He knew that here was the most likely place to find the evidence that he sought.

They walked up over the slope, the ground covered with long coarse grass and sedges. Here was the village, a collection of grassy mounds and walls half-buried in the ground. As they examined them, they discovered underground tunnels roofed with slabs of rock, all covered with growing turf. More recognizable as dwelling places were beehive-shaped stone huts, again covered with green turf. To one side of the village lay the stone wall remains of St Ronan's Chapel and the small cell where the Saint had lived. Behind this was the graveyard with memorial stones protruding through the thick mass of ground cover made up of yellow-flowered silverweed and an assortment of grasses.

'So this was the place where that ancient island race lived and survived for so long. Look over there,' he said as he pointed to some lines of low banks. 'There are the remains of their cultivated fields, their lazy beds, like the ones we saw on Handa.'

'Yes, I remember them. Quite remarkable that people could live here for so long. I find it all fascinating,' and she went off towards them, wanting to explore everything in sight like an excited young schoolgirl.

Sean examined the area around the gravestones. He saw them first near the largest headstone of the last inhabitants. Several small spheres lay deep in the grass. He picked one up and examined it. The size of a new penny and incredibly light, it shone with an intensity that surprised him considering its colour of dark grey. 'These were just what Toni asked me to look for,' he said to himself. 'So they have been here, but not recently, these things are too deeply buried within the grass.' Again he felt that pang of fear in his stomach as the dreadful reality of what he had found struck home. He searched around and found more in several different and scattered places around the village. Shona saw him picking up pieces from the ground.

'What have you got there?' she asked.

He tried to appear casual and unconcerned.

'Oh just a few pieces of metal. They seem incongruous here on this remote place, probably left over from some scientific study.'

She seemed satisfied but wanted to see what he had found. He took one of the eleven pieces he had collected out of his pocket and gave it to her. She examined it closely.

'Never seen anything like this before. Look at how it shines, almost a pink hue in places.'

He nodded and said, 'I'll take some pieces back for analysis by my colleagues. Never know what we have found.'

She seemed satisfied and they continued their exploration of the island with its seals, birds and breathtaking beauty.

The sun was low on the horizon before they had eaten their simple meal of beans and potatoes cooked on a small primus stone and supplemented with lettuce and raw carrots. They were tired but decided on a last walk across the boulder-strewn peninsula before opting for their sleeping bags on the hard floor of the tent. It was 11.00 p.m. before they returned and with their arms around each other they looked out to the west as the last flicker of the evening sky lit up the shallow cumulous cloud with an orange-red tinge. A seal popped up its large grey head, barely discernible against the darkening sky and a flock of oystercatchers and redshanks cried out their long piping trill as a farewell to the day.

Shona slept soundly but Sean lay awake listening to her deep breathing, almost in motion with the sound of the waves on the shore. The only other sound to disturb the night were the wails and groans from the seals on the western shore of the peninsula. He dozed for a while, thinking of the significance of those fragments of metal stored in a polythene bag only a few feet away.

He was fully awake quickly as he heard a gentle buzzing noise and a slight vibration through the ground. A great feeling of fear swept over him as he saw a glow of light underneath the tent-flap and just faintly showing through the thin fabric. The tent was on the south side of the wall and as he lay on the side facing up the hill towards the village, he knew that the light was coming from that direction. He looked at his watch, 1.30 a.m. God, how frightened he felt but he had to see what was there. Shona was still sleeping soundly. 'Thank goodness,' he said to himself. 'She can perhaps escape all this.' He was partly clothed and slipped out of the tent and put on his boots. He could see the light pulsating gently over the crest of the hill, he edged forward over the uneven ground, stumbling over the boulders as he went. As he neared the top of the hill the buzzing became louder and there was a definite trembling of the earth beneath him. Suddenly there just to the east of the village was an astonishing sight: an intense light of great brightness some twenty feet across was pulsating slowly and portraying enormous energy. Sean lay on the grass just watching, mesmerized and enthralled by the spectacle which he saw clearly was not of the world he knew. The walls of the old chapel and the gravestones stood out starkly against the mysterious brightness. The edges of the light were blurred and he could see no definite object within it. There was no solid craft discernible, nor was there anything he could see that was causing it. The buzzing suddenly increased in tempo and above the light there appeared a great beam of energy, blue in colour, forming a sort of tunnel that disappeared upwards to infinity. The intense blob of light moved slowly at first and then with increasing high speed, hurtled up the tunnel. The earth shook for just a second and he likened the sight to white hot metal coming

192

out of a huge blast furnace but without the sparks. And then it was all gone, quietness returned and the earth was still. For a moment he lay there confused in mind but gradually his fears subsided and he felt a strange inner strength guide him through a process of thought that brought back sanity and truth. He realized that he had just witnessed an event of great beauty, whose meaning was not frightening in itself, just awesome within the context of the real world. Now he could accept and believe in the truth of an alien force as described by Toni Angelini and it brought back all the memories of his encounter with a similar force those years ago off the coast of Florida.

He slipped back into the tent and she barely stirred, oblivious to the momentous happenings of the night. He lay awake for a short time, but then fell into a deep sleep.

The next day dawned bright and clear, the anti-cyclone had built up and a long period of settled weather looked assured. Sean felt elated and happy, his fears had abated to the point where it was just an apprehension of the unknown that concerned him. Even some of the unknown was revealing itself and he was content in the situation he found himself. Only the mountain to explore and then it will be over. His main worry now was Shona. If he took her to the mountain would she be in any danger? Toni had not mentioned or hinted at abduction by these visitors from another world. Sean wrestled with the problem in his mind and decided to put off a final decision.

'Good morning, did you sleep well?' she asked as she raised her head from beneath the cover of her sleeping bag.

'Yes, very well,' he replied, relieved that she had seemingly seen and heard nothing.

He opened the tent flap and the sun streamed in, catching her hair and making it glow with warmth and beauty. 'God, I don't want to lose her,' he said to himself. 'She is just beautiful and all I have ever wanted.' He had a hurried breakfast and was anxious to investigate the site of the past night's events.

'I'm just going up to the village to look for more of those pieces of metal. Be back shortly,' and with that he hurried off up the slope.

She yelled after him, 'Don't go now, we can look for them later.'

He shouted back, 'I can save time now, we want to explore the south coast during the day.'

His words trailed away with the wind and she was left to tidy up.

Just behind the chapel the vegetation was flattened in the shape of a circle and within it Sean picked up more pieces of strange metal. Three indentations on the ground, some four inches deep and six inches across, were set equidistant near the circumference of the circle. He walked the distance between them and counted out 15 paces, about 22 feet.

'See, that didn't take long,' he called loudly as he neared the tent.

'Yes, and leave me to clear up,' she said in a matter-of-fact way. 'Anyway did you find much?'

'No,' he lied, 'just a couple more small pieces to add to the collection.'

They spent the day exploring the cliffs and caves of the south coast and, just as on Handa, they marvelled at the sight of thousands of sea birds nesting in huge colonies on the rock edges. They discovered the strange wavy scratches left by the claws of St Ronan's monsters on the rocks of a place called Leac Na Sgrob.

'Nothing but a geological fault,' laughed Sean.

'Strange though,' was all she said.

The days passed blissfully. They watched the seals on Fianuis, Sean explaining, 'North Rona has 9,000 Atlantic grey seals, that's something like eight per cent of the world's population of this quite rare seal,' adding, 'you know it's not surprising that Rona is an ancient word meaning seal.'

They sat amongst the pink thrift, the hostile and restless sea washing over the outlying rocks and skerries, giving a sense of timelessness to the scene. Shona, her thoughts of a stable future with this man whom she loved and who had given her a sense of purpose to her life; and Sean, whose mind was now preoccupied with the meaning of what he had seen and with the task that still lay ahead.

The Corona picked them up on schedule two days later, having achieved everything they set out to find. They had explored the Island of Seals thoroughly and had each found the love and companionship that had been missing in their lives for so long. They both agreed that Shona would give notice to leave her job after their search for the Arctic bramble on Beinn a' Ghlo and then they would get married in December. Hamish welcomed them back on board.

'You picked a good time to visit Rona, the weather being so calm and bright. Did you see everything you wanted?'

'Everything, what a place,' Sean replied, adding to himself, 'if you only knew the whole story.'

'How about you. Did you get all the gannets you wanted?' Shona asked with a note of sadness.

She didn't really approve of killing so many birds just to be consumed as a delicacy.

'Och aye, we got plenty but we will be back again in August when they're bigger.'

His cheerfulness showed on his rugged sun-tanned face. Both of them marvelled at the sheer determination and fortitude that men like Hamish possessed to enable them to endure the hardships of fishing the waters of the north Atlantic in winter when the weather was extremely harsh and forbidding, for even in summer the seas could be terrifying and hostile.

Sean innocently asked the skipper when they were alone for a moment whether he or his men had ever seen strange lights in these northern latitudes.

'Och, funny you should ask that question. One of my men said he thought he saw a light three nights ago over in your direction, but we were anchored to the west of Sula so he didn't get a good look. We often see the lights in the sky called the northern lights or borealis, that's probably what he saw. Why do you ask? Did you see them?'

195

Hamish seemed pleased to tell him of his knowledge of the aurora borealis.

'Oh, I just wondered whether you ever saw those so-called "northern lights" I have never seen them. We certainly didn't see them the other night, we were fast asleep, far too tired.'

He lied, glad that he had confirmation of what he had seen but pleased that it was too far away for them to recognize it for what it really was.

They said their goodbyes to the crew at Port of Ness and to each other at Glasgow airport.

'Take care, Sean and don't forget I will love you for ever. Come and stay the night at my place when you return in 10 days' time. Fly up and we'll use my car to go to Braemar, stay at The Dell as before and spend the days exploring the slopes of the mountain looking for our bramble.'

She had clearly thought it all out and he was pleased.

'Fine, that sounds great. We'll find the Arctic bramble I know. Take care my darling, I love you.'

His flight departure was being called and they kissed hurriedly and then parted. She waved and was gone as he hurried down one of those anonymous glass corridors of a modern airport terminal. Within his mind he had resolved the problem and conflicting issues about Shona visiting the mountain with him. Despite his interest in her, Toni had not suggested that any harm would come to either of them, just a reference to his own life changing, but that could mean anything. No, if these craft are visiting for a peaceful purpose, as Toni had indicated, it should be safe. Certainly he had come to no harm on North Rona. His conscious was clear and, anyway, his love for Shona was such that their life was now together in everything they did and she would know about his secret before long, he would see to that.

He had two weeks back in the office, a time luckily when all was quiet, no traumas and no big problems that needed his full attention. He wrote out in his own freehand a full report on his experience on North Rona and packaged up the 34 fragments of strange metal he had collected, 11 of the older pieces in one packet and the 23 new pieces in another. He waited for the call. It came late on a Friday afternoon.

'Is that Sean Foster?'

It was not Toni Angelini's voice.

'Yes, speaking,' he replied.

'Have you got a report for Toni Angelini?'

'Yes, and some pieces.'

'Meet me at two p.m., same place as you met Toni, tomorrow. OK?'

'OK, but how will I recognize you?' he responded.

'Don't worry, I will recognize you and will introduce myself as Sam. Just put your report in a brown envelope and bring your packages, see you tomorrow,' and with that he hung up.

'That seems easy,' thought Sean.

It was as the next day. He was waiting at Gatwick's information desk. A tall, well-dressed, slim man with a thin face, narrow pointed chin and wearing dark glasses, came up to him.

'I am Sam, Sean,' was all he said and he took the small parcels held in a plastic bag and the brown envelope.

Not even a thank you or a handshake and he was gone. Sean was happy in a way it was over so quickly and he had no doubts that this man was Toni's agent. The parcels had lain in a corner of his room and his mind became obsessed with their impact and meaning. He was glad they had gone.

Time seemed to stand still for two weeks before eventually he found himself in her arms once more. He liked her little semi-detached house set in a quiet position just under the Kilpatrick Hills, north of Glasgow. He didn't have time to be introduced to anyone as they were off early in the morning after his arrival to Braemar.

'I'll introduce you to my friends when we return in a few days,' she had said.

The sun was already above the mountains and gaining strength as they set off up the long track to Loch Loch just under Beinn a' Ghlo. Sean knew of some rare alpine plants that grew on a limestone outcrop in the area and he was keen to show these to her; but this was to be after their search for the bramble on the mountain. It was going to be a long, long day and they had deliberately set off very early at dawn to enable them to properly explore the immense corries and rocky slopes of Beinn a' Ghlo, remote and boundless.

They said little as they climbed up the southern slope across the wet bog and boulder-strewn moor. The bracken was still bright green, contrasting pleasantly with the blue waters of Loch Loch and the shades of brown and white of heather and rock. The snow had melted from the deep corries and as they climbed even higher, they heard the plaintive echoing cries of the curlew and plover that had returned to their upland haunts to nest and raise their young. Above them the wide skies were filling almost imperceptibly with fluffy white clouds like balls of cotton wool moving slowly over a canvas of blue.

'It won't be long before the sun disappears altogether and we're under a solid cloud cover with occasional showers,' he said as they sat for a moment to feel the atmosphere and take in the view.

'Never mind, it's still beautiful and thank goodness we came early when the sun was out. Look at the sun's light as it traverses the hillside and brings out all the colours. Just breathtaking.' She jumped up, startled as a mountain hare suddenly ran past them and took cover behind some distant rocks. 'Come on,' she said, 'let's get up to the corrie past that little waterfall.'

'OK, might as well get as high as we can and search for the flower, now before the inevitable mist comes down.'

He was certain the clouds would lower as the afternoon wore on and he noted it was almost noon already. He felt a sense of foreboding as they climbed up through a deep cleft in the rock where a cataract of water tumbled over the rocks, 'No sunlight ever reaches this place,' he thought as he scrambled over the wet slippery surface. She was well

198

above him climbing higher into the circular hollow on the mountain.

'This looks like a good place for the plant,' she shouted down at him.

'Come on up, there's a lovely view down the valley'.

He had briefed her carefully on the likely habitat and sites for the Arctic bramble and had shown her some colour photographs of it taken in Norway. 'Maybe she'll find it first,' he thought as he quickened his pace up the mountain.

They stood there awhile locked in each other's arms, the steep dark sides of the huge hollow closing around and giving them an uncanny feeling of magnificence and awe. The sun had finally ceased to shine, covered over by cloud, and the first signs of mist appeared over the sharp edges of the corrie crest. It was as if time stood still and the whole place had a sense of chilling eeriness. She shivered.

Come on, it's creepy here. Let's search for the bramble.'

All his fears came back and he just wanted to return to the warmth and hospitality of the hotel.

'OK, I'll look here, you search that patch of vegetation over there.'

He didn't really expect to find it, after all it was well over 100 years since it was last found here.

Twenty minutes passed, twenty minutes in which the mist started to tumble down over the black cliffs of the corrie and small droplets of water formed on their clothing like dew in the early morning. Occasionally it brightened for a moment and a fitful sun shone weakly through the all-enveloping cloud.

Suddenly she shouted, 'Sean, quick over here, a bramble with red flowers.'

She sounded excited and he leapt over the ground a short distance to her side. He looked down between some moss-covered boulders and sure enough there it was; a small creeping bramble growing among the rocks. It was almost past flowering, but he recognized it instantly with its few bright red flowers and many more dark red fruits and with leaves, each with three leaflets edged with rust brown. Here was that plant that had haunted him like a passion ever since as a young boy he had read about it in one of his floras. He was as excited as she was and for a time he busied himself taking photographs whenever the light improved. 'Well done, well done,' he kept repeating to himself.

Meanwhile, Shona had wandered perhaps a hundred yards away to sit down on a patch of soft grass and unpack their flask and sandwiches. She was happy to watch him in his excitement and exultation. 'So this is the man I am going to marry in a few months' time,' she mused. 'He really is everything I ever wanted and we share so very, very much.'

The light had suddenly brightened and he was taking a last set of pictures when he felt the rocks tremble and his ears were filled with a loud buzzing noise.

'God, they're here again,' he yelled aloud, fear gripping his whole body in a panic of alarm and terror.

His mouth turned dry and his tongue felt rough and parched. He rose and looked towards Shona and saw that tunnel of light again descending from the sky and enveloping her in its tremendous brightness. His legs started trembling uncontrollably.

'Sean, Sean . . .,' she screamed, her voice echoing across the surrounding crags.

Sean was beside himself with fear and distress. There she was disappearing, her screams deadened by the buzzing noise and the rumbling of the ground. He tried to run towards her but his feet were like lead and he was held fast by some powerful force. Just as on North Rona, the area of maximum brightness which had engulfed her, hurtled skywards up the tunnel and a few seconds later all was gone. Peace and quiet returned to that desolate place. His mobility regained, he frantically searched the place where just a few moments ago she had sat happy and laughing, but there was no sign of her. Sean knew then that she was gone forever. Angelini, he was sure, had planned this all along and they had abducted her.

He sat down and cried, his heart utterly crushed with despair, the remains of their lunch all around him; a small piece of the Arctic bramble still clutched in his hand. The mist of the mountain enveloped him in his tragedy and mingled with the tears rolling down his face.

EPILOGUE

The reader will wish to know what happened to the main characters.

Sean

Sean reported the disappearance of Shona to the police. He told them everything that happened on the Mountain of Mist, but did not mention anything about North Rona or Toni Angelini. He would tell the whole story only if he were accused of a crime and brought to court. The police at first did not believe a word of his story and for a few days he was kept under arrest, but with no body and no evidence against him he was released without charge and Shona became just a missing person on their files. Small fragments of metal were recovered from Beinn a' Ghlo and a forensic report on them was prepared. When this found that the substance was made up of an alloy of zinc and iron, whose specific combination was not known to be manufactured on earth, the credibility of Sean's story was given some support and copies of the files were sent to the Government.

Sean himself lost interest in flying and the Royal Air Force. His career prospects suffered because of what had happened and his personal integrity had sustained a great blow. He retired several years after the incident and with a gratuity and small pension awarded to him for his years in the service, he was able to buy a small cottage on the west coast of Scotland. Here he lives a quiet and frugal existence alone with nature and still pining at the loss of his beloved companion.

Shona

Her body was never found and only Sean knew positively that she was no longer on this earth. Many years later he was made aware of a notice in the personal columns of an English newspaper. It said simply:

> Sean. All is peace and beauty here. *Rubus arcticus* grows in profusion. You will be with me soon – Shona.

He pondered over the word 'soon'. Typical of Shona, he thought and recalled the many times they had talked about life and death, and how time meant so little in comparison to eternity. Even a normal life span was but a fleeting moment in time and space.

He tried to trace who had placed the notice but to no avail as cash had been paid with a false address. Somehow he suspected what had happened. They had visited again, or were they already here?

Toni Angelini

Sean never heard from Toni again. To this day he is still mystified as to who Toni was and who he represented. Toni Angelini was obviously well-integrated into the society we live in. Sean was intrigued by his revelations of 'black holes' and a dimension now known as 'singularity' but he remains bitter and believes that this mysterious person was responsible for the loss of his loved one.

There was a mysterious sequel to the story of Toni. Sean had occasionally heard from his co-pilot, Bob Harding, who was with him during the Bermuda Triangle incident. Some years later just before leaving the Royal Air Force he had a Christmas card and letter from him. In the letter he mentioned meeting a mysterious man who called himself Roberto who seemed to know about 'their incident' and kept pestering him to join him in a business venture. Sean immediately contacted Bob by phone and from his description he knew that Toni and Roberto were one and the same person. He did not elaborate on his own story except to say that Roberto had also contacted him. Harding told Sean that he had traced Roberto, who until recently lived as an apparent recluse on an island called Saturna, one of the Gulf Islands between Vancouver Island and mainland Canada. He, Harding, lived near Seattle in north west USA and had often fished for big salmon amongst the Gulf Islands and he had some fishing friends amongst the community there. One, called Johnnie from the small settlement of Genoa Bay, had told him that he had met the so called Roberto while fishing the waters around Saturna and had struck up a slight friendship. Johnnie described him as a very intelligent but strange man who lived a solitary and ascetic lifestyle. Anyway, the latest information was that Roberto had disappeared and Johnnie had not seen him for several years and suspected that he had died.

So who was Toni, and where did he come from?

The UFO Phenomenon

Much has been written about UFOs. Whether you are a believer or a sceptic, here are a few facts relevant to this story:

In 1976, during his election campaign, Jimmy Carter revealed that together with his colleagues he himself had seen an UFO watching them and had vowed then that if he became president he would make available to the American public details about UFO sightings. He did not fulfil this pledge and was clearly prevented from doing so by others.

On 27 November 1978 a statement from the astronaut, Gordon Cooper, was read out at the United Nations and revealed that he had seen UFOs at great altitudes over Germany in 1951. Later in another letter to the United Nations he sets out his beliefs of extraterrestrial vehicles and their crews who visit us from other planets.

In an interview conducted in Los Angeles in 1995, Gordon Cooper spoke about his sighting of a disc-shaped craft, 30–40 foot in diameter, that landed some 200 yards from him at the end of the runway at Wright-Patterson Air Force Base (Dayton, Ohio, USA) in the 1950s. He was testing some new landing gear at the time and his colleagues were filming the tests when the UFO appeared. Cooper's film crew couldn't believe their eyes and rushed towards the strange craft with their cameras still rolling. As they got near to it, the UFO took off, making no noise whatsoever, and Cooper and his crew assumed that it was propelled by some type of electromagnetic system using the Earth's magnetic field.

For many years there have been rumours of alien craft and even bodies stored in a so-called 'Blue Room' at Wright-Patterson Air Force base and at other bases such as Langley and MacDill. Senator Barry Goldwater, is on the record as having written many times to senior officials seeking access to the facility at Wright-Patterson where UFO material is said to be stored but his requests have been repeatedly denied. In October 1981, Goldwater wrote that he had given up trying to gain access to the 'Blue Room', adding that he did not know who had such access, or what was contained in it.

In 1979 a high level NASA official who helped to design the Apollo spacecraft confirmed the sightings by Neil Armstrong of UFOs on the moon, and this was corroborated by Soviet scientists.

In 1987 Admiral of the Fleet, the Lord Hill-Norton in the Foreward to a book *Above Top Secret,* revealed that he believed that there is proof of a worldwide cover-up of the UFO phenomenon.

In 1996, British daily papers carried accounts of mysterious lights and explosions seen by many people beyond the Outer Hebrides of Scotland. Searches by RAF Nimrod aircraft costing some £200,000 revealed nothing, nor did sophisticated radar devices pick anything up. Extensive inquiries and investigations by many people revealed little of consequence and the mystery remains unexplained. Again on the 23 September 1997, bright lights and 'fireballs' were seen across the western isles and the police, coastguards and the RAF received many calls from people who saw them.

Mexico is the centre of many UFO visitations ever since the solar eclipse of 11 July 1991. On that day a strange object appeared in the sky and was seen by many people in Mexico City and nearby towns. since that date many more sighting have been made of UFOs over the deserts, towns and cities of the country. During Air Force flypasts on Mexico's independence day, UFOs have regularly appeared within the military formations flying in a manner that defies the abilities of any known aircraft. These, of course, have been witnessed by huge crowds of people and have been captured on video tape. It has been argued that the ancient Mayan people of some 1,200 years ago, who were great mathematicians, forecast the eclipse of 1991 and indicated that this would be a harbinger of revelations that would change the world. Clearly these revelations are continuing to be confirmed.

On 10 August 1997, just as this book was completed, *The Mail on Sunday* gave details of an account by Air Marshal Sir Peter Horsley of how he met a visitor from another planet in a London flat in 1954. Sir Peter Horsley had a distinguished service career as equerry to the Duke of Edinburgh and finally as Deputy Commander-in-Chief of RAF Strike Command in 1973. His extraordinary testimony and his uncompromising belief in flying saucers was concluded, 'I believe he was here to observe us ... I don't care what people think; it really happened.' Another account of this meeting was given in *The Sunday Times* of the 2 November 1997. Was the man he met the same Toni Angelini?

Finally, President Clinton is now on record as having a great interest in the truth about UFOs. Do they really exist?

ACKNOWLEDGEMENTS

Thank you Jean Crask, Diana Howell, Bessie Webb and especially Joy Preen for your help and encouragement during the writing of this book. Thank you also Rory Millikin of Calgary, Canada, for your important contribution and to Fiona Cruttenden for her patience in deciphering an illegible script.

I am grateful to Hebridean Island Cruises Limited of Skipton, Yorkshire for their permission to include my experiences of the *Hebridean Princess*. Finally to my friends; Frank Wootton, my appreciation for the striking painting used as a cover for the book, and to Sir Neil Wheeler for writing the Foreword.

BIBLIOGRAPHY

Timothy Good, *Above Top Secret*, Harper Collins, 1993.

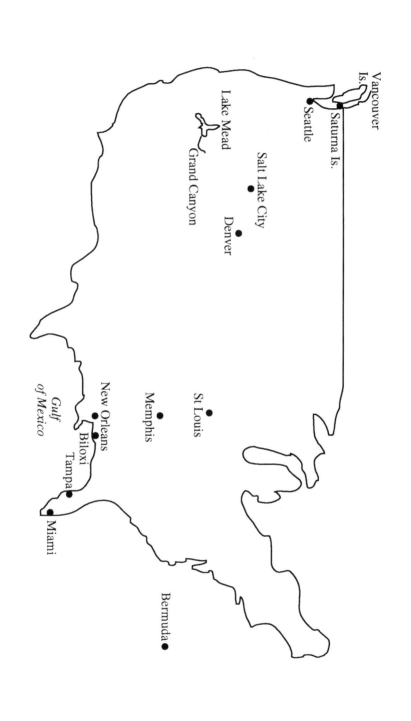